Heather

AN EDINBURGH LADY

By

JEAN LUCAS

With every good wish
Jean M. Lucas.

Cover Design: Ricardo Insua-Cao

Note for Librarians: A cataloguing record for this book is available from Library and Archives Canada at www.collectionscanada.ca/amicus/index-e.html

ISBN 1-4120-9536-0

Printed in Victoria, BC, Canada. Printed on paper with minimum 30% recycled fibre. Trafford's print shop runs on "green energy" from solar, wind and other environmentally-friendly power sources.

PUBLISHING™

Offices in Canada, USA, Ireland and UK

Book sales for North America and international:
Trafford Publishing, 6E–2333 Government St.,
Victoria, BC V8T 4P4 CANADA
phone 250 383 6864 (toll-free 1 888 232 4444)
fax 250 383 6804; email to orders@trafford.com

Book sales in Europe:
Trafford Publishing (UK) Limited, 9 Park End Street, 2nd Floor
Oxford, UK OX1 1HH UNITED KINGDOM
phone 44 (0)1865 722 113 (local rate 0845 230 9601)
facsimile 44 (0)1865 722 868; info.uk@trafford.com

Order online at:
trafford.com/06-1291

10 9 8 7 6 5 4 3 2 1

Dedication and Acknowledgments:

For Lucille and Geoff

Who persuaded me to write the novel.

I am grateful, above all, to Lucille and Geoffrey Campey, the former for having most generously made her research on the emigration of Scots to Canada available for me to draw upon, and the latter for his patience with my amateur efforts on the computer, and his unstinting advice. To both, my gratitude for encouraging me to accompany them to Canada on three occasions, and for their critical commentary on the unfolding story.

To others, my sister, Sheila Scarr, who expunged many of my lingering errors, to Ricardo Insua-Cao, who captured the spirit of early Pictou in his painting; to Andrew Wasielewski, who put the final technology in place; and to many friends and relatives, who encouraged me to persevere, goes my heartfelt gratitude.

There are many real people, and a few real events in this book, but the situations in which they found themselves and their relationships are a figment of my imagination. I apologise in advance for writing in the modern idiom, rather than in nineteenth -century language, which would have been less readily under-stood. Should I have made any historical blunders, they are entirely my responsibility, although I have striven to be as accurate as I can.

Jean M. Lucas

List of Chapters

Prologue

Jean Lucas

PROLOGUE

Standing proudly on its small hill, with gravestones clustered round it, the white-walled wooden church was shaded by tall pine-trees, screening out much of the sun.

The coffin, carried by six bearers, had been borne from the lych-gate along a well-worn path to join the many mourners inside, as the Minister raised his sonorous voice: "I am the Resurrection and the Life, saith the Lord . . ."

Hillary shivered in the cold church. Her Mother glanced anxiously at her. Had it been right to bring the child, at 13 easily the youngest mourner in the packed gathering of family and dignitaries? But Alexander Thomson had been her Great-Uncle and a prominent figure in Quebec. It was right to show respect.

While the long service, with its address detailing all the many attributes and offices held by the high-ranking British Government servant dragged on, Hillary's attention focussed on the human reference to Alexander's late wife, Isabella, whose death ten years earlier, said the spokesman, he had never ceased to mourn.

Hillary, of course, had no memory of ever meeting Great-Aunt Isabella, and when Uncle Alexander had visited their home in Pictou, as he had from time to time, it had been a subject too painful to mention.

Nevertheless, when the mourners later clustered round the grave, Hillary, lingering at the rear, read the inscription on Isabella's tombstone:

"Mrs Isabella (Liddel) Thomson, 1788 – 1846, beloved wife of Alexander Thomson, a dearly-loved Edinburgh lady, who leaves behind a well-watered garden in Cape Breton."

Why Liddel? Why Edinburgh? Why Cape Breton? And above all, why a garden, well-watered or otherwise?

She duly asked Mama, but that lady merely said, "She was a lady who helped many people. You had better ask your Uncle Neil. He lived with them for a time." And left it at that.

* * *

Years later, when Hillary, now Mrs. Blyth, with teenage children of her own, and a column to fill in the Pictou Gazette, was on holiday in Quebec, she paid another visit to the Church, to put flowers on Great-Uncle Alexander's grave. The Churchyard had become somewhat overgrown, for a newer Church had been opened as the City grew, and most people were now buried there, the old one being used occasionally when a family vault had to be opened. The churchyard was even more over-shadowed by the pine trees. While Great Uncle Alexander's inscription was still clear, that on Isabella's stone had faded. It was necessary to scrape bits of moss away with her fingernail to decipher it fully, and this time she wrote it down.

Why a well-watered garden? Her curiosity and her professional interest were aroused. It could be a story worth investigating. . . .And she had better hurry up. Uncle Neil, a respected doctor, was himself growing old.

Chapter 1 - Reading the Will

What can one <u>do</u> with widowhood?

On 5th May 1824, the afternoon sun shafted through the leaded windows of the Liddel home in Glasgow, lightening the room, normally a dark one with panelled walls and heavy drapery. Despite herself, Isabella's mood lightened also.

Although she felt a profound sense of shock and loss at her husband, William's unexpected, sudden death from a heart attack at only 43, she was already beginning to realise that, for her at 38, life would still go on. How was she to use the remaining years, which could well be another thirty-eight? William's pre-occupation with business had led to her spending long hours alone, without the solace of children, and with only a few infrequent visits to her family, two days' travel away. Of course she had had the house and servants to manage, and there were social gatherings to be attended or to organise.

Isabella, a brown-eyed lady of medium height, and a neat, slender figure, was not improved by the deep black attire in which she was arrayed. She had thick brown hair brushed smooth and coiled, and a creamy skin. Though not conventionally pretty, her eyes sparkled with liveliness and her demeanour was by no means crushed by recent events.

Theirs had been a satisfactory marriage, she thought, typical of the arranged unions of her modestly aristocratic class. The newly rich merchants looked for wives among established society, hostesses who would contribute to their social standing, while they concentrated on making money. The partnership had worked admirably. They had rarely had a cross word, each fulfilling their appointed role, always polite and respectful in their dealings with one another. Love and passion had not featured, except fleetingly in the early days, but liking and mutual regard ensured success.

They had been happy together.

Now it had all disintegrated.

The Church, ever since her son, Euan's death, had featured largely in her present life, providing comfort, explanation and understanding, and demanding good works and her talent for organisation in return. Perhaps that was the way she could bring meaning to her existence.

What did other widows do? They mostly had children, she thought, through whose lives they lived vicariously. They perhaps had grandchildren to pamper. If they were rich enough they sponsored the arts, presiding over salons and entertaining musicians or painters.

Her year's mourning, she thought, would probably be a preparation for the exercise of her skills and energy on behalf of the Church in the decades ahead. Already the funeral feast, which she had expertly arranged, was consumed, and the menfolk had gathered in the Library ready to hear the Will, she herself and her sister, Louisa, being the only females present.

Mr. Briggs of Archibald, Tennant and Son adjusted his pince-nez, cleared his throat and launched forth. It was a simple tale . . . "all that I possess to my beloved wife, Isabella Margaret Liddel, in gratitude for her devotion and patience during our life together . . ."

It was over. William's family took their leave, unsurprised at the outcome. William and Isabella had always been a close partnership, never having more than the one, ailing child, whose death at five years old had left them without the expanding family that was the habit of their contemporaries.

William's nephews, each prosperous in a chosen profession, wondered what would happen to William's business? His partner, Edward Mortimer, over in Pictou, Nova Scotia, had died three years earlier. There was no partner left and therefore, no-one to continue the business. It would have to be sold, the nephews considered. That should leave Isabella well provided for, and she might well sell the prestigious Glasgow property and move to Edinburgh to be nearer her family.

Sister Louisa, before departing with her husband on the following day, urged Isabella to come to her home on a long visit "to recover from the shock" as she put it. While appreciative of the kind offer, Isabella thought this was the last thing she would do. She must not allow her life to be taken over, or to drift away in mournful despair, as some other widows did. She must accept that the first phase was over, but the second phase was yet to come. Purposeful action would give her the greatest satisfaction – but action for what, exactly?

Mr. Briggs, plump, smug and be-whiskered, was much less sanguine than the nephews had been about the state of affairs left by William Thomson. He explained his concerns when Isabella visited his office in Blytheswood Square in her carriage the following day.

"My dear Mrs. Liddel," he bowed over her black-gloved hand, and settled her in a chair before an imposing oak desk. "Everything is yours, " he continued, "But the size of the estate is a matter of conjecture. Indeed, I cannot discover what tangible assets, apart from your house, Mr. Liddel has left."

"But the timber trade prospered," Isabella protested. "We were always contributing to charity; we lived and entertained well; we had the house, the stables, the servants."

"True indeed," agreed Mr. Briggs. "However, your husband's death was untimely and unexpected. Tradesmen will press for their bills to be settled. Your inheritance depends on the business. The death of the proprietor of a business causes problems. Confidence wanes, particularly when there is no heir to carry it on."

Isabella's mind flew briefly to the small, wasted body of the son who had died in infancy, but she struggled to regain composure. There had been no more children.

"I have a little money of my own," she said, "But surely I could sell the house and live in a smaller property?"

"The house belongs to the estate," the solicitor replied. "When the partnership was broken by Edward Mortimer's death, your husband operated alone as a private company. The house was not registered in joint names. It will take time to settle, of course, but in the meantime you may be well advised to restrain your current expenses, to live quietly for a while until we can establish what is due to the estate, as well as what is claimed from it."

"I shall of course live modestly during my mourning," she answered. "Nothing else would be fitting, but I shall want to be kept apprised of what is happening to the business and the estate. I am not to be shielded from it; I may not be able to manage the timber trade, but I am perfectly capable of managing my personal affairs. Should we not engage professional advice for the business?"

"Professional help will cost money," countered Mr. Briggs. "I think you may safely leave matters with us."

Isabella's chin tilted upwards, and there was a glint in her eye as she surveyed the benevolent but bumbling Mr. Briggs.

"I shall make enquiries," she responded briskly, "and see you again in five days' time. That will be Tuesday," she added. "Is ten o'clock convenient?"

Mr. Briggs felt the situation escaping from his control. Widows did not normally behave in this fashion. They wept, they dabbed their eyes with lace-trimmed, tear-sodden handkerchiefs, they clutched at their sons or daughters or sisters for comfort.

"Certainly," he muttered weakly. "I may have further light to shed on the matter by then, as I have an appointment to visit the timber yard on Monday."

Isabella rose, rustling her stiff skirts as she turned, extended her hand again to show there was no ill-will, and was escorted out by the clerk.

She had no clear idea what to do, except that she did not intend to spend the next thirty-eight years as a destitute widow, which future Mr. Briggs seemed to have designed for her. She would start her enquiries with Thomas Mortimer, whose uncle, Edward, had been William's business partner. She believed him to reside somewhere in the city, remembering that he and his wife had visited to dine with herself and William soon after Edward's death.

* * *

Her sleuthing proved not too difficult. She paid a state visit to Liddel's Timber Yard in the commercial and dock area of the City. Here all was bustle and activity. Her husband's office clerk provided Thomas Mortimer's direction, and was anxious to know about the future of the timber operation. Sympathising with his concern, Isabella could only advise him to discuss this with Mr. Briggs, but she also promised to raise the matter herself when she saw the solicitor on Tuesday. She asked who was now in charge of the Pictou end of the business, and was told that Mr. Bruce Cameron managed the North American yards.

She then penned a note advising Thomas Mortimer that she would call on the following day, sending it with her footman and instructions to await a reply.

When Thomas Mortimer's reply, expressing sympathy at William's death, and the willingness of Agnes and himself to receive Isabella on Saturday afternoon came to hand, she considered her tactics. She needed more information about her husband's purchase of Edward Mortimer's estate, about the property in Pictou, about the traffic between the two countries and if possible a recommendation on who to consult for financial advice. A touch of dissembling might be in order.

The confident approach, which had succeeded with Mr. Briggs might alienate Thomas Mortimer, for females were presumed to seek guidance from their masculine relations. An appeal to his greater worldly knowledge might flatter him into bestowing his assistance, particularly if Isabella's entree into Glasgow society could be offered to benefit his wife.

She journeyed to the more modest suburb where Thomas Mortimer lived. After the pleasantries, the offer of tea was accepted, although Isabella noted that Thomas Mortimer had a glass of wine at his elbow. He had a rather florid complexion for a young man, and his neck-cloth was carelessly tied. She asked him about Pictou. He had visited his Uncle Edward there some six years ago, he said, having worked his passage outward and back on a timber ship. But he preferred his work in a counting-house in Glasgow and the predictability of life in Scotland with his long-time sweetheart to the rough environs of Nova Scotia, he said.

If Isabella thought this a tame approach, she was too well-bred to betray surprise.

"Is life very rough there?" she asked.

"Well, I thought so. However, Uncle Edward loved Pictou," Thomas reminisced. "He had become someone very important, after his early start as a clerk in Halifax in the late 1780s. He just knew everyone. He used to negotiate the purchase of timber from the settlers as they felled it to expand their farms. Mostly it was in small lots, and of course they had to transport it, or pay for transport to the wharves. Why, in one week he would ship timber to the value of £500, and he is said to have loaded 80 vessels in one year. He had some fisheries interests too. And of course he dabbled in politics, and was especially keen on education. He backed the Pictou Academy financially, and some called him 'the King of Pictou.' He was quite a local benefactor and sometimes gave people credit to help them out, though he would never do that for anyone other than a fellow- Scot."

"Did he only trust the Scots?" queried Isabella.

"Well, who would trust an Irishman?" countered Thomas. "As for the English, he felt they were driving the Scots out of their own country. No, it was Scots or nothing when Uncle Edward did credit business. He knew they would pay back when they could."

There was a momentary pause, while Isabella digested this, "And did they pay back?" she asked, knowing much might depend upon the reply.

"They didn't all get the chance. Uncle Edward died and your husband bought the business into his. I wasn't prepared to go out there again and sort out the mess, so William Liddel bought the real estate, the wharves, timber yards and buildings, including the Stone House on the Harbour, and the business, which by then dominated trade between the New World and the Clyde. I should think he got a good bargain. I don't wish to speak ill of the dead, but William Liddel was known to be strong and fierce in business matters. When the estate was settled, it left enough for Mrs. Mortimer to live on when she returned to Aberdeen."

Isabella thought her husband's generosity to the Mortimers might prove the cause of her own penury, and yet it sounded as if there was real value in the Nova Scotian side of the enterprise. Should she confess her problems, and seek Thomas's help? He seemed a sensible man. Then caution took the upper hand, and she decided against it.

He was a Mortimer and not a Liddel, after all.

She turned to Agnes, but out of the corner of her eye, caught Thomas looking at her with a speculative gaze. He was taking another gulp of his wine.

"You are members of St. Cuthbert's parish here, are you not?" she asked.

The shy Agnes stumbled a little in her reply. "We go to Church most Sundays," she said, seeking reassurance from her husband. He confirmed that they did, volunteering that Pastor Griffiths was a famous preacher. They talked a little of Isabella's work in her own parish, and she enquired whether they took an active part in the life of St. Cuthberts? Apparently not, for his work in the counting-house kept him very busy, he said. Isabella marked him down again for his lack of voluntary effort.

"What sort of work do you do?" she asked. He was hoping for promotion soon, he said, but it was the Partners who made the decisions, advised the private clients and kept the most interesting work to themselves.

"Who are your Principals?" enquired Isabella and he offered a letter-heading which listed the names. One or two she recognised, but she sensed that he was becoming wary at the pointed nature of her questions.

"I may find I have to go to Nova Scotia myself," said Isabella. "My husband's death, like your Uncle's, has left matters in some confusion."

He stirred uneasily. "Surely it's not a job for a lady!" he said. "The timber trade is man's work. Of course Mortimer and Liddel had it all organised. It was a great benefit to the settlers to have a ready market, and the growing economy of the new world depended largely on timber. You would not know where to start."

Isabella did not appreciate the patronising nature of this last remark. "I have started with you!" she said rather sharply. "Naturally I may need to hire professional assistance, but no-one other than myself seems to appreciate the need to proceed speedily."

Agnes rushed gallantly into the breach. "Tell Mrs. Liddel about your voyage," she suggested. "It may be helpful to her, if she should decide to go."

He was only too willing, and the wine was fuelling his loquacity. It had been a turbulent crossing. The ships were now more modern, he said, and often made the journey in four weeks, if the winds were favourable. The cabin passengers now had every comfort, with good quality food, prepared by the ship's cook, and served by their Cabin Steward, for their passage costs of between £10 and £15.

"Were there any female passengers on your ship?" asked Isabella.

"Only in steerage," he answered, "and they were emigrating with their families."

Steerage also was better now than it had been at one time, with greater height for the passengers between decks, usually towards the rear of the ship, and more care given to their comfort and safety. Steerage fares were normally £4 to £5, but the passengers "found for themselves". They would bring bread, biscuits, flour, oatmeal, sugar, molasses and tea on board. The ship provided fire and water. Most of them ate very little meat. Often the ships, which brought timber to Scotland took emigrants on the return journey. That was where the profit came in. A journey would be costed to deliver timber with the return trip empty. But if passengers could be found, the journey could be made to pay quite handsomely. Whole families went sometimes. If they were going for good, they took some amazing possessions with them in their bundles, varying from family heirlooms to seed potatoes to start their new crops.

Isabella listened with close attention. The journey did not sound too arduous, and might be very interesting, she thought.

She judged it time to take her leave, and thanked the couple for their kind assistance, promising Agnes a card for a future party when she had put off her black gloves.

She did not really like Thomas Mortimer. He seemed slothful and possibly addicted to drinking. As for that reference to "not a job for a lady", she thought him typical of that group of men who assumed themselves to be innately superior to any female. Well, she would prove him wrong and prejudiced!

On the return carriage journey, Isabella looked again at the list of Principals. One of the Partners, whose name she had recognised, was a member of her own Parish Congregation. She did not know him well, but surely a respected Presbyterian worshipper would be safe to apply to for assistance. She could consult the Pastor on Sunday. Perhaps this Mr. Goodrich might even be at the Evening Service tomorrow. The congregation would pray for William, of course, and that would give her an opening to follow up her enquiry.

Suddenly, Isabella was smitten with remorse. She had spent the last two days in schemes and machinations, and her dear William had only been buried for three days! She resolved to visit the grave next day, refresh the flowers and pray for William's good sense and guidance to be passed down to her through the Will of the Lord.

Arriving home, and settled in her window-seat, looking out over the peaceful Glasgow Square, she began to daydream about the sea-voyage and the far-off land across the ocean. She had surprised herself with that spontaneous suggestion that she might need to go to Nova Scotia herself. It looked as though William Liddel might have taken over the debts due to Edward Mortimer when he bought his partner's share of the business. That would mean the debts would continue to be due to herself, as the only beneficiary of the estate, and there was the matter of the wharves and timber yards in Nova Scotia, too. Presumably Mr. Briggs would be selling those.

Her financial future was of concern of course, but perhaps more enthralling was the possibility of a great adventure, which few females among her contemporaries were in a position to experience. A sensation of excitement began to stimulate her thoughts and give thrilling urgency to her plans. Perhaps widowhood would not be so very bad, after all!

Chapter 2 - Isabella's Plans

Tuesday's meeting with Mr. Briggs was far from re-assuring. The subsequent investigations into William's estate, although establishing the purchase of many of Edward Mortimer's interests in Pictou, also revealed debts of over £50,000 with the St. Petersburg Companies with which William Liddel had carried on the larger portion of his timber trade. There was a depressing list of small losses on virtually every cargo carried. The ship *Thetis* featured often. Isabella wondered why William had carried on trading if the voyages had been so unprofitable. She supposed long-term contracts might have been entered into. Again, the bottom had fallen out of the Baltic market when the Government imposed tariffs during the Napoleonic Wars. It was all too true that the business appeared to be insolvent.

There was, however, Mortimer's List, which he showed to her, which bore the names of 49 people who owed money to Edward Mortimer, and thus to William Liddel, who had bought Mortimer's interests. Extensive credit had had to be given to people who were emigrants and had little capital, but were building up enterprises in the new territories, and there were in Nova Scotia and Cape Breton these names of people who had not yet paid their due debts. There was also, listed in immaculate copper-plate writing, the land holdings in Pictou which had been transferred to W. Liddel from Mortimer's estate. Among the debtors listed, the man who owed the largest sum, virtually £1,000, was Alexander Thomson, described as a trader, but there were many others whose names proclaimed their Scottish origin, and the sums outstanding ranged from as little as 13s 6d to £480.

Mr. Briggs, disclosing the existence of the list, proposed to write to all the people concerned, although first he would have to find out from colleagues in Nova Scotia some addresses for them.

"It would take too long, and you cannot be sure they would reply," was Isabella's comment. Mr. Briggs looked pained.

"Can't you send someone out to pursue the debts?" was her next question. Mr. Briggs thought up a number of convincing reasons why this would not be possible – reasons convincing to himself at any rate. Isabella grew very impatient.

"Give it to me, then," she snapped, and Mr. Briggs reluctantly handed it over. Armed with Mortimer's List, the conviction was growing stronger in Isabella's mind that she would have to go to Nova Scotia to reclaim her rights. Then she remembered the Glasgow business. "The clerk is very anxious to know about the future of Liddel's Timber Yard," she said. "I have referred him to you."

"Yes, well, it will have to be sold. I don't anticipate trouble finding a buyer, because the business here is sound. You will leave that to us, I presume," he added with some sarcasm. "It will then be up to the purchaser to decide whether he can continue to employ the men."

* * *

Isabella then sought an appointment with Mr. Goodrich, one of the Principals of Thomas Mortimer's firm, who had been approached by her Pastor and agreed to advise her.

"Financially, I am likely to be very badly off," she explained. "My interview with Mr. Briggs, our lawyer, has confirmed that my husband's debts on the St. Petersburg side of the timber trade are likely to swallow up all the profits on the Pictou side. As I understand it, my husband paid over a lot of capital to his partner,

Edward Mortimer's estate quite recently, and there has been no time between the two deaths to get a return on that capital."

Mr. Goodrich, a distinguished, silver-haired, smooth-shaven figure, sympathised. "It is always a problem when one death succeeds another so rapidly. It happens with duties on some big estates, as you will know. But you have those purchased assets to sell, I presume."

"I believe so, but I have no idea what they may be worth."

"Well, the price put upon them at purchase will give us some idea. The problem will be to realise them either at that price or an enhanced price. I would only caution you that it is always more difficult dealing with property overseas."

"I have asked Mr. Briggs to send someone to Pictou, but he is talking about months of enquiries and letter-writing. I was wondering whether to go myself."

"There is no reason why not. You would need to employ valuers and professional people when you got there, but at least you would be able to make a better personal assessment of what the property might be worth."

Isabella was grateful for Mr. Goodrich. Apart from freely giving his advice, he was not being patronising to her as a female, but treating her as of equal intelligence.

"I have also discovered a list of debts owing to Edward Mortimer, and which was bought in by my husband with the rest of the property. Those also need to be pursued. One or two are quite large, although most are quite small.   There are names, but no addresses, and of course, some people may have moved on."

Mr. Goodrich pursed his lips and looked very dubious.

"Mrs. Liddel, I should not give you this advice, because such debts technically would also belong to your husband's estate. However, it seems very unlikely that all of them could be recovered, and in any case, any attempt to do so would be bound to subject the settlement of the estate to intolerable delay.

Better perhaps to divorce them from the other assets.   See if you can have them extinguished as uncollectable.   Get the estate settled, and then perhaps try and recover them later if you can."

Isabella also looked doubtful. "I am assured that Scots always settle their debts, or Edward Mortimer would not have lent them money in the first place. But I don't think Mr. Briggs is going to succeed from Glasgow in getting the money back."

"Then let him issue instructions to sell and realise the main assets, and wind up the estate. If it turns out that the debts exceed the assets and your husband was insolvent, then you will have nothing, except perhaps half the proceeds of the furniture and effects in your house, and the possible expectations from Mortimer's List. On the other hand, as you were not joined with the business, you cannot be pursued for your husband's debts. I am sorry for you, but I believe it will be best for your solicitor to seek all legal means to retrieve what he may on your behalf, and then to declare the insolvency, however unpleasant that may sound."

Isabella asked a few more questions, thanked him for his kindness in explaining the situation so clearly, and came to the conclusion that it would not, after all, be in her interests to rush over to Pictou immediately to seek redress from the debtors. She would try and get the List excluded from the settlement, and in the meantime deal with those household matters, which required urgent attention.

* * *

First there was the house to be disposed of, and a new home to be sought.

Once Isabella had determined to reduce her household, she set about it in her usual methodical way. She would see all the servants individually after morning prayers. Her dilemma would be explained while they were all together, and then she would discuss their personal situation with each of them.

One female and one male servant would have to be kept for the time being. If the stables were closed, she would still need a man to summon her a hack, to close the shutters, to carry coals, to light the lamps, to answer the door and maintain her status. She would still need a cook, or a housemaid who could cook. She would dispense with her dresser, after learning to manage her own hair. Luckily the new styles were smoother and simpler. She might be able to hire a country girl cheaply, for about £8 a year, to give assistance with washing, ironing and grate-cleaning.

When she eventually visited Nova Scotia, which she was determined to do one day, to try and retrieve the Mortimer debts, then the country girl could maid her. What skills would she need in the new world? In rough territory it might be as well to learn some of the work females normally did. One would not wish to be too dependent. Perhaps she would take a few lessons before Cook departed.

Planning her future restored her spirits as practical matters always did. It was not poor William's fault if she was in financial trouble. He had afforded her every comfort while he was alive, and she would not fall into a melancholy now that he was dead. Nor would she hang on the sleeve of her family. To be beholden to her sister and brother-in-law was not to be considered for a moment.

She would salvage all she could, use her small private means to remain well-dressed and of superior appearance, and trust in the Lord!

She resolved to rent a small house in Edinburgh. Her family lived in Dalkeith, just south of the city, and would be a support while she sought the right spot in which to live. Dalkeith, little more than a large village, had a main street of cottages and a few shops, while the larger stone houses, set in their own grounds, clustered round it. Brother-in-law, Henry, was a gentleman, farming in a leisured fashion, and owner of a neat property. Although she knew sister Louisa was quite willing to offer a permanent refuge, Isabella was determined it should only be temporary, foreseeing the involvement in a still growing family as more of a burden than an enjoyment, when she intended to devote her time and efforts to the Church.

"But you may meet someone and marry again," suggested Louisa.

Isabella shook her head. "It is not my intention," she answered. "Impecunious widows are not first sought after for matrimony, and I have had my opportunity as a wife and mother. It is time I helped others."

Her brother-in-law was equally frank, but considerably more tactless.

"You need a husband, Isabella," he said. "Women on their own, and particularly those without a husband's income, can have no life worth living. You're a pretty woman, and a capable one. You should control your husband's household, and do your good works with that!"

Isabella fought down an urge to retaliate. She knew they would try their best to find her a second husband, whatever she said. She shook her head, and said, "I would rather be remembered for something I had done myself, than something done merely as an appendage of a husband.".

Louisa looked scandalised. "But, dearest, you were quite happy with William. You could be equally happy with someone else, I am sure."

Henry was severely disapproving. "There's little opportunity for ladies to achieve fame. Notoriety perhaps, as actresses or mistresses, but that's not your ambition, I trust."

"Of course not! I merely meant that, as a human being, with a reasonable brain, I should be putting it to use in the service of humanity. Interesting professions are not open to us females, but we can always find fulfilment in voluntary work."

"What voluntary work?"

"I don't quite know. It would be Christian-based, I think. But I would truly wish to be independent, and to serve my cause whole-heartedly, without being restricted by duties at home."

"Not possible!" dismissed Henry, "nor desirable!"

Isabella left it at that. She was benefitting from their hospitality, after all.

* * *

House-hunting was not easy. Journeys into Edinburgh via stage-coach and putting up at lodgings while advertisements were perused and followed up on foot were time-consuming and wearisome. Eventually, however, fortune smiled and what seemed an ideal house in a genteel neighbourhood was advertised in The Edinburgh Evening Courant. Isabella took a hansom cab to be early on the scene. It had a dainty colourful front garden, a yellow front door with a brass knocker, and a bow window. A widow was moving to live with her sister, and wanted to rent for an income. The two ladies struck an instantaneous bargain, and Isabella had a new home, with just enough room for herself and her maid.

She did not regard it as a "come-down" from her big mansion in Glasgow. No-one knew her here. It was the start of her new life. With no army of servants to oversee, no prestige dinners to organise, no round of social visits to consider, she could spend her days as she wished, in prayer and contemplation or in organising Church activities. She would be free!

Louisa and her husband surprisingly accepted her announcement, merely assuring themselves that the rent was within her means, that the neighbourhood was respectable and that she would not be moving until the end of the month. This was because a dinner-party to which John Sutherland had been invited was to be held the following week. Privately they were relieved that she was renting instead of buying, as the former could more easily be changed again than the latter.

For her part, Isabella could auction her heavy furniture and her silver, yielding some capital, while the pretty chintzes and smaller fitments which would come with her new furnished property would be congenial. She had some visiting cards printed with her new address – a last token of her old and grander style.

In the meantime she had written to her cousin, Helen Creighton, who had been married about three years ago to David Creighton, originally from Dundee, but now a merchant in Pictou. She had enclosed a copy of Mortimer's List, and asked if Helen knew any of the people mentioned, and whether she could assist in tracing any of the money owing.

* * *

The proposed dinner party organised by Louisa and Henry duly took place. Isabella, at Louisa's instigation, felt it appropriate to lighten her mourning with a becoming lace fichu over her black silk dress.

There were eight people in all. Louisa had balanced her table well and set it with gleaming silver and sparkling glass. On her right was John Sutherland, a lawyer, with whom Isabella was already slightly acquainted, as he had had business dealings with her husband. He was unmarried, and a distant cousin of the noble Duke.

Isabella was on John Sutherland's right, and her own right-hand neighbour was the Member of Parliament for Berwickshire, whom she had not met before. Opposite were the Member's wife, an angular lady, who kept an eagle eye on her husband's predilection for the fairer sex, and the party was completed by a country squire and his lady, the Frobishers, not remarkable for their conversational prowess, but due for an invitation.

Isabella's skills at making the Frobishers feel comfortable had been exercised during the pre-dinner assembly over sherry, and she first felt it incumbent on her, while the first course was served, to draw out the Member of Parliament's opinions on the day's issues. He was willing to oblige, and favoured her with a long discussion on the price of cereal crops, about which the Berwickshire farmers were perennially concerned.

She managed to direct his mind to British North America, about which he knew little, but was prepared to pontificate, and all she gleaned was that a Select Committee was to be established to look into conditions on the emigrant ships.

His wife intervened, as the M.P's third glass of wine emboldened him to press Isabella's hand and bestow a knowing wink at her, while he described the plight of some of the emigrants, and Isabella turned quite thankfully to John Sutherland.

He was a tall man, austere of countenance, compared with the florid MP, and with keen and penetrating dark eyes, set under bushy brows. She knew him to have originally succeeded his father, who was a lawyer in Dornoch, dealing with some of the larger estates in Sutherland and Easter Ross. She asked him if he still maintained an office there.

"Yes," he replied, "but it is the lesser side of my current business. There are many absentee landlords and my base in Edinburgh enables me to meet many clients here in the City."

She knew him to have an interest in opera, and enquired first about the latest professional production to have visited Edinburgh, where St.Cecilia's Hall in Niddry Wynd was often used for performances. Although having lived quietly for the past year, she had seen "Israel in Egypt" by Handel in Glasgow and was able to discuss this oratorio with him.

"You must allow me to include you in my next opera party," he offered, but Isabella, while expressing thanks, demurred.

"I may be going away soon," she volunteered. "My cousin, Helen, lives in Pictou in Nova Scotia, and I am thinking of visiting her."

"You are surely not thinking of carrying on William's business yourself," he asked in some surprise.

"No, no, it is merely a visit. The business is virtually wound up, but I might mix the visit with a few outstanding matters. I shall be back before the winter, and I shall then embark on some charitable and church work in Edinburgh. I have acquired a little house, you know."

He did not know, but sought her direction, and seemed anxious they should not lose touch. Louisa chipped in,

"Tell Isabella about your choir, John. I am sure she would be an asset if you could persuade her to join."

"Are you a singer?" he asked, again surprised.

"Not really," she answered, "But I take part in any Church set pieces, the anthems and formal music."

"Soprano?" It was more a statement than question, for she had a light, clear voice.

"Yes, but never solo. I am too shy."

"You are not shy. A more accomplished lady I have never met!"

She accepted the compliment with grace, "You are too kind, but there is a great difference between being at ease in company, and being prepared to put oneself forward at a public spectacle."

He acknowledged this. "But you would be prepared, perhaps, to join in our rehearsals and take a chorus part, in Handel, for instance?"

She hesitated. "Perhaps. We must wait and see, when I return from Nova Scotia."

The conversation became general, and the meal ended with the ladies withdrawing and the gentlemen circulating the port and brandy.

"Well?" queried Louisa, after the tea-tray had appeared, and her sister was conveying cups to their guests. "Did you like him?"

"He was very agreeable," replied Isabella. "Do you know of what faith he is?"

"Why, Presbyterian of course. I know you would never look at anyone otherwise."

"It is not so much important to me of what faith, but certainly that a person should have faith – enough to move mountains – is vital," Isabella replied.

"Oh, you are too wrapped up in religion!"

"It is my choice," responded Isabella, "And now my vocation."

Louisa could not counter that, but she was not dissatisfied with her evening's work.

* * *

After returning to Glasgow to settle her affairs and arrange the removal or sale of her portable property, Isabella honoured her promise to Agnes Mortimer, whose husband, Thomas, had provided some information about his Uncle Edward's business, and took her to a Musical Soiree, introducing her to some of the ladies who represented the cream of Glasgow Society. Most were surprised that Isabella was leaving Glasgow. She would be missed, they said, as they accepted the little address cards, but behind their fans smiled discreet, knowing smiles, as William Mortimer's business losses were commonly discussed over their husband's after-dinner port.

The Glasgow Christian Aid Society, when she resigned from their Ladies' Committee, hoped she would continue her good work in Edinburgh, where the Society was sadly lacking in ability and expertise, but Isabella took this with a substantial pinch of salt, as the rivalry between the two cities was notorious. They were continually striving to eclipse one another, and invariably quarrelling when supposedly committed to a common cause.

The plans for Cook to train Isabella in the mysteries of cooking had met with less success. "You'll not be wanting to get your hands stained with the fruit, or cut with my sharp knives, Missus," she said. "And in any case, it's not fitting, for the likes of you to be slaving away in the hot kitchen." However, Isabella found Cook a prestigious post with a senior Churchman's household, and was rewarded with a few hand-written cards of Cook's most successful recipes.

The Butler had proved a stumbling block. He seemed to think that, at his age, it was his due to be pensioned off in retirement. Isabella explained that this was not possible, and referred him smartly to Mr. Briggs, the solicitor. Eventually, he accepted a glowing reference, and an introduction to Sir Henry Percy's household.

She was lucky with the country girl. Her footman's younger sister was desirous of obtaining a position, and on being interviewed, proved to be an eager, energetic young person, rejoicing in the name of Joanna.

When Isabella was almost ready to leave Glasgow for good, the expected letter arrived in Helen Creighton's sloping handwriting. Much of the letter described her new family, the two little boys of her marriage, and the boy and girl of her new husband's first marriage. She was preoccupied that the measles, then sweeping Pictou, would engulf them all.

"However, you must come and visit us," she urged. "Pictou is normally a healthy town. We have a splendid harbour, and there is constant coming and going of shipping from Britain. We are about one hundred miles by road from Halifax (one hundred and fifty by sea), and the mail goes three times a week, which is better than in parts of Scotland. Our town continues to grow, as settlers from round about bring in their produce. Of course, the winters are long and hard, but when the ice forms, people travel by sledge instead. I have a lovely piano, which cost £60, and came from Liverpool, and it is my hope that the children will learn to play and become musical. Alas, there is little in the way of society here, like we used to enjoy in Dundee, but the people are very pleasant and friendly. I miss not having many female friends, and it would bring great joy if you could come.

David's father, Archibald Creighton, comes most years to oversee the Pictou side of the business, and he is due out from Dundee on *The British King* this year, sailing on 28th May. He would be happy to escort you, I know, if you can obtain a passage.

I am in no way connected with business and do not like to ask David, as some of the people on your list may well be friends of his, or customers at least. I truly think it would best if you were to come and see this country for yourself. It is very different from our big cities in Scotland – not worse, but different! Do come, dear Isabel,
Your loving cousin,
Helen."

The Insolvency Hearing took place. Mortimer's List was excluded as being of doubtful value, or none at all. Nothing now stood in her way. After a few week's stay at the little house in Edinburgh, and two years after she became a widow, Isabella and Joanna prepared to set off on their travels to discover the New World.

Chapter 3 – Isabella's Atlantic voyage

Isabella set sail on *The British King* from Dundee on 28th May 1826. The *King* was a top quality ship, recently built, and the cabin quarters were relatively spacious and well-appointed.

Archibald Creighton proved a helpful, avuncular guide. "You'll be sick as a parrot, at first," he said. "And so will your maid, so no help there! But keep your heads down, breathe some fresh air as soon as you can, and you'll soon get your sea legs and be all right."

He proved a true prophet. Though the wind was barely brisk, no sooner did they leave the shelter of the harbour than the ship began to lift with the swell, sink down again, lurch a little, sway a little, creak a little, dip a little, and Isabella left the rail to go below.

It was a full forty-eight hours before she was able to totter back to the sunlit deck, and to take a constitutional around it, noting the coops of chickens, from which their future meals would come. The British King, she learned from the Captain, was 90ft. long, 23 ft. wide, and some 15ft deep. She seemed a small enough craft in which to tackle the mighty ocean, and her sails, spread to catch the best of the breeze, were all they had to power the ship along. The breeze remained fresh, and the coast of Scotland, which they had rounded before setting course for their Atlantic run, was fast disappearing from sight. A ship passed homeward-bound, somewhat lower in the water, because of her heavy timber load. The two ships exchanged greetings with loud "halloos", and the running up of signal flags. There might be rivalry in the pursuit of cargo, but they were comrades in the constant battle against the elements. On the skill of the Captain and his crew the lives of all aboard depended. The Captain was also known as the Master, and his word was law.

Soon the Captain called all the steerage passengers on deck, lining them up as if on parade, and performed a roll-call in search of any "strayed sheep". Many of them had boarded at Aberdeen, where the ship had anchored for half a day while the families with their packages and bundles had been loaded, had gone through the customs procedures and had found space for themselves and their belongings in the dark hold of the ship. Others had been picked up at Cromarty.

While they stood in line and answered to their names, the crew searched the rest of the ship in case there were stowaways. The steerage passengers seemed a respectable group, fifty-five of them, of whom the oldest was seventy, and the youngest, a babe in arms. There were twenty children, and Isabella worried whether they were getting any schooling on board, and considered whether she might seek permission to hold a Sabbath School, such as she had run in the days before her marriage.

The Captain readily gave permission, saying also that public worship would take place at 12 noon on the Sabbath. Consequently all convened, young and old, master and crew (except the helmsman) around the Capstan, which served as a reading desk.

The service was conducted by the Episcopal Minister from Cruden, who was leading several of his flock to the New World, while a Free Churchman read the Lesson. Somehow, the open air, and the broad expanse of ocean upon which this tiny ship was but a speck, inspired a sense of awe, and it was with a sense of special purpose that the Almighty's help and guidance were devoutly sought.

Isabella read her Bible with a particular zeal. It was her first great adventure in an otherwise sheltered life, and she little knew what terrors the voyage might have in store, or what her eventual destiny would be.

Great excitement was caused by a pod of whales accompanying the ship for several miles. They were so close an active man could have jumped upon their backs – had they stayed still long enough! Some dived contemptuously beneath the ship and came up the other side, but unlike Moby Dick of Pacific Ocean fame, which had sunk a whaling ship a few years earlier, they were young and playful, and had no evil intent. They rolled and plunged, and sported playfully, leaping and turning to flash their white undersides, and seemingly showing no fear.

The wind blew hard astern for two or three days, the ship making fast progress, eight or nine knots an hour, as the Captain told Mr. Creighton, who duly conveyed the information to Isabella, together with the intelligence that there was to be a Concert on Friday evening after Dinner. There was a Piper aboard, and someone who played the tambourine. Everyone was to give a turn. Isabella begged to be excused, but Joanna had been urged by one of the sailors to join in a saucy duet, and, her mistress raising no objection, giggled her way through the song.

The Ship's Captain was an excellent and steady man. He talked mainly with Mr. Creighton, over their evening glass of brandy, but made an opportunity to seek out Isabella to ensure that she was entirely comfortable. He also paid regular visits to the steerage quarters. He and Isabella also met, in any event, nightly at dinner, and she was reassured by his matter-of-fact way of dealing with the hazards of the sea. He had crossed the Atlantic more than fifty times, and instead of alarming his passengers with the more exciting and hair-raising tales of narrow escapes, concentrated on the familiarity of it all.

"You may see ice-bergs soon," he warned. "They break off the ice-caps further North and float southward. It's a bit early for the big ones. Indeed I hope you do see one, for they look beautiful with the sun shining on them. They can be dangerous, for two-thirds of the berg is under water, so we may have to alter course, to give them a wide berth."

Sure enough, a fairly big berg, looking about the size of Edinburgh Castle, was spotted on the horizon, and as it was passed at a distance, it seemingly altered shape until one could imagine it as a row of town houses instead, with tall chimneys and steps in front.

One day, after the halfway point of the voyage had been passed, a family of dolphins entertained the passengers. Some of the men tried to catch them, but they were disdainful of the hook, and instead came across a shoal of herring, which resulted in a lively chase. The dolphins pursued, and the herrings scattered, leaping half-in and half-out of the water, in the manner of flying fish, but they could not last long, and the dolphins overtook them and feasted copiously.

Isabella spent part of each day preparing for her Sabbath School. Some of the teenage children she coached in little tasks, the others she rehearsed together in a hymn or sacred song. Consequently the Sabbath School became a participating performance for the children, who quickly learned to perform well, and were watched, and even applauded by their elders.

She also wrote two long letters to her sister and William's nephew to tell them of life on board. They would be conveyed back to Scotland by the next ship to leave Pictou, but at least it would let them know that she had reached port safely.

She chatted with many of the wives of the steerage passengers too. They had brought many of their chattels with them to start life afresh, cooking pots, a sieve and fire-irons for example. Many had been lured away by pressure from members of the family who had gone before, enticed by tales of land to be had for the asking, and fearful too of tales of others back home who had been evicted by their landlords.

The women had little choice in the matter. If Jock or Robert decided to go, it was for them to uproot their very existence and go with him, but they anticipated hardship and years of uncertainty. Better the devil you know, than the devil you don't, seemed to be their attitude, though they were fearful of the unknown. For many, however, the enforced, comparative idleness on board ship, after years of child-bearing and sheaf-stooking and weaving and bread-making and milking and threshing, was a benefit. They stood up straighter and stronger, and sat around in the sunshine, enjoying the change of air.

"It must be worth it," comforted Isabella. "I never heard tell of folk returning to Scotland, except for a visit or a funeral, and most say life is better, and more free in the New World."
The Cruden folk were most easily comforted, for they had their pastor with them and several neighbours and friends. They would be able to support one another.

Isabella found every twilight fascinating, as the light faded gradually until only a last thin streak of brighter sky remained on the horizon. Yet still the ship ploughed on across the boundless depths of the sea, bearing its tiny group of souls afloat in a vast black world, until the moon came up and the stars shone comfortingly.

They were visited by birds daily. The "Mother Carey" bird, or storm petrel, fluttered constantly about, having come from the Banks of Newfoundland, hundreds of miles away. The sunshine became a scarce commodity once they reached the Banks, for fog closed in, a grey, fluffy, damp and eerie mantle, and the ship was constantly sounding its klaxon to give warning to the French and English fishing boats, which were about. Soundings also had to be taken, first in fifty fathoms of water, soon reducing to forty, to make sure they were in no danger of running aground. The fog lasted for two days, but then a breeze sprang up, and the passengers could wave to the fishing boats, and at last the mournful warning siren could be still.

The breeze soon became a gale, accompanied by heavy rain, and for about two hours the ship was under storm sail.

"Do not be uneasy," said Mr. Creighton. "We have plenty of sea-room." In fact he quite seemed to enjoy the storm and the mighty seas, staying on deck throughout it all, though in fact the worst was soon over.

Below in steerage, there was no such enjoyment, as the passengers had to sit on the floor, and hold on, one to the other, while their possessions, pots, pans, trunks, tables and chairs, were breaking adrift and tumbling from side to side, and even over them.

Isabella lay down on her bunk and prayed silently.

But the end was in sight. On the twenty-first day since leaving Scotland, the "Land Ho!" call signalled the first sight of Cape Breton Island. There was a high, rocky shore, and little inlets leading to well-forested land. As the winds grew calmer, once the ship was in the shelter of the estuary, and with a channel to negotiate, her progress slowed, but Pictou was reached on the twenty-fourth day in the morning. As the town came into view, Isabella could see crowds on the waterfront and on the quay, for news of the ship's progress had preceded her, by the sort of bush telegraph employed by seafarers and those whose living depends upon it.

The *British King* sirened her approach, and the pilot came out to guide her in.

* * *

Isabella took a polite leave of the Captain, and Joanna a tearful one from her new-found sailor friend. Mr. Creighton busied himself with ensuring that all their baggage and bandboxes were assembled, ready to be carried ashore, and the gangway was soon positioned.

Helen Creighton clung to her cousin's arm as soon as she disembarked. "It is so good to see you," she enthused. "I am sure we are going to have a wonderful time. It is so brave of you to come all this way. I know you will like Pictou."

Isabella saw a small town, with houses terraced above the harbour on a gently sloping hillside. There was a bustling water-front, with fishing gear prominent upon it, and space for several ships like *The British King* to tie up. There seemed to be a chandler's shop, and was that the timber yard, with sheds on a second quay, where the Mortimer and Liddel business was based? She knew there were three rivers emptying their waters into the sea from the range of steeper hills in sight beyond the town.

David, having greeted his father, was now bowing over her hand, welcoming her to Pictou, and escorting her to a carriage and pair, which was intended to convey them to the house. The luggage was piled into a hand-cart to follow.

The steerage passengers had disembarked, but looked a little lost; some of them had been greeted by friends, but the Cruden group stood together looking uncertain, until a man of somewhat under medium height, and distinguished by a shock of reddish hair and a neatly-trimmed reddish beard, went up to them. She did not know it then, but this was Isabella's first glimpse of Alexander Thomson, the man whom she believed to be her chief creditor on Mortimer's List.

The little procession moved up the hill to the Creighton home, a neat pink-washed town house, fronting directly on to the street, with carriage-lamps on each side of the pedimented doorway.

"We're an upside-down house," chattered Helen. "Your bed-chamber and ours are up two flights of stairs, because we have the salon and the dining-room on the first floor, where there is space and the best sea-view, while the maids and the children have the ground-floor and the basement, and can easily get to the back-garden. I hope you will be comfortable.   There will be hot water brought up to you, as I'm sure you'd like to wash, and then, do join us in the morning-room, one floor down."

Isabella's bedchamber was comfortably furnished, with a vase of fresh flowers on a polished pine table by the window, which looked over the sea, and an easy chair from which to enjoy the view. A bed and wash-stand, a pier glass, and a large pine wardrobe completed the furnishings, and a fire-place currently stood empty with a screen before it, as the weather was warm. She used the pier glass to check her appearance. Still arrayed in the loathsome black, she felt a strong urge to add colour. Perhaps a lavender scarf, or even a pink one! No-one knew William here. She could lighten the mourning, a symbol of release from the old life, although her black dresses were far from worn out. Her luggage had not yet come up, so she washed her hands only, re-arranged her fichu and her hair, and went down to her hosts.

"We have arranged a welcome Soiree for Saturday," explained Helen. "There are so many people we want you to meet, and now that we have the piano, we thought a little music would be just the thing. Pictou has very little in the way of entertainment or culture, but David and I thought we should give a lead, and I know you were always famous at organising parties, so we will put our heads together, and give a good one! Besides, it's a famous way of knowing who's who at an early stage, and you never know, but someone may give a party back again, which we can go to! In fact, the MacFarlanes had almost decided to do so, the last time I heard."

When Isabella and Archibald had drunk some tea, and retailed their experiences on the journey, and she had arranged with David that he would see that her letters went back by the next ship, they explored the house together, and went to meet the children.

Chapter 4 - The Quarrel

Alexander Thomson's General Store was situated on the edge of the small town of Pictou, with a piece of rough ground in front of it, the more easily to accommodate the carts and traps which their owners would need to transport the heavier items of equipment. It was very much geared to the needs of immigrants, offering tools and equipment as well as bulk supplies of seed and animal feed, to see the livestock through the long, harsh winters. Other shops would supply day-to-day food and clothing, but Alexander carried a wide range of heavy-duty wear, and he sold things that were traded in for other goods, as well as imported via the ships that frequented Pictou Harbour.

His family had been among the earliest settlers in 1803 when Lord Selkirk had offered parcels of land to encourage immigrants, and Alexander had been sixteen when the family left Morayshire in Scotland. At first they went to Prince Edward Island, but eighteen months later his father had enough money to make a down payment on a farm in Digby, Nova Scotia, where he raised beef. William the Pioneer, now retired, but still hale and hearty at the age of 66, was a firm advocate of emigration for the Scottish people, and he worked unofficially as an emigration agent, helping new arrivals to get started, and sometimes selling them land. For some years now Alexander had had sole responsibility both for helping emigrants and running his store. As a result of his work and the fresh influxes of immigrants arriving from Scotland and elsewhere, the business was thriving, and he was on the verge of establishing a new venture in the buying and selling of land.

The mornings were busy, and two customers were already in the store when Isabella arrived, alone, for her business was confidential, and it would not be appropriate to discuss it in front of either Helen or her maid, Joanna.

"Duncan, offer the lady a chair," was Alexander's curt request to his somewhat vacant-looking assistant. This youth set a high stool for Isabella, dusting the seat with his sleeve, before she sat down.

Perched upon this, Isabella had leisure to look around her. She observed a man of less than medium height, dressed in a suit of roughly woven cloth, if the jacket hung on a hook behind him was his, and which he had replaced with a grey, shapeless but functional overall. She thought he might be the same man she had seen two nights ago at the harbour talking to the Cruden immigrants, but could not be sure. He had reddish hair, and a pencil propped behind his right ear. His manner was brisk and alert, and he had an easy familiarity with his customers, with one of whom he had been joking. To the other, he seemed to be giving advice, before writing the result of his conversation in a large, black ledger, which lay open on the counter. The store was crammed with all types of goods, but they were tidily disposed, and the shelves bore prices clearly marked in black ink. Eventually, when Isabella was becoming irritated with the long wait, which she was not used to, both customers left, and the shop owner turned to greet her.

"Mrs. Liddel?" he enquired. "I believe you are staying with Mrs. Creighton and arrived by *The British King* on Tuesday."

She acknowledged this and asked if they could be private, as she had something to discuss with him.

"Assuredly. Duncan, put the sign up and go and tidy up the warehouse."

Alexander's penetrating gaze was assessing Isabella as the youth left the store. She was obviously an upper-class lady in her fine black dress, with gloved hands, and a jewelled comb in her hair beneath the fashionable jet-trimmed bonnet. He suspected that she had never done a day's hard work in her life. He would hear what she had to say, but he was determined not to be out-faced by anyone, however grand she might think herself!

Isabella produced Mortimer's List and explained that she had been widowed two years ago, and left in very reduced circumstances, but had found that sums due to Edward Mortimer were still outstanding after her husband had bought out his business. She was here to pursue the sums due, chief of which was £1,000 owed by Alexander himself.

Alexander felt himself becoming so incensed, partly by her distantly haughty manner, and partly by the accusation that he owed money, that he found it difficult to say politely, "But I have paid Mortimer back years ago. Your list must be out of date."

"I believe not," Isabella said regally. "The Accountants could find no trace of re-payments."

"Well, they wouldn't necessarily. I paid him in cut timber, three huge loads, which were shipped direct to Scotland."

"Do you have receipts?"

Alexander could contain himself no longer and exploded into a furious rage. "I don't need receipts, Madam! My word is my bond, and always has been. When I did business with Edward Mortimer, who was a fine man and did much to help Pictou through its early years, we had a gentleman's agreement that I would pay him that way. It's what a lot of people do here. Clearing land and founding a new town is an expensive business. People need credit and capital to operate. I give credit to people myself, to Scots only, naturally. They pay back."

"Then perhaps you could look at my list, and see who else will pay back . . ." Even as she made the suggestion,, Isabella knew she had made a mistake. It seemed to make the man even more angry, if that were possible.

"Look at your list! Why should I?" he almost shouted. "Why should I help you dun poor people who may be customers and friends of mine, just to fund the life of a privileged Edinburgh lady?"

"I don't have a privileged Edinburgh lifestyle. I've had to give up my big house and all my servants and move away when William's business became insolvent." she defended herself clumsily.

"Of course!" he sneered, "Put your people out of work! Pay them a pittance anyway, but make sure you still have your silk dresses while they have nothing!"

"My decisions in Scotland have absolutely nothing to do with the matter," said Isabel haughtily, and putting on her icy tone to match, "It is debts from this country I am talking about."

Alexander's voice grew rougher also and more contemptuous, "If you had the slightest idea what you are talking about . . . do you know how cold and hungry and desperate people are when they arrive on these shores? Do you know how they have to work like navvies cutting down forests before they can even grow enough to eat? Do you know they need credit for their first spade, their first seeds, their first animals?"

"But debts must be honoured and paid back!" expostulated Isabella.

"Of course they must be paid back, but in something of use to the community. We don't treasure sovereigns here; we treasure people, and we help one another when we can."

"Oh, it's hopeless!" said Isabella, beginning to feel tears of injustice spring into her eyes, and plunging blindly towards the door, the stool falling over as her skirt swept it aside. She felt bitterly humiliated, and by a mere tradesman! It had cost her some determination and swallowing of pride before she had even visited the shop. She had never been addressed in such terms before. It was horrifying and humiliating!

Alexander unlocked the door to let her pass through, his face still thunderous. There was a customer waiting outside, to whom he was obliged to attend, which he did mechanically, having been shaken himself by the ferocity of his own attack.

Meanwhile Isabella could hardly see where she was going. She tripped and slowed her headlong flight, pausing in a porch a little distance away to find her handkerchief, mop her eyes, blow her nose, and compose herself. She was thus hidden from view, when Alexander opened the store door again to see what had happened to her. He wondered where she could have gone. He had made her cry, not a very gentlemanly thing to do. He began to regret his own conduct.

Because his own anger was rapidly evaporating, he acknowledged that he had been extremely rude, and to a lady who was a visitor to Pictou. She had traversed an ocean to obtain her rightful dues. His prejudices, Scottish touchiness, and the flaring of temper not uncommon in red-heads had carried him beyond the line of proper behaviour. She might have been haughty in her manner, but that did not excuse his own reaction. He must apologise and seek to mend his relationship with her, if that were possible, and the signs were not propitious.

Isabella had naturally poured out the story of her distress to the Creightons, who soothed her, and tried to make her feel better. They felt upset themselves at this rift with someone they respected.

Alexander's contrite note was carried by Duncan to the Creighton household later that afternoon. Isabella, now calmer, opened it, approved the square black handwriting, and read:

"Mr. Alexander Thomson presents his compliments to Mrs. Isabella Liddel and craves forgiveness for his abominable rudeness to her this morning. He apologises unreservedly."

"Very proper," said Mr. Creighton Senior, when this missive was handed to him to peruse.

Alexander had judged that formality would be more acceptable to a high-born lady than a simple, "I'm sorry." He was right.

Helen, who did not want her party compromised by the absence of a favoured guest, also thought that Alexander must be truly sorry, and she had never heard of him losing his temper like that before. Her husband, who felt that he should have briefed Isabella before this about people in Pictou, thought Isabella should accept the apology. Mr. Archibald went so far as to say that it would only serve to make people think her too high in the instep if she failed to respond.

Her own mortification also having subsided, Isabella, in her neat script, wrote:

"Mrs. Isabella Liddel thanks Mr. Alexander Thomson for his apology, which she is pleased to accept. She regrets that her tactlessness in broaching the subject of the conversation was the cause of the disagreement."

This was despatched to the General Store by messenger. Alexander received it with some satisfaction, and resolved to consult urgently with his father about the second stage of his plan, which was the re-establishment of friendly relations.

David Creighton remedied his earlier omission, and put his wife's cousin in possession of a few material facts before the Soiree.

"Isabella, the Thomsons are one of the oldest families in Pictou. William the Pioneer came over in 1803. He first went to Charlottetown, I think, and after a short while moved to Digby, where he raised beef.   Then in 1808, he sold his cattle to a Government official, but it turned out he had been dealing with an imposter, probably set on to him by the Scottish land agent, who had been responsible for raising his rent in the first place, and who was resentful of the success William had had. Other people were following him out here from Morayshire by then.   Because of the loss of his cattle, William was unable to meet the next payment on his farm, and it was re-possessed, and he ended up in great disgrace in a debtor's prison in Halifax.

By working all the hours God gave, his two sons, Alexander and Nathaniel, with some assistance from the younger brothers, cleared new land for another farm, and raised enough money for him to be released, and he re-established himself on his present farm in Pictou. He doesn't go out much now, because he's somewhat crippled with rheumatism, but he does want to meet you, and has asked if you would wait on him at Maple Tree Grove on Monday. You'll like him, Isabella. He has done a lot for the County, advises immigrants on jobs in local farms and business, and sells them allotments from his acres of wilderness land. He and Alexander are both strong advocates of emigration from Scotland. They believe it has brought Scots great freedoms, affluence and dignity, and William has always done what he could to help new arrivals get the best possible start.

In view of his father's problems, I can assure you that the very last thing Alexander would do is to allow a debt to be outstanding. I believe you may have seen Alexander meeting the boat on Monday. He wouldn't let any new arrivals languish with nowhere to go. Nathaniel does much the same in Cape Breton. Things are even worse, there, of course. The main town is very small, and there are no roads to the settlements, so everything has to go by boat. There are neither clergymen nor Churches, and Nathaniel acts as Lay Preacher."

"No Churches!" said Isabella, scandalised, "How do the people go on, for burials and christenings?"

"I don't quite know. I believe Nathaniel sets out on a sort of pilgrimage once or twice a year, and presumably he deals with it then, though of course burials won't wait, but he could hold a memorial service or something."

The conversation gave Isabella food for thought. The glimmering of an idea was beginning to form in her mind. She would certainly like to meet William the Pioneer, even if he was Alexander's father. She intimated that she would be willing to wait on him on Monday.

* * *

In the meantime, the Soiree proved a great success. About twenty people assembled, and feasted on a variety of buffet dishes, followed by creams and jellies in the first floor dining room, and then adjourned to the

Salon, when they sat on low chairs in a semi-circle round the esteemed piano.

Isabella extended two chilly fingers to Alexander when he arrived and greeted his hosts. He bowed in the approved manner, and passed through the reception area, but later sought her out, brought her a glass of ratafia, and said, "It is peace, then! Thank you for your note."

"I want to ask you about Cape Breton," said Isabella, suffering some embarrassment and changing the subject. "Is it true there are no Churches at all at any of the settlements?"

He replied that there were one or two small Roman Catholic Churches along the Western shore of Cape Breton, for example at Judique, but no Presbyterian Churches at all, and only an occasional service held in a log cabin at Mabou. Otherwise, there were no priests, no schools, and only his brother, Nathaniel , to support the people. "The trouble is that the people mostly only speak Gaelic, and it never seems to have been possible to get a Gaelic Minister to come out. The people are especially poor, too. There's nothing like the store I run, for instance, to give credit and supply tools. I think the people are very much sunk in their own low esteem, and exist in much the same state they were in their homeland, often the Western Isles, rather than improving their lot."

"You said something to me this morning, which struck home," pursued Isabella. "You said, "It must be paid back, but in something of use to the community." What did you mean?"

"Mrs. Liddel, I don't mean to preach at you again. I thought we were going to let bygones be bygones. I suggest you ask my father, when you meet him."

With that, and the exchange of a few further pleasantries, he moved away, and by the time the music started, had left the house, thereby missing a spirited rendering of a concerto by his hostess, and Isabella's party piece, when she played and sang a Shakespearean ballad.

* * *

On the following day, a great commotion arose in the harbour, which they could hear from the house. From her upstairs bedchamber window, Isabella could see people assembling on the quayside, and the masts of a tall ship approaching the anchorage. Helen suggested they go down and take a look at the incoming ship.

There was something splendid about the sight, not only the physical grandeur of the vessel with sails set, but the fact that she also had crossed the same ocean Isabella had crossed only a few days before. Hopefully she had had a similar lucky crossing, though they learned later that the storm which had rattled *The British King* had hit the *Thetis* rather harder, having built up to almost hurricane force and caught the ship on the Banks of Newfoundland, which was very bad luck. There were six large families emigrating from the Highlands and Islands, and a few single men. Most had relatives to meet them, which accounted for the 90 or so souls congregating in the harbour. The mood was jubilant and boisterous, except for one sad young couple, Ian and Margaret Campbell.

Ian's elderly father, James, had fallen ill on the voyage, and was now literally at death's door. Far too weak to be moved, Ian had stayed with him on board, while Margaret ran hither and thither, asking everyone if there was a Church of Scotland Minister who could administer a blessing. Pictou's Presbyterian Minister happened to be away on Church business, but Alexander Thomson, as a lay reader, offered his services to Margaret and went with her on board.

The crowd melted away, except for a few standing silently, waiting to see if anything happened. It was a short time only, before Alexander returned, sombre-faced, to say that James Campbell had just died. He had done what he could, and would now arrange for a coffin to be taken on to the ship.

Isabella was shocked. "Can I be of comfort to the poor woman?" she asked.

"It's her husband's father. They're together now, and a comfort to one another, I believe. Better leave them be."

"Why is there no Minister to bring comfort to the dying?" she exclaimed.

"Our Pictou Minister is away on Church business. I can only say that it's lucky the *Thetis* did not arrive at Cape Breton!" responded Alexander. "As I told you yesterday, there isn't a proper Church nor Minister on the whole island – permanently!"

Since she had heard the same thing from David Creighton, Isabella knew it to be true, and a second visitation of her idea stirred again in her mind.

Chapter 5 - William the Pioneer

"So you've quarrelled with my son and heir, have ye, lassie?" was William the Pioneer's first greeting to Isabella, when she arrived by David's carriage at the Maple Tree Grove farm on Monday.

Isabella blushed, and felt the colour suffuse her cheeks. She would not be disconcerted. "We had a disagreement," she acknowledged. "Perhaps I was too abrupt."

"Ye got him on the raw, nae dout! It ain't good for a merchant to have a jailbird for a father, without being accused of welshing on a debt hisself!"

Isabella was non-plussed again. Was this embarrassing old man referring to his being in jail? As if he read her thoughts, William's next words confirmed them. "Aye, I spent eighteen long months in the Halifax Penitentiary when things went sour eighteen years ago. But the boys got me out, and I made another fortune, so I'm not complaining."

He surveyed the wonderful view from his hill-top farmhouse. "I believe in living high," he said. "Up here, I'm like the stag – monarch of all the glens!"

"It's a magnificent view," agreed Isabella. From the window she could see a close circle of small trees, presumably the maples which gave the farm its name. On either side were meadows, grazed by cattle, with a rim of dark conifers where the forest closed in again. The ground sloped away in front of the house, and there was a wide panorama of sea and coastline. She also noted and commented with admiration on the room's cast iron fireplace, which was adorned with the Scottish thistle.

"Aye," he said. "We brought those with us in 1803 – two of them --and all our brass candlesticks! Bella wouldn't leave them behind. But the boy's honest through and through," went on the old man. "If he says he paid back, he paid back. I brought them all up as God-fearing Presbyterians. You can trust his every word."

"So David Creighton confirms," said Isabella, "And in truth, I believe it was all a mistake, and I'm extremely sorry I didn't know that when I spoke to your son. Apparently, he paid his last consignment of timber to Mortimer, only a few weeks before his death, and the figures never got back to Scotland. It makes me very hesitant to approach the other names, in case some of them paid back too."

"Ye should'na have to," said the old man. "Get a man to do the dirty work. Nay, let me take a look at yr list."

Isabella produced Mortimer's List, which was permanently tucked in her reticule, and William perched a pair of rimless spectacles on his nose, and ran his finger down it.

"Galbraith!" he said, "Now he mun pay ye. He's rich as Croesus with that great saw-mill working night and day. He's £480, I see, plus a couple of year's interest. And Tammy McGilvray --- he's come good. It's fair water on his land and the crops have prospered the last two years, besides what he makes from the fishing . . . leave it with me!"

"No, no, Sir, you must not," stammered Isabella.

"I shan't do much of it myself," admitted William, "but I'm still something of a power in the land, and I'll put the word out ye're to be paid. It will work with

Galbraith, or if not, Alexander will get it. He could find enough on Master Galbraith to put <u>him</u> in jail, nae dout! Ye won't get it all, of course. Some of the little 'uns can't raise it even yet, but they might, given a year or two."

"Sir, you must not ask Alexander. It would not be fitting!"

"Alexander will do as he's bid," growled the family patriarch. "Anyway, he's sorry he flew at ye, and he needs to make that good. Has he said so?"

"Yes, he wrote, and we met at Helen's Soiree. He apologised for his ill temper."

"So I should think," said William. "And ye a lady come all this way from Bonnie Scotland to see us! Ye live in Edinburgh, they say."

"Indeed I do, Sir, though it is only recently that I have rented a small home there. When I was married, I lived in Glasgow with my husband, William Liddel."

"Liddel and Mortimer have done well for Pictou. I'm reet sorry that they've both passed away. They were both youngish men. Ye've been left with debts, mebbe?"

"I owe nothing now, but the business was declared insolvent and there was nothing left," said Isabella. "However, I have a small private income to live on, but I have had to cut down on my way of living, and I see no reason to leave debts which are due to me uncollected, if I can clear the matter up."

"Ye shouldna have to worry yr pretty head with business matters. Couldn't your lawyer see to it?"

"Mr. Briggs didn't seem to see there was an urgency about it – and to be frank, I doubted whether he would deal with it at all."

"Haven't you any family to see to it?"

This was getting personal. Isabella liked the old man. It was true that his direct manner was disconcerting, but there was kindliness in his face. His whiskers were white now, where once they might have been red like his son's. His eyes were piercing, as if they saw through the surface into the very soul. They were overhung by heavy lids and bushy brows, while the white hair had receded, leaving a high domed forehead, a little lined, but impressive. Some men age well, and William the Pioneer was one of those. The power that once must have filled his large frame was slipping away, for he stooped now and found it painful to rise, but the mental force was still strong. Isabella was not sure she liked his inquisition. She hesitated, and William sensed this and immediately changed the subject.

"Now I believe you've got a fancy to see Cape Breton," he said.

"I understand that they have no Churches nor Ministers to see to their needs," responded Isabella.

"Tha's reet! It's the Gaelic, of course. They're mostly puir folk from the Isles and Gaelic speakers with little English. They'd have to have a Gaelic-speaking preacher, and they'd have to have him paid for in advance until the settlements can raise the money to keep him."

"I believe I might be able to help," Isabella offered. "I could start a Ladies' Aid in Edinburgh with that specific object, and if some of the debtors here could pay in kind, provide timber or stone to build a Church, well, that would be a beginning."

"Ye'd need a deep begging bowl, lassie. These projects don't come cheap. Why don't you pay the island a visit to see for yourself what you're taking on?"

She saw the sense in this argument. "How would I get there?"

"There's a small local coastal packet, sailing three times a week. After that it's a row-boat and walk. Alexander can take you!"

"No. I can't have that," she demurred. "Alexander's busy."

"Well, he should take a holiday! He always goes once in the Summer to help Nathaniel on his rounds. So they can both take you! Any other problems?"

"You'd fix them if I had!" laughed Isabella, swept along on the tide of the old man's enthusiasm.

"Ye'll need shoes. You can't wear those pretty slippers on Cape Breton's rocks! Get Alexander to find you a pair of boy's boots."

Isabella thought it time for her to change the subject. Alexander seemed to be cropping up at every sentence end. "Sir, David Creighton says you went first to Digby, Nova Scotia, and set up an Agricultural Society there. What is that, if you please?"

William the Pioneer was pleased at her interest. "I won't bore you with the detail," he said, "but all over England and in Scotland too, there were new ideas in farming being introduced. Ye'll have heard of Coke of Norfolk, mebbe, or Jethro Tull? They had ideas about land drainage, and drilling the seed, instead of scattering it, and sowing in winter, to bring the crops on earlier. Well, we have to be careful about winter crops here because the winter is so long and the summer so short, and very little spring, but through the Agricultural Society we could promote some new ideas."

"I suppose poor crofters had not enough knowledge to experiment."

"True. That's why so many of them stay puir. When Lord Selkirk first got me out here, he knew I could bring experience to bear to show the backwoodsmen what it was possible to do. We did well enough in Nova Scotia and P.E.I, but I daresay ye'll find Cape Breton very backward."

"Alexander says the repayment of the loans must put something back into the community. What is it he means, do you think?"

William the Pioneer paused for thought. "It's like the seed-corn, I think. Ye mun ne'er eat the seed-corn. Ye mun plough the land, and sow the seed, and then ye'll get eating corn, 'n more seed-corn, and straw to make beds for the animals an'all. So a loan or credit mun be paid back, but the interest and the profits mun go to the community to provide more growth, an' then everyone gets richer. At least I think that's what he means. He's quite a thinker is our Alex."

"I was surprised to see him working in the store."

"Och, he's built up a fine business there. He's skimped and saved, living behind the shop and staying single, and he's going into land purchase, the noo! I often wonder whether it would have turned out so well if he'd gone to St Andrews, as we meant him to."

"The University?" queried Isabella, a little surprised, for it was the sons of the aristocracy who tended to patronise such higher education establishments.

"The very same! He had the brain, but we lacked the siller. I was suddenly faced with a rent increase from Patrick Younger, who was Lord Moray's farm manager in 1803, and I was alive to any opening when Lord Selkirk offered to let me supervise some of his farms at Belfast in Prince Edward Island. So I came out here to an assured start, and Alexander came with me as the eldest. Nathaniel finished his schooling and came out later too, and glad I was to have the both of them when the sky caved in. It put them both back off course a good five years getting me out of trouble, and I owe them a lot."

A tinkling bell sounded in another part of the house. "Ye'll stay for evening prayers," suggested the old man. "And ye'll meet Bella and some of the other children – those that aren't married, that is. We had seven altogether. After that we'll have supper."

"I'll stay for prayers, but not for supper," decided Isabella. "Helen will be expecting me back, and I still have their carriage."

She talked to Bella after the simple Presbyterian prayer service, attended by servants and family. "We have nearly the same name," said the older lady. "I was baptised Isabel, but everyone began to call me Bella." Isabella sympathised, and said she hated to be called by a shortened name.

"Aye, Alexander is just the same. He wouldn't answer to Alex, even as quite a little boy. It was lovely to have him to see us yesterday. He's very busy you know, with the ships and the store, and though we see more of him in the winter, it's only an occasional visit at this time of year."

Strange, thought Isabella! William the Pioneer had said nothing about seeing Alexander! But, of course, he had known about the quarrel, so he must have done!

The suspicion occurred to her that this visit to Cape Breton had been sorted out between the two men. No matter, it was what she wanted to do.

* * *

The next day Isabella visited Alexander's General Store again, to enquire when he was intending to go to Cape Breton, and whether he had any boys' boots in stock which might fit her and Joanna. Alexander suggested leaving on the following Monday, and they were likely to be away a week, but flatly refused to take Joanna too. "The boat won't hold more than three," he said; "two of us to row and one passenger. I couldn't take the weight of another person, anyway. And travel light if you're coming. One piece of luggage only!"

It was not very gracious, Isabella thought, but William the Pioneer had obviously not thought she could want a maid. It was only her own afterthought that had suggested it. She asked about the boots, and was shown a couple of pairs. "That's all we have, but they'll probably do." They were exceedingly ugly, and would probably be extremely uncomfortable. However, for walking on rough terrain, they would undoubtedly be better than her town shoes. "I'll take a pair," she decided, and thought she'd better purchase some socks too.

He arranged to fetch her from the Creightons, and escort her to the coastal packet on Monday morning. In the meantime, he had an article about the island, published by the Pictou Gazette, which he would lend her, so that she would be in some way prepared. "It won't be a picnic," he warned. "You're pioneering now!"

"And bring some lotion or ointment," he added, as he ushered her out of the doors, this time holding them open and offering his hand. "The black flies will be fierce!"

She asked Helen later what she should take as presents, presuming they would be staying at people's homes for the night. "Soap, perhaps," suggested Helen, "or candles or linen. I daresay they'd be glad of anything." So they went shopping to see what Pictou could offer Cape Breton, and found a good many little necessities which they thought would be welcome.

* * *

Isabella had also asked David Creighton to take her down to the Stone House and the Mortimer/Liddel wharves in the Harbour. She would be interested to see the property, which she should have inherited as the successful arm of her husband's business.

He readily agreed, and they walked down the hill on Thursday morning, past the passenger terminal to the Commercial Dock.

Hoists were working busily, swinging bales of timber into the holds of two ships. Stevedores were guiding and stacking the wood in the holds, securing it with rope and tackle so that the load would not shift on the voyage.

There was much shouting and continual bustle, as carts with more loads of timber kept arriving to check in at the small office, were directed to the weighing point, and had their loads recorded. Isabella asked for Bruce Cameron and an unmistakably Scottish figure emerged to greet her; he had the red hair of the Scot, too, and sported a tartan waistcoat.

"Mrs. Liddel! I heard you were in Pictou. Welcome to the wharf!"

"Are these ships bound for Scotland?" Isabella wanted to know.

"Indeed, yes. They're both Glasgow-bound tomorrow and the day after for the Liddel Wharf as it used to be before your husband died. We have to complete loading, and then they have to be provisioned, and any lighter cargo and passengers picked up. Then we have a Leith ship and a Dundee ship due as soon as these two have moved out."

"You're very busy then?"

"We never stop. May I just say how sorry we were to lose Mr. Liddel two years back. I did write at the time, but we all offer our sympathy."

Isabella warmed to the man. He was so jolly and competent and straightforward.

"That's very good of you," she said. "I remember your letter. It was a great shock at the time, and there were so many financial problems. I know the wharves had to be sold. Who owns them now?"

"Well," he said. "We were all upset and concerned that they might fall into the wrong hands. So we formed a company of local business people who put up the money to buy them. We paid slightly over the asking price to make sure we got the business. The town depends on this trade. The Company calls itself the Pictou Timber Progressive, the PTP. I was appointed their Manager, and I'm a shareholder too, as are you, Mr. Creighton, I believe. Mind you, Ma'am, we have no complaints about Mr. Liddel, or Mr. Mortimer before him. They both did their best for the town, but we couldn't afford for someone else to come in and raise their prices at our expense."

David confirmed that he held shares in the company, as did most other prosperous persons in the Town, including the Thomsons.

"Shall I take you round the Stone House?" offered Bruce Cameron. "We bought that too to be our Head Office and warehouse."

They entered the old building, built of warm, red stone, and mounted a wide staircase from the lower warehouse section to the Upper Floor.

"When Mr. Liddel came over, this was his office, and this was his chair," said Mr. Cameron, ushering her into a large, light, square room overlooking the waterfront. On the wall facing the windows, William's portrait hung. Its painted eyes seemed to lock on to hers, and wherever she stood in the room, they seemed to survey her in an approving way, as if glad to see her in Pictou. She remembered the picture being painted. It had been a good likeness and William had been pleased with it. The other portrait seemed to be of Edward Mortimer, a companion piece.

"I'm glad you've kept them there," she said.

"They'll always be there, Ma'am. They're part of the history of this company and the history of our Town."

Isabella was glad she had come. In a way she also felt part of Pictou, knowing that its prosperity had so depended on these two Scotsmen, and their contribution continued to be acknowledged so strongly.

She felt tears fill her eyes, and hastily made her farewells before sentiment overwhelmed her.

Jean Lucas

"Do you think there are any books in your Library about Pictou?" she asked David as they walked up the hill. "I should so much like to understand more about the town."

Chapter 6 - Cape Breton

Alexander and Isabella were met at Mabou Quayside in the late afternoon, after a day on the bustling little packet boat, by his brother, Nathaniel, a slightly taller and more blond edition of the Thomson family. A very large canvas bag, Alexander's knapsack, and Isabella's small cloak-bag comprised their luggage, the canvas bag being deposited in the Harbourmaster's office, to be collected again the following day.

They walked – a distance of nearly two miles – to the farmhouse home of Nathaniel and his wife, Minette, a pretty dark-haired lady of French origin, who had already produced two pert little dark-haired boys, and whose third child was in the offing.

The little boys danced round their Uncle, expecting a present, and were not disappointed, Alexander teasing them until he eventually undid the straps of the knapsack and gave them two wooden toys.

The house was single-storey clapboard, an advanced design for those times, and Isabella learned that the components had all been carried from Pictou, and assembled by Nathaniel and his brothers on the spot. It consisted of two spacious rooms, one the sleeping quarters and the other a living area with open fireplace, huge wooden table, chairs, stools and a dresser.

"You can share my bed," generously offered Minette. We will have the children with us, of course, and the boys can make themselves comfortable in here."

Isabella could not remember sharing a bed with a stranger in her life, not even her sisters, and her husband had used his dressing-room as often as not, but she assured her hostess that she was sure she would be very comfortable. The article on Cape Breton that Alexander had lent her had referred to the Gaelic settlers usually occupying one room cabins, built of rough-hewn timber, with a wood fire and a primitive chimney through which the smoke could escape. However, pioneering required sacrifice. Glasgow seemed suddenly sophisticated in its standards, even artificial, perhaps. Here people were warm and welcoming, simple in their habits, owning little, but willing to share what they had. There was no point in standing on ceremony; she had to adapt, be grateful, and give back equal warmth.

"Eat a hearty breakfast," advised Alexander, the following morning, "As we'll get nothing else till tomorrow evening."

Isabella took the advice, for the buckwheat cakes and fresh milk and butter were very good, but Minette pressed a small packet into her hand before they set off, saying it would be a tasty nuncheon for the three of them. She would expect them in a few days' time, and in the meantime was going to teach the elder boy the arts of milking. The child looked barely five, but was obviously keen to try and regarded it as a treat.

They walked back to the harbour, collected the canvas bag, and transferred themselves to a small rowing boat for the local trips to the settlements. The two men had donned shorts of a military cut and bush shirts, with stetson-like hats, acquired last year from a pedlar visiting Pictou, Alexander said. He had thought them just the thing for their annual expedition.

Isabella had judged a long-sleeved white cotton blouse with a high, frilled neckline, and her long black skirt suitable, and had prepared for sea breezes with a light scarf tied round her head. She hoped it wouldn't rain. There was indeed a parasol in the cloak-bag, but it would look ridiculous!

Once she was settled on a cushion in the bows, the boy's boots were discarded, and she prepared to enjoy her trip. Alexander took the first pair of oars, with Nathaniel behind him. They rowed smoothly and firmly, and in practised harmony, and the boat literally sped through the waves.

She understood that they were aiming for the Gut of Canso, which was some 80 miles distant, and once out of the harbour they turned West and South-West. There were two stopping places en route, at Judique and Ship Harbour, places where Nathaniel knew there were friends to accommodate them for the night. Judique had been first settled by the French, who were in turn driven out by the British in the mid eighteenth century, and then from 1790 the Gaelic-speaking Highlanders and Islanders, many of whom were Roman Catholics, had settled. The later group, living nearer the coast, were Presbyterians, he thought, from the Isle of Lewis.

The sun was hot. They did not converse. Isabella looked about her, but the coast-line was rather dull, with forests down to the cliff-edge, a few rocky outcrops, a few sea-birds, and that was all. She looked instead at Alexander. They were sitting very close, their knees almost touching. She tried leaning back, but that was no better. She became conscious of a strong physical current between them.

With his sleeves rolled up, she could see powerful muscles working in Alexander's forearms, their downy red hair bright in the sunshine. Sweat was dripping from his forehead. She rummaged in her cloak-bag and passed him a face towel. He rested his oars, quickly used it, and gave her a word of thanks and a sudden smile.

Isabella reflected that it was the very first time she had seen him smile --- a normally dour face transformed by the grin. Her heart beat a little more rapidly. She wanted to look away, but could not, her senses overpowered by the realisation that this man could stir her emotions to a powerful degree.

For his part, bending again to the oars, Alexander's eyes were focussed on Isabella's slender ankles and grey-stockinged feet. She had moved back, but that merely dangled the feet even more tantalisingly in front of him. He wanted to hold them, caress them, tickle them, feel them twist and wriggle in his hands. It was ridiculous! He was not even attracted to her – and yet he was. She looked younger, more vulnerable, yes, prettier in the white and black. He might have to carry her to the shore. The prospect pleased him. His breath came a little faster – not that anyone would notice, for he was already breathing hard from the exertion of rowing.

Isabella had at last wrenched her gaze away. How would they get to the shore? The men had sensibly come bare-legged, presumably to leap out of the boat and haul it in. Perhaps there would be a jetty, or one of them would have to carry her. She felt a sense of pleasurable anticipation -- and then a shiver of revulsion. How could she, a mature widow who was to devote her life to good works, be so disturbed by a man, not of her class, a man she didn't even like!

Alexander noted the shiver. "You can't be cold," he said.

"No, no. A goose walked over my grave!"
He laughed at the old saying, but didn't believe a word of it. Was she blushing?

Isabella had felt the colour surge into her cheeks. She bent her head to hide the tell-tale stain, and felt in the bag again, this time offering him a drink. He shook his head. She liked the laugh. People were different when they laughed. Certainly different from when they were in a towering rage.

"Have you truly forgiven me?" It seemed as though he was reading her thoughts.

"Yes, of course. It's behind us. I don't want to think of it ever again!"

"Good!" The simple syllable established a new relationship, a companionship on offer – nothing more.

But it was something more. As they left the boat – there was a small jetty to which a couple of other boats were tied - and began the long climb up a rocky path to the settlement, Alexander went first, and put out a hand now and then to grasp hers and help her up to the next more level stage. Then the hand needed to support her elbow as the boy's boots failed to find a footing, and eventually her waist at a particular fissure in the path. Nathaniel was a few steps behind with the cloak-bag. But if the arm round her waist lingered a fraction too long, the sense of its pressure remained with her much, much longer than that.

It was a relief – and yet not a relief – when they reached the first cabin, and Alexander spoke to a woman in Gaelic, drawing Isabella forward to be introduced.

"I'm leaving you with Mary," he said. "She has a little English. We'll go on further until we find what arrangements have been made, and then I'll come back."

* * *

By next morning the magic had totally disappeared. Isabella had spent a wakeful night in Mary's cabin, her mind a jumble of new experiences – and emotions! In the morning, she prayed vehemently to be restored to calmness, to her duty and vocation.

She took so long, and Alexander was so impatient to be off, that he became irritated by what he suspected were her devotions, and consulted his time-piece ostentatiously when she appeared. He had cut and fashioned a stout stick to assist her on the downward trek, and made sure Nathaniel took the first pair of oars on the next and subsequent stages of their journey, with a muttered comment that his weight was more effective at the stern.

Isabella didn't believe a word of it, but honoured him for a wise decision.

It was hot again, but the little black flies which had been so troublesome on land the previous evening, seemingly attracted by the white blouse, were nowhere to be seen.

Nathaniel had discarded the bush shirt in favour of a singlet. Even so, the pace they kept up made him perspire furiously.

"We do it like this," he explained, "because we get the rowing over in the cooler part of the day, and then we get to talk to people in the afternoon, and take a service in the evening. Did you enjoy yesterday's wedding?"

"It was unexpected and unusual. I was surprised that someone not a full Minister could perform the ceremony."

"Oh, I have the Government licence to do civil marriages, and register births and deaths in this part of Cape Breton. They pay me a pittance, but it all helps. There's another chap over in Sydney Harbour who does that side of the island. We don't do many weddings," he went on, "but those two came over as teenagers, and it's been expected they'd hitch up. There's really no-one else for them!"

"Mary was telling me they'd all had a building "bee" to make them a cabin, and then a sewing bee to stitch the blanket pieces and the quilted pieces together, and the bride has been collecting goose down and feathers for a whole year. She said that every family had contributed a dish to the wedding feast."

"We did well from that. Oatcakes and smoked fish were pressed upon us, and I think we're going to have a break somewhere, and have a splendid lunch!"

The effort of talking and rowing was too much, and they fell silent for the rest of the journey. When they stopped after a couple of hours, they pulled up on to the beach in a sandy cove. This time Isabella did have to be carried ashore, but Nathaniel was deputed to fulfil this task.

Isabella had admired the community spirit, which had led the Judique Presbyterians to pull together for the wedding, and took an early opportunity of asking Alexander if he thought they would do the same to build a Church.

"I know they want one," he said, "and I believe they would build it. What I doubt is whether the community is big enough to sustain it." Nathaniel also doubted it, and wondered whether they could join with a neighbouring "parish".

"Certainly to share a Minister they could, but the Minister would have to do the travelling, and there's at present only access by boat. However, a Church building would be a big step forward. It can be used for all sorts of things – harvest suppers, for instance. The people would provide the work, I believe, if we could supply wood."

"There's plenty of wood around," said Nathaniel.

"Yes, but no sawmill. You could build the bottom part with logs, but I believe you'd need proper timber for the roof."

After they had consumed the gifts of food, and taken a drink from their water-bottle, the men disappeared one by one into the forest, and Isabella began to consider where she could perform her own toilet. A large rocky outcrop seemed to offer the best cover, and she made her way to its shelter, returning barefoot, with her stockings rolled up into a ball in her hand.

"Going native?" quizzed Alexander.

"Why not?" she countered lightly. "There are no Edinburgh fuss-pots out here."

In truth, she had shed in less than a fortnight many of the in-built customs and manners, which had been bred into her. They were simply inappropriate and useless in this new society.

When they reached the boat's mooring, she bunched up her skirts and paddled out to it. The cool water soothed her feet, as well as washing them clean. Nathaniel lifted her up to the boat, and she settled once again in her seat.

She studied the younger brother. He was a taller, slighter figure than Alexander, with his colouring more a tawny blond. He was already very tanned from working in the fields, and his eyes, of the same brilliant blue, seemed to be set more deeply. His face was more lined, as he constantly screwed up his eyes against the bright sunlight.

When they landed at the next little jetty, Alexander handed her the stick, and also the cloak-bag. "You'll have to be your own porter, today," he said. "Nat and I have brought goods for the homesteads." So that was what was in the big canvas bag, which had accompanied them all the way from Pictou!

Nathaniel objected. "You can't do that," he said. "And anyway, I don't want to carry your scythes and axes! Leave them be, and someone can come down with a hand-cart in the morning."

Isabella appreciated his chivalry, for the cloak-bag was quite heavy. The brothers glared at one another for a moment before Alexander gave way. Isabella sensed it was not the usual outcome. He took the cloak-bag himself, but left her with the stick.

This little place was called Ship Harbour, although Isabella thought it would have to be a very small ship, which used the tiny jetty. Perhaps ships stood out in the bay and passengers and goods were rowed ashore.

As it happened, they had only gone a few hundred yards, when they met two youths coming down the path with a hand-cart. Word had obviously preceded them, and they were expected. Alexander turned back with the boys, and Nathaniel and Isabella tramped on.

"Did he tell you what he preached about last night?" asked Nathaniel.

"No – and I didn't understand a word."

"You wouldn't, as it was in Gaelic. It was all about temptation, and how to resist it. A good spiel!"

Although she had not understood it, Isabella had been impressed by the sermon. Alexander had spoken well, with a powerful, resonant voice, which echoed a little in the clearing between the woods. He had mounted a small stage, which the villagers had nailed together from lengths of wood, of which there was a plentiful supply. He had used gesture well, not too frequently, but punching home a point, and throwing both arms wide once or twice. She admired the delivery very much, and thought it contrasted well with some of the staid Churchmen back home.

* * *

Ship Harbour was almost a repeat performance of Judique, except that there was no wedding, only a joint Baptism of half-a-dozen infants up to the age of about three. Alexander spoke again, this time throwing in a few sentences in English, for her benefit. He referred to the Edinburgh Lady, who had come to see for herself life on Cape Breton, and how she might consider their needs for Churches and Clergy, and whether her Scots friends could help their far-flung community. There was a stir of interest and ripple of sounds of approval.

The axes and spades were apparently a provision for the next village undertaking, which was to clear a wide strip of forest to make a new field. They went to see the site. Already much of the undergrowth had been hacked away, and the brushwood stacked in big heaps to dry out, ready for burning. This left tall trees, mostly coniferous, which would need axe work and rope guidance to make them fall the right way. Once felled, they would be chained and dragged to an assembly point by two slow-moving, but powerful oxen, the only beasts most communities had to work with.

That left the stumps. For the smaller trees, the spades and pick-axes were needed to loosen the roots, with the oxen brought back to heave them out, if possible. Most of the bigger stumps were left to rot, and the surrounding ground worked and planted with potatoes, usually used as a first crop to cleanse the soil, or mangolds, which would feed the beasts. It was back-breaking work, and the pay-back might take some years, but the harrow could then cultivate the cleared ground, and more varied crops be sown.

This community had pigs and hens, so their diet was more varied. They had fresh water from a spring, and a brisk stream, which was carving its own path to the sea. The older men were in deep conversation with Alexander, presumably discussing the transport of the timber, which would help to pay for the project, and pay back the cost of the equipment, which he had advanced to them on credit. Isabella began to see how the local economy worked, and she was deeply impressed.

The women, said Nathaniel, were more concerned about the children. While back in Scotland Presbyterian schools were established to educate children in religion and the skills with which to read the Bible, few of the Cape Breton elders could read or write but they passionately wanted their children to be taught how to do so.

There was no school, and while no-one expected children to be in school in the summer, the winter would arrive in late September, or the first week in October. While they got some outdoor exercise, there were long, dark nights, and in the depths of the season it was too cold to be outdoors. They needed books, or play-things with a learning content.

Isabella took all this in. She herself was concerned with the spiritual needs, first and foremost. The basis of life was belief that there was a Being who had created the earth, from which man drew benefit, and whose rules for society needed to be obeyed. This was the very structure required by any community, and if this were in place, all else would follow.

She felt this simple theory somewhat wrecked when they reached River Inhabitants the next day. The place had no name, but was an extended settlement on the banks of a substantial river, which flowed into a bay round the next headland.

They had a tricky delta to negotiate with the boat, but eventually landed, and found their land journey much easier and flatter. There was an ox-cart to meet them, as the bush telegraph had indicated that a lady was in the party. Alexander suggested that Isabella should take the boat cushion, as the seat in the cart was likely to be hard. He walked beside her while Nathaniel went ahead, talking to the youth who had brought the cart down for them. It was easier walking with the cloak-bag and haversack also in the cart, but very slow!

The flies were worse by the river. It wound its way between the trees, but the path on one side of it was quite wide enough for the cart, and had obviously been maintained. The first settlement was poverty-stricken, the homes looking down-at-heel, the children dirty, the women slatternly. Everyone came out to give a greeting, and among the women were two who were probably native, members of a small Mic Mac Indian tribe.

Was there a tribe on Cape Breton? Isabella enquired of Alexander.

"No, I believe not. I think these come from the Mainland. Sometimes the younger men go lumbering to the summer camps to earn money. They may bring back a wife, a woman anyway; these women understand trapping and hunting in a way the Scots don't, so they are an asset in using furs and pelts."

"And they are accepted?"

"Oh, yes.　Language is a difficulty, of course."

"Are there fish in the river?"

"Plenty!　But the water this far down tends to be foul, as it's used as a drain as well. The better village is farther up than this, above the pollution, but probably the cause of it."

He left her at one point, to go into a humble, dishevelled hovel, at the invitation of a bedraggled female with her child.　He caught up with Isabella and the ox-cart up about a mile further on.　"Faugh!　It was disgusting!" he said.

"Why?"

"The woman cares nothing for the home, and that is unusual.　The man is a lazy good-for-nothing, who won't do a hand's turn.　He got used to idleness with a little poaching and illicit whisky distilling in the islands where they came from.　There are often tinkers, who scratch a bare living in the Scottish glens, eking out the potato harvest with a dash of sheep-stealing.　Now they live like animals; indeed the animals share the cabin, as there's no barn.　Without the will to work their existence is no better here than it was back home.　Instead of buckling to and improving their lot, they spend their time in laments and hankering for their homeland."

"But, what about the children?"

"They will be even worse, I fear.　Bad parenting produces worse children.　But I am afraid disease will overtake many of them before they reach adulthood."

"Is there nothing to be done about it?"

"Very little. The whole community here is sullen and discontented, arguing with one another instead of pulling together. Perhaps a resident Minister could help, but it would be an uphill struggle. There is a problem too in the way that, without a structured religion, there is a tendency to revert to paganism, even witchcraft."

Isabella was horrified. "But surely we are centuries away from that!"

"In the cities, of course. But in the country, people are so close to the elements that they tend to worship false gods if they don't get the true gospel. And Cape Breton is so backward and remote. However, you'll see the contrast when we get to the next place."

It was as he said. Four miles further upstream, they came upon a second village, but the clearings were extensive here, as the ground had been worked for years. The homes were neater, and one even had a flower garden, something she had not seen before, and she was delighted to know that this was where she was to stay.

"We're leaving you here for two nights," said Alexander. "I believe you have a headache, and I know you have blistered feet, and we will be walking ten miles tomorrow over the hill and down to the next valley, which is Canso. There's nothing there you haven't already seen, and so I think it will be better if you rest, and talk to people here; some of them speak some English."

Isabella acquiesced. Her face and hands were becoming tanned from the sun, but its heat was causing a thumping pain in her head, and she would be glad to lie down.

Alexander was concerned; he had argued with his father that it was not a suitable journey for a woman, but had been over-borne. William the Pioneer was possibly thinking that, if his own Bella had borne hardship uncomplainingly in the first decade of the century, then Isabella could cope with it too. He insisted that if the lady was to help Cape Breton, she must see it for herself. How else could she describe its needs when she got back home and sought to raise funds for it? This was a great opportunity to bring Presbyterianism to the people of the island. Alexander knew that this was what Isabella had in mind. What he did not know was whether she had the tenacity, the contacts, the ability to carry it out.

* * *

Isabella's hostess at the upper village of River Inhabitants was a lady with eight children, Elizabeth MacBride. Elizabeth was a veritable Viking of a woman, half a head taller than Alexander and towering above Isabella. Her hair, still predominantly golden, but peppered with grey, was caught up in a comb on top of her head, where a traditional cap was perched. Her cambric blouse, sleeves rolled up, was secured at the neck with what looked like a nappy pin, and her long, dark skirt was protected with a sackcloth apron, similarly fastened.

She smiled warmly at Isabella and, wiping her hands on the apron, gave a little bob of greeting. Isabella glanced round the room. Apparently the children slept in wooden bunks stacked two and two round the walls like so many shelves, and climbed upon a wooden stool to tuck themselves into the upper berths.

There was no husband to be seen, so Isabella was offered the family bed in a sort of alcove while Elizabeth busied herself at the open fire, stirring a meat and vegetable stew for the evening meal.

The atmosphere was warm and Isabella tired, and she soon fell fast asleep under the feather coverlet, getting up only in time to receive her plateful of "lobby" and a bannock of bread. Mercifully, her headache had gone.

She was amazed on going outside to find a huge congregation assembling, hungry for the Word. Alexander explained that they had not planned on visiting the Bras d'Or Lake settlements this trip, but that news had reached them somehow, and the settlements had come to them! Whole families had trekked many miles to River Inhabitants to take part in the service, bringing very small children with them. There might be one perched on the father's shoulders, and another cradled in the mother's arms, with a third or a fourth, clutching their hands and walking themselves. There was a natural slope, leading up from the river, and they ranged in settlement groups, sitting on the grass, quiet and expectant.

Isabella had been provided with a chair near the baptismal table, and watched as the baptisms took place. First, each family brought its children, mostly quiet and some sleeping, to be held out, given their names, touched with the Holy Water and blessed. Nathaniel performed the ceremony, while Alexander acted as scribe, writing all the details in the official Record. Often the exact birth-dates were not known, the month only being remembered. He assigned them a date anyway. Every child must have a birthday!

After the baptisms and prayers, Alexander spoke, again in Gaelic. It is a most musical language and the cadences rose and fell in a spell-binding way. She did not know what he said, though she picked up a reference to herself and her visit, and somehow she knew that the message was Hope. The audience was so moved that they began to applaud as he finished. Alexander stilled the applause with his uplifted hand, and began a prayer.

Isabella's eyes filled with tears.   She felt a tremendous surge of admiration that these two men should leave their store and farm at a busy time of the year, should travel such distances, should give such needed service with true eloquence, should offer such inspiration, show such devotion to their mission.   She took her own silent vow that the people, who had responded and made up this tremendous audience, should have the reward of churches of their own Faith, and Ministers to preach in them.

Isabella Liddel had found her Cause!

Chapter 7 - The Garden

The following day, having been urged by her hostess to rest, Isabella found a suitable spot for her stool, and put the parasol to use to shelter her face from the sun. She had no sketching block with her, or she would like to have attempted to picture the scene.

She noted that a small area of the river had been staked off, and this seemed to be the community's bathing pool, mothers and toddlers in the morning, children later. She thought of joining the mothers' group, but the idea of stripping naked, even to refresh her sticky body, did not appeal. She would persevere with the lavender water she had brought with her. No-one else had such inhibitions, and judging from the laughter, the bathing-pool was obviously a popular meeting and chattering-point. She did, however, venture to reach down from the bank to wash some of her underwear (usually Joanna's task), and leave the white, lace-trimmed garments to dry on a hot rock in the sun.

She went to explore the village. Most of the men were working in the small fields, with the boys, whose task seemed to be stone-picking, a monotonous job and a never-ending one, judging from the piles of stones at each field corner. The hay in one field was being cut by scythes and laid out to dry. The potatoes were in flower; the corn looked strong. There were the beginnings of prosperity here, unlike the lower village where apathy seemed to reign. One small field pastured a few animals. They were tethered to ensure that each ate only a limited amount, and would be moved the next day. A few people spoke to her; she smiled but could not reply if the greeting was in Gaelic.

She admired Elizabeth's flowers. In halting English the woman said she loved colours. They needed a lot of water. Most people didn't bother. The children fetched the water from the river. She saved the flower seeds to plant again next year.

Sure enough, about six o'clock, when the sun was dipping down behind the pines, the group of eight children lined up, in age order, each with two pails or containers. They marched to the river, the eldest supervising, and then walked back with the pails full of river water. Isabella took the saucepans of water from the youngest one, and joined the parade. Some water was for household use but the rest was carefully poured round the plants, which had been wilting, and were much refreshed by the drink. Then the children had their supper, Elizabeth told them an episode of a serial story she was making up as she went along, and all but the two eldest went to bed.

Isabella resolved to describe the little scene to Alexander. He might like it for a sermon. The flowers were the beauties of life, the pleasure beyond the mere practical, but they needed nurturing and watering well to flourish in difficult, barren soil. The scriptures were the water and nourishment to feed the souls of the people. She decided she could use the illustration herself if she talked to the ladies of Edinburgh, whether Alexander wanted to quote it or not.

The next morning Nathaniel and Alexander had returned by nine-thirty, having started their trek at seven, and Elizabeth prepared a "dish o' tay" for them. Isabella made her farewells and on impulse gave her cameo brooch to Elizabeth as a memento and replacement for the nappy-pin, together with thanks for her hospitality. The brothers sent Isabella ahead with the luggage behind the ambling ox, while they had a dip in the river, and said they would catch her up.

They wanted to make the return trip to Mabou in two days, with only one overnight stop at Long Point which could be reached in a couple of hours, but leaving a very long sea trip for the final day. Isabella wished she could help, and said so.

"Fiddlesticks," boasted Nathaniel, who wanted to get back to his farm and family. "We've gone further than that in a day."

"Isabella can help," suggested Alexander. "She can serenade us. Rowing is damned boring, and a tune will help."

Isabella could hardly refuse, but she little welcomed the idea. "I can only sing hymns," she said, trying, unsuccessfully, to deflect the suggestion.

"No, you can't. What about that piece I missed on Saturday?"

She acknowledged this, but said it was more suited to the drawing room than the open sea. He refused to countenance this excuse. "We'll have that as an hors d'oeuvre, and some sea shanties for the main course. Don't tell me you didn't have them at every concert on the ship coming over!"

She did manage to have a couple of serious conversations during the stop-over at Long Point. They discussed with Nathaniel the kind of Minister she should look for, as a first pioneering person for Cape Breton, and she asked Alexander, when she got him on his own, where he had learned his oratory, and his mastery of Gaelic.

"The language is natural. I spoke it with my cousins as a child in the Highlands, although English was more common in Morayshire, and one doesn't forget. As for the speaking, I think I always liked debating and declaiming at school. If we did a play or recitation, I was always in the forefront. In fact, I think I was in the forefront of most things, except learning!"

"Your father says you should have gone to St. Andrews."

"Yes, well, I might have done, but I didn't. I might have gone into politics, but I didn't. So you could say preaching is a natural extension of that. I only do it because it's needed. I don't have any vocation."

Any idea she might have had about his undertaking the Ministry himself was dissipated. "What is your vocation?" she asked instead.

"I don't know. I think I organise, and make things happen. I'm not really a businessman, because I don't worship money for its own sake. I just like to have enough to do useful things with it. Perhaps I'm a jack of all trades, and master of none."

"I think you're a master preacher."

"You can't tell! I spoke in Gaelic!"

"I can tell. It was very moving. It made up my mind for me that I really want to help provide a Ministry for Cape Breton. The sermon was about Hope, wasn't it?"
"That would be truly wonderful. But it would be a gigantic effort. And yes, the sermon was about Hope."

"I knew it! I am prepared to commit myself to Cape Breton. I want to talk to your father again about ways and means."

"I know he'll want to see you."

* * *

The visit to Long Point repeated the established process of the other visits, except that this time there were two burial places to be blessed, and two families to comfort. One of the men had been elderly, but the other was young. He had developed some affliction of the lungs, and despite the nursing care of his mother had passed away. His loss was deeply mourned, not only for himself, but because the family was the poorer in earning power through his loss. Both Alexander and Nathaniel spent time in consolation, while Isabella held the woman's hand and murmured sympathetically, but she would not be comforted, and the wailing and sobbing went on for hours, as was the way of the people of the Isles.

They left early in the morning, but there had been a change in the weather. The sun still shone, but a breeze had sprung up. It was much cooler, and Isabella needed to wrap her shawl closely round her.

After some urging, she sang *When daisies pied and violets blue*, from the Winter's Tale, and as an encore, *It was a lover and his lass*. She found she could sing to an audience of only two, and began to enjoy herself, letting the tune out with a will, as if to fill an auditorium. She needed to, for the sky, which was becoming overcast, was her only ceiling, and the breeze was carrying her words away.

"More, more," urged Nathaniel.

She wasn't sure if she could remember all the words, but she launched into *The Skye Boat Song*, with the brothers humming the chorus; then *Bobby Shaftoe*, from the repertoire of the sailors on *The British King*.

"We're in for a rain-storm," said Alexander, who had been watching the weather anxiously. Overhead the sky had turned a sombre grey, with only a small patch of blue left in the distance. The woods were almost black in the gathering gloom. "Better beach, and use the tarpaulin, I think."

Nathaniel assented, and they turned the boat towards a small patch of shingle under a cliff. Hardly had they pulled the boat out of the water, Isabella helping to drag it ashore, than the raindrops started. A big tarpaulin was stretched over the boat, and all three crouched on the bottom of the boat, with the tarpaulin stretched over them, and anchored with stones and a spike or two in case it blew away.

The rain was falling heavily now, beating noisily on the sheeting.

"Remember 1824?" asked Nathaniel of his brother.

"Do I not! We had a most unseasonable summer," explained Alexander to Isabella. "Although we had oilskins, we got soaked practically every day, and one storm was so bad, we had to beach, struggle to put the tarpaulin up, and huddle inside for a day and a night until the gale blew out." Alexander passed round a flask, from which Nathaniel drank, and passed it to Isabella.

"What's in it?" she asked suspiciously.

"Whisky! Do you good if you're chilled." She took the flask; she had never drunk from a bottle before, but then she had done many things in the last week she had never done before. She spluttered a little as the fiery liquid trickled down her throat, and wiped the rim before handing it back. She was warmer already in the confined space.

"The Scots and the Irish will set up a still as soon as there's grain growing," joked Nathaniel. "We're not short of the hard stuff, though the best comes over on the ships."

"I hope the gale blows out quickly today," said Isabella. "We haven't too much time, have we? And quite a way to go."

"I think this will only be a shower," Nathaniel prophesied optimistically. "I believe I saw it clearing behind the big cloud. We would perhaps have rowed through it on our own, but we can't have you drenched and catching cold. Tell us about your new house, Isabella."

Isabella described the pretty cottage she had found and its situation in Edinburgh, and said she was looking forward to seeing it again.

"Do you go back immediately?" asked Alexander. They had only been a week together, but the camaraderie between the three had become strong as they shared the privations and experiences.

"I must spend a little more time with Helen, but yes, I will ask David to book me a cabin on a ship going back in a week or so's time. I am anxious to start organising my fund-raising."

The beat of the rain seemed to be lessening. Nathaniel stuck his head out, and said, "It's passing. Five minutes or so, I reckon."

Isabella thought of Elizabeth's garden, and hoped that was being watered too. On the other hand, the cut hay would do better without any rain.

She described the garden, and the little parade of children whose task was to water it. "Subject for a sermon?" she asked Alexander. He agreed. "I would like to see gardens all over Cape Breton," she went on. "Perhaps I shall, one day."

"When the people have a little more leisure," he agreed. "Will you come back, do you think? I do hope you will."

"I think I must come and see all the Churches when they are built," she replied, gaily. "If I can brave the sea crossing."

They were able to resume the journey then. The passing storm had left a head-wind as its legacy, which would slow them down, and make rowing more arduous. Alexander checked his time-piece. They would be hard-pressed to complete the journey before nightfall.

Hours passed, and fortunately there was no more rain. They passed through the narrow strait that separated Port Hood Island from the mainland.

They had eaten the small amount of food they had brought with them, and there was no more. The men, who had been rowing for hours, were perforce adopting a slower pace. Despite more singing, they were tiring, she knew.

"It will be a moonlit landfall," said Nathaniel.

"How far to go?" she asked.

"Three, four miles."

Mercifully, the wind had eased at last, but she was still cold with the evening chill.

Alexander passed his flask round again.

She refused, thinking they needed it more than she did. She added a few more items of clothing round her shoulders and crouched lower in the boat. It had been an amazing journey, one she would remember always. She thought Edinburgh would seem tame after this. The pioneering effort of so many families, some successful, some not, was astonishing. They deserved all the support she could muster, and the Mother Country of Scotland should provide it. After all, it was the conditions there which were causing most emigrants to escape, whether voluntarily or from sheer economic necessity, or compulsion, as in the Islands. The Churches, she recognised, were also blame-worthy. They had made no real effort to send emissaries abroad, to see for themselves what was happening, as she had done. They had largely washed their hands of their people, except for local leaders like the pastor on *The British King* who had accompanied his flock.

When their boat crept eventually into Mabou Harbour, the daylight had almost gone, and the pine-clad hills looked black. The moon itself lurked behind a lacy film of almost transparent cloud. The lighthouse was aglow, and there was a pin-prick of light from an oil-lamp in the Harbour-Master's window. As the brothers wearily tied up, and they all mounted the seaweed-slippery harbour steps, hand in hand, he came out to greet them. "Left it a bit late, Master Nat, haven't you?" he said, and drew them indoors for a nightcap.

A retired sea-captain, ruddy of face and hospitable by nature, he bade them welcome and offered refreshment. Isabella thankfully accepted the strong brew from a brown earthenware teapot while the men downed ale from a similar jug. A kind of oatcake and jam were offered too. Phineas, a widower, claimed to be a dab hand with a skillet, but not at any other form of cooking. While they supped, he entertained them with one of his many sea-faring tales, this one featuring a ghostly barque bearing down on a lone fisherman as night was falling over the bay.

Isabella's eyelids were drooping from weariness, and Alexander, dog-tired himself, was nevertheless concerned enough to ask if she felt well enough to go on. She assented, but negotiated with the harbour-master to leave the cloak-bag with him, until they caught the packet boat in the morning. She could sleep in her petticoat tonight, rather than carry that pesky bag two miles to the farm!

They linked arms for mutual support as they left the Harbour, and embarked on the two-mile walk up from the bay, warmer now for the drinks they had consumed. Anyone looking out would have doubted the evidence of their own eyes, as two lay preachers, with a woman sandwiched between them, swung their way down the lane, singing *The Skye Boat Song* softly in harmony as they went.

* * *

Alexander and Isabella were back to catch the packet boat by 8 am, having wolfed virtually all the food in Minette's pantry, and leaving Nat to catch up on the milking.

Alexander had foreseen this last day's journey as a potentially difficult trip, for he had rarely been alone with Isabella since the first day, having interposed his brother between them. In the event, however, it was easier than he had expected. He had himself well in hand, and she was quite different, enthusing over the island and its people, planning her work in Edinburgh, and seeing him, he thought, as a partner in this enterprise.

When the packet drew clear of the harbour, Isabella produced the hated boy's boots from her cloak-bag, having resumed her own French slippers, and flung one of them out to sea. "I am so glad to see the last of you!" she cried. He took the other from her: "Pooh! That was nothing of a throw!" he said, and hurled the other in a curving arc astern. "There, we've deprived some poor boy of a good pair of boots."

They laughed. It reminded her of something she meant to ask. "Why do you employ that boy, Duncan? He's not really of much help, is he?"

"He fetches and carries. I actually employ him because no-one else will. He's a bit simple, and can be frightening if he gets in a fit – but luckily those are becoming less frequent. It's a problem here. If you can't work, you don't earn. If you don't earn, you don't eat. And he really comes with his mother. She is my stand-by if I have to go away. In fact, she's been minding the store this past week. Anything difficult has to be left, of course, but she's got a good memory, and she will remember to tell me, and they can serve the straightforward purchases."

"However," he went on, "I really will have to think about the future carefully. If I go into land purchase, and even perhaps into organising immigrants to come from Scotland, I'll be away much more frequently, and I'll either have to sell the store or put in a manager. I don't intend to be tied to it for ever."

Isabella picked up on the second point: "Organising immigrants from Scotland. What can you mean?"

"Well, haphazard immigration is not much of a success. It's hit or miss. Sometimes a success, but sometimes a miss and a mess, in that people are too isolated, and find they're little better off, starting from scratch with only the skills they know. Far better to come like the Cruden party from your ship, several families who are neighbours,with their Pastor. They have a ready-made group, and provided they can get the land, and a little capital, they will have no problem getting going. Better, for example, than poor Ian and Margaret Campbell from the later ship, having lost their father and left the rest of their family behind, who were then dependent on strangers."

"Did you help them?"

"Yes, of course. Father has leased them a patch of cleared land, and I've provided tools on credit. They'll have a little house up before the winter, I trust, and they'll be able to grow a few things before the end of the summer."

"The wind is pretty brisk," said Isabella. "I think I'll have to go below. Don't come if you'd rather stay on deck." He acquiesced in this arrangement. It was better so. He reflected on how much Isabella had changed in one short week. All the starchiness and hauteur were gone. She was a warm human being now. He hoped she would not revert, once she returned to her Edinburgh circle. He would miss her company. She was the one woman he had met with whom he could talk and match intelligence with intelligence. Strange how his own views had changed, too, since that disastrous first meeting.

On docking, he walked Isabella with her cloak-bag to the Creighton's home. There were cries of joy on seeing her safely back, and he was invited to return later for dinner, an offer readily accepted.

Isabella, meantime, luxuriated in the best bath she had ever had, with water constantly brought up the two flights of stairs by the faithful Joanna.

They recounted their adventures over dinner, laughing over the boat sing-song and the boy's boots, now consigned to the briny. David Creighton said he thought William the Pioneer had been busy, for several packets had arrived for her. Helen marvelled at the change in her cousin; she was relaxed, brown, amusing, light-hearted, enthusiastic, gay. She looked at Alexander too, more chatty, tanned, at ease with her father-in-law, but wary, she thought, of Isabella, though he did beg her to sing again after dinner, "that pretty song you sang in the boat." Her performance was animated, rather than stilted, which it had been at the Soiree.

Archibald Creighton broached the subject of their return. "Do you wish to come back with me?" he asked Isabella. "There's a ship due in next week, on which I intend to book passage. Helen wants you to stay longer, and perhaps you will, but if you want company on the voyage, I fear I have to go."

She did not hesitate. "Yes, I must go back. I have work to do."

* * *

The visit to see William the Pioneer was arranged for the Friday. David Creighton's carriage was lent for Isabella, and they picked up Alexander on the way. He complained that he had been busier than ever in the store, after the week away.

Bella and William Thomson greeted them both warmly. "And how were dear Nat and his family?" asked Bella, with grandmotherly concern.

"Very well. The boys are growing, and Minette was teaching Neil to help with the milking."

"She'd better be careful. One flick with a cow's tail would send him flying!"

They went into prayers, where servants and family were ranged reverently round the room. The table was covered with a lace cloth, with candles flickering in their brass candlesticks on either side of the big, black family Bible. There were readings and formal prayers, during which William gave thanks that his son and Mrs. Liddel had returned safely from their visit to Cape Breton. Isabella could understand the source of Alexander's eloquence and his convictions.

After supper, when Isabella recounted her impressions of the island, and the sing-song and the boy's boots were laughed over again, William, Alexander and Isabella withdrew to talk over the implications of the visit.

First, William produced Mortimer's List. Isabella thanked him for the reminders, which had produced the six packets she had received at the Creightons. He asked which they were, and said he understood Galbraith's banker's draft would be with her in the morning. "Several want to pay in kind," he said. "Shall we go through them?"

"Before we do that, Sir, I must tell you that I have quite decided that I must use the money to help build Churches on Cape Breton," said Isabella. "I am going to go back to Scotland, and will use my best endeavours to raise more money, so that a Minister can be employed to start a ministry on Cape Breton; then I shall carry on raising more money to provide more Ministers."

"Hold your horses, lassie," said William. "Ye go too fast for my poor brain. Alexander, what d'ye think of that for a scheme."

"I think Isabella has no need to be so generous, Sir. I believe, in any case, it is better for communities to put the effort in themselves – with help, of course."

"But we should use the money promised in kind over here," said Isabella. "Loads of timber and a litter of piglets are no use to me in Scotland!"

They laughed. "True, dear lady," said William. "But you will have expenses yourself. You cannot travel the length and breadth of Scotland raising money, and not have the wherewithal to pay for yr lodging or yr coach fare."

"Do not despise the timber," said Alexander. "It is a very valuable resource. We can build a log church, with pine trunks laid end to end on top of each other, cutting niches into them where the cross members will fit. And piglets grow into bacon."

"I believe a lot of the money can be raised in Edinburgh itself, Sir," said Isabella, "And I shall play off the needs of Cape Breton against some of the schemes the Glasgow Aid Society has embarked on, which I cannot think are wise. Of course, I am prepared to travel when need be, or send other people on my behalf. Letters will work, too, I believe."

"Aye, but the money from Mortimer's List is yours," insisted William. "I did not attempt to get it back for you on Cape Breton's behalf, but because I believe Scots should never welsh on their debts, and I will have no slur on the Scottish character."

"A solution, perhaps, Sir," suggested Alexander. "We could be the Trustees of Isabella's Nova Scotian monies, and turn the "In Kind" payments to good use, while the cash should be remitted to her in Scotland, as it becomes available. We may add interest too if the debt is outstanding too long."

"Like the seed corn!" Isabella liked the concept. "Eat some, sow some, and use the chaff for bedding."

"Exactly like the seed corn; put something back into the community." Alexander agreed. "It will be cheaper too. If we get timber, it can be processed here, and shipped to Cape Breton for roofing your Churches. The local people should provide the labour as their contribution to their own benefit. You will provide the Gaelic-speaking Clergy to minister through the Churches. Nat and Father and I will administer the operation and collect the monies on your behalf. It is a partnership."

"I knew he would find an answer," said Isabella, "Your son, Sir, is a very clever man."

When they had gone, William discussed the matter with his wife. "I'd got at the back of my mind the idea that a week in feminine company would do Alexander no harm," he said. "What think you?"

"I think they like one another," said Bella slowly, "but it is not very practical. She will be in Scotland; he is over here. Besides, say what you might, there's a huge social difference."

"Social differences may matter in Scotland. They don't here. Anyway, I think it did him good. He'd got too set in his ways, and I don't want him a confirmed bachelor."

"Nat's providing the next generation, so that's taken care of," said Mrs. Thomson. "I reckon he can do as he pleases."

"And he probably will!"

Book II - 1826 - 1827

Chapter 8 - Edinburgh Again

The *Thetis* had returned to Pictou, after collecting a consignment of timber further up the coast, and Archibald Creighton and Isabella booked their passage on her. She was loading up even more timber at Pictou, and it looked like being a slow crossing as she was heavily laden.

Alexander determined not to see Isabella off. He preferred to leave the hand-waving to Helen, but he waited on Isabella for a morning visit the day before she left.

"I'll write and report progress," she said. "I am so anxious to get started."

"Will you do something for me?" he asked. "I have been thinking for some time that I am becoming out of touch with what is happening in Scotland, and any articles which you could send me from The Scotsman or any other Edinburgh papers would be very useful, particularly anything to do with emigration."

"Of course, I will," she responded. "But correspondence will be delayed during the winter, I presume."

"There are no passages after October, usually until April. The ice will close in."

"I'll try and write before then," she promised. "There will be a letter for Helen as soon as I land, of course to say that I've arrived."

"I'll keep you advised of what monies have come in from your list. I don't know how long it may be before we meet again, but I want to say how privileged I feel to have met you, Isabella, and how sorry I am that you must leave so soon."

The words were formal, but the intent look that accompanied them was not. Alexander's eyes were focussed on Isabella's face, striving to drink in every detail that he might remember her by. He could not tell when, if ever, he would see her again. She was also affected by the moment, but replied, as lightly as she could, "And I am so grateful to you for introducing me to Cape Breton, and showing me what I must do with my life."

They shook hands briefly, and he raised her right hand to his lips before turning abruptly and clattering down the stairs to the front door. She heard it close sharply and went to the window to watch him walk quickly down the street. He did not look back.

Helen said, "He is a really good man, Isabella. Do you like him better now?"

"I like him very well, and I like his father very well too. They have been really helpful to me."

This was not quite what Helen meant, but she realised there were no confidences to be offered, and let the subject drop.

* * *

All went well for the first part of the journey. Isabella had leisure to write a diary of their progress for Helen, and to plan various schemes for starting an Edinburgh Ladies' Association, under the general auspices of the Glasgow North America Colonial Society. The sketching block was put to good use also, as she found subjects in the seabirds, the sailing ships which passed them, and even some members of the crew. She made friends with Captain John Smith, the regular Captain of the ship, and they discussed the routes, the weather to be expected, the problems of the emigrants, including the unfortunate Ian and Margaret Campbell.

Captain Smith knew Alexander of course. His cargo often included packing cases of equipment destined for him, and he had in his cabin business letters from Alexander ordering supplies from merchants in Dundee. Isabella explained that her own purchase of the boy's boots from Alexander's store had been less than successful, and found their way to a watery grave. Captain Smith had not been on Cape Breton, passing always to the west of it on his way to Pictou, but he listened with interest to Isabella's descriptions of the island, its settlers, and its deficiencies in religious observance. Like most sea captains, who pitted their brains and their ships against the elements, he was of a religious persuasion himself.

The end of the voyage was less tranquil. Storms were battering the North of Scotland, and Isabella and Joanna were ill once more. Even Archibald Creighton said it was the worst weather he had known, and retreated to his bunk. The ship, weighed down with its timber load, battled its way through, though they were in sight of perilous rocks and treacherous islands most of the way. A shipwreck would have been a disaster, for the people of Cape Breton as well as herself, Isabella thought. Luckily, they had an experienced Captain and a hard-working crew.

She felt very relieved when they reached port, and after a simple coach journey she reached her little house in Edinburgh once again.

Letter from Isabella Liddel to Alexander Thomson
September 1826

Dear Alexander,

Is it permitted to use your first name?   I am persuaded that conventions in the New World are not so rigid as in the old, where I have reverted to the formal Mrs. Liddel!

My first efforts at promoting the Edinburgh Ladies' Association have every expectation of success.   I felt that black would not be appropriate for my visits – too dismal when we hope to promote hope and enthusiasm!   I therefore ordered a very pretty dove-grey silk with matching hat and parasol, and set off on my first visit to Lady Stanhope.   My card-case carried new cards elegantly engraved with my name, new address and (with their permission) "Glasgow Colonial Society" inscribed in italicised, but small letters beneath.

I intended to leave the card should Lady Stanhope not be at home, or too much engaged to receive me, and I scribbled briefly on the reverse of the card, the occasion on which we last met.   Fortunately she was at home and willing to receive, and so I trod up one pair of marble stairs in the wake of the footman, who flung back the double doors and announced my name.   I thought she looked momentarily puzzled, but I put on my most charming smile and said, "Your ladyship, it is so good to see you again."   She met my effusiveness with a slight (and chilly) inclination of her head, but I retrieved the situation, and talked of her daughter's home and family until she unbent, and I came to the purpose of my visit.

"I have just returned from Cape Breton in our North American colonies," I said, "and it is interesting to see how well our pioneers are coping with their difficult work of forestry and farming in a completely virgin land. They are Gaelic speakers, most of them, and they suffer severely because they lack the guidance of our Faith.   Do you know that, while prayers might be said in private homes, there is no Church, and no Ministry?   There is nowhere for people to come together and worship, and no religious instruction given to the children.   Schools are virtually non-existent too."

She replied that she knew the Glasgow Colonial Society did good work in our overseas territories, and I replied that I thought our Scots people who had emigrated to Cape Breton, had a particular claim on assistance from Scotland's capital.   She agreed and I said that I hoped to organise a meeting of ladies who might come together to promote practical assistance.   I offered the suggestion that Edinburgh could (and should) not be outclassed by Glasgow, and that we should need a President and Chairman to head the campaign.   She withdrew a little at the word "campaign", and I said I hardly had in mind the excesses of Georgiana, Duchess of Devonshire, but that Christian generosity to the Scots in Cape Breton was such a worthy cause, that it could only reflect credit on those who lent their name.   I would do the work of canvassing for support, I said, if she could recommend some friends and acquaintances I might approach.

She duly obliged, and I came away with half-a-dozen names from her address book <u>and</u> a letter of introduction.   I hope to see them soon, and make an assessment of those whose help it may be possible to enlist in a practical way, and those who will give money only.   Then I will write to Lady Stanhope, and invite her to chair (and perhaps host) our initial meeting.

I had an interesting experience yesterday. A small group of the ladies I hope to interest in Committee work gathered at the house of Mrs. Macdonald.   I thought it would be useful to rehearse my speech about Cape Breton to them. I launched forth, describing our journey and the villages we went to, including that poverty-stricken one at River Inhabitants. (I think, by the way, that you may have shielded me from some of the worst ones!)

I described the christenings and the need for permanent Ministers, though stressing the value of the work you and Nathaniel do voluntarily. I said how pleased that huge audience, who had come such a long way to hear you, were to know that we hoped to build a Church. But my spirits were dashed when I asked for questions, and all they wanted to know about were, one, had I really travelled for a whole week alone with two men? Two, were there wolves in Cape Breton? And three, why had the Government not built roads for the people?

I shall seriously need to revise my presentation. St. Mary's Wives Fellowship have asked me to talk to their Group, and I have promised to do so, if we can take a Collection for Cape Breton mission. Are there wolves, Alexander?

I must stop now, as my pen is becoming scratchy and needs mending, but I will write again when I have further progress to report. I describe myself, though humbly, as Cape Breton's special envoy to Scotland!

Isabella Liddel.

P.S. I enclose some pages from "The Scotsman."

By the same post David and Helen Creighton received an "arrived safely and thank you" letter from Mr. Archibald Creighton. "I was well entertained on the journey home by your cousin, Isabella," he wrote. "What a change from the lady I travelled out with! Then she was demure, conventional, teaching Sunday School and fairly withdrawn. On the way back she was full of excitement, busy planning her schedules, bubbling over with bright ideas. She tried to involve me in some of these, and I weakened sufficiently to say I would help her form a fund-raising group in Dundee. Pictou seems to have done her a power of good."

* * *

Before Isabella received Alexander's reply to her letter at the end of October, she had renewed acquaintance with John Sutherland, who had invited her to join his party in a box at the opera. The suave Edinburgh lawyer was pleasantly surprised on meeting Isabella again. Her demure and serious demeanour at Louisa's dinner-table had been replaced by a sparkle and open-ness, which he had not noticed before. And she was out of mourning!

He teased her gently about this. What was it about Nova Scotia that had so captivated her? She said she had enjoyed her trip to Pictou, met many new people, retrieved some of her outstanding debts, and spent a week visiting Cape Breton Island. She had even learned to sing solo, she responded, equally lightly, "on a boat in the middle of the ocean, with a storm blowing up."

"Then you certainly qualify to join my choir," he insisted, and she found it a very satisfying activity. The proceedings were not too formal; they practised weekly under the tutelage of an excellent conductor, and were to give a performance of a Handel piece at Christmas. Very often the party would break up into smaller groups for a visit to an eating-house nearby, or to someone's home. There was much jollity and amusement. By hook or crook, John Sutherland would contrive that he and Isabella were in the same group, and it was natural for him to escort her home afterwards.

She did not want to offer him too much encouragement, for her heart was set on Cape Breton and her mission to build Churches there.   Moreover, when she talked about Cape Breton to individuals or Church groups, Alexander's image was always present in her mind.   She fell into a reverie.

Her first meeting with Alexander had been the source of tears; she had patronised him and he had been angry.   Her second, at the Creightons, had mended fences; her interview with William the Pioneer had shown him in his family setting.   Her week with him and his brother on Cape Breton had shown him to be capable and considerate.   He was capable of huge physical effort; he was also vehement in his disgust at the feckless families' existence at Riverside Inhabitants. The inspiring way he had preached to the families on the banks of the river in the upper village had moved her to tears again, and showed her the way she must go.   Their final day and night had been both funny and frightening, in almost equal parts.   A bond had been created which she would find it difficult or impossible to break.   Despite the whole Atlantic Ocean billowing between them, she felt close to him, aware of a greater intimacy than she had known with anyone before.

She had tried John Sutherland on whether he might be prepared to help with her campaign, but he had proved evasive, saying merely that there must be far better people than he to help her, but he would try and think of someone who could be a Treasurer for her.   She sensed, however, that he was not truly sympathetic to her cause.

Another concern of Isabella's at this time was the situation of her maid, Joanna. She had taken the girl fresh from the country, and realized on their journeys to and from Pictou that, although strong, willing and eager to learn, Joanna had had little opportunity to acquire refinements proper to a lady's household.   She could not set a table and wait upon it in the correct manner; her cooking was limited to plain fare, and she rarely read anything, even the headlines in the newspaper, and so had little awareness of the customs of society or its fashions. She went to Church, of course, and her morals were beyond reproach.

Normally a girl, such as Joanna at seventeen, would have gone as a between-maid or scullery-maid in a bigger household and learned from the cook, the butler and her fellow-servants. It would have been an apprenticeship.

As it was, Isabella felt that she ought to try and provide some of the experiences and education which Joanna lacked. Indeed, while mistresses did not normally concern themselves with the social lives of their servants, she ought to make sure that the girl had suitable opportunities for recreation on her afternoon off. It probably behoved her to be generous also in giving her the time off to visit her family. If she took Joanna to Glasgow with her, the girl would probably meet her brother, who had been Isabella's former footman. She determined to do this and then, when she went away again, give Joanna money to return home for a visit. In the meantime she would look around for some opportunities to offer her further training. Probably the girl would marry rather than attain the servants' highest position, that of parlourmaid or ladies' maid, but she would marry better if she moved in a wider circle.

Mistress and maid had shared the experiences of the ship and the New World, and often talked of them over a cup of tea in the kitchen when their garden tidying had been accomplished together. Joanna was good at gardening, and apart from digging could distinguish weeds from plants. Isabella introduced the subject of reading one day. Joanna looked shame-faced.

"It takes me so long, Ma'am," she said. "I know you have lots of books, but it would take me a year to read even one!"

"Then I shall have to find you something you would like and find exciting," said Isabella. "I don't think a religious book would be right to start with, nor even a magazine, although that could be our next stage. I will find a book, which we could start reading together, and then you can finish it on your own. I will find a cookery book which we could read and then practise the recipes."

Having established that Joanna was willing, even eager, to try this regime, she began to look about her for a household or organisation which could offer some training.

* * *

Alexander Thomson to Isabella Liddel
September 21st 1826

Dear Isabella,

Your letter reached me this morning. I hasten to reply since the return ship leaves the day after tomorrow, and may possibly be the last one out this year.

It was a joy to hear from you, and I am delighted that your eloquence (and your new dress) evoked a favourable response from Lady Stanhope. I should like to have seen the dress, for you were often in black in Pictou. You had to exercise much tact, no doubt, to secure her ladyship's patronage, but you seem very skilled in the art of flattering these people. My blunt tongue would have failed, I know.

On the other hand, plain-speaking has brought in another five of your debts, and £360.4s 2d reposes in your account in Pictou, earning interest! (King, Falconer, Taylor, Dickson and Grant) if you want to tick them off your list. This brings the total of payments up to 26, which is more than half-way, and I have promises of more to come. My father wishes me to say that he thinks Finlayson (£191.19s 5d) should be written off. The poor fellow has fallen ill and may not last the year out. He has been in distress that he could not pay, and Father thinks it would ease his mind, and that of his wife, if the debt could be written off. Will you let me know your wishes in this matter?

Life goes on quietly here. My mother has been down, with my sister, and given my apartment a going-over! Everything was taken out, beaten, washed, shaken and dusted. Piles of papers were deposited in the store, and I was instructed to sort them out between customers. My cupboards were relentlessly emptied and some of their contents thrown away, as likely to poison me, if consumed. It is very good of them, and I feel somewhat ashamed that they thought it needful. But my excuse is that I am busy in the summer when the ships come in, and I suppose I have neglected things.

There is no news yet of Minette's confinement. Nat was hoping for a girl. It cannot be long now.

Your visit here has stirred things up socially. The MacFarlanes held their party a month after the Creighton Soiree, and cleared their rooms for dancing. We were a trifle cramped for reeling, and some of us need lessons before we attempt it again, but there is already talk of the young people getting up a fortnightly dance, urged on by my younger sisters from Maple Tree Grove."

He paused, mended his pen, and reflected that so far the letter had flowed quite smoothly. She would be interested, he felt sure, but he longed to discuss with her more important matters than small town gossip. He looked forward to reading the articles she had sent, and continued:

"For what it is worth, speeches should, I think, start from a relation of what the audience knows from its own experience. For example, 'what would you feel if your child had no name, no birthday and no Christian sponsors?' Then go on to why there is a need to provide these things, and the broader concept that you have in mind. Use the questions you receive on one occasion, to incorporate as part of your next talk. This will mean different questions at your next meeting, and will give you some variety in the speech, which can become repetitious and monotonous to you if you deliver the same thing each time.

As for your compromised reputation, I hope you told them that your escorts were God-fearing preachers, and behaved with the utmost propriety – most of the time!

There probably are wolves on Cape Breton, but generally they are shy of man, and will be able to find plenty of food in summer, so I was not worried about them. A greater source of danger is the black bear, which is strong and powerful and objects to strangers in its territory. You must never run away, but stand stock-still and face him down, and he will be the one to shamble away. Nerve-wracking, but true! I haven't had the occasion to try it myself, fortunately.

What were the excesses of Georgiana, Duchess of Devonshire? She campaigned, I believe for the Whigs, (or was it the Tories?), but must be long dead now.

Your faith in Captain John Smith was justified. He is a splendid fellow, but I regret that you had to endure such a severe storm on your way home. It must be a deterrent to a return visit, which I know Helen (and I) would very much like.

May I wish you all success in your canvassing and fund-raising.
Your partner in this enterprise,
Alexander"

It would have to do. He would work out a much better letter for the Spring. In the meantime, her letter secured a place in his inside pocket, as a precious memento to be taken out and read again time after time.

* * *

Isabella received Alexander's letter with a good deal of pleasure. His advice on speeches was sound, she thought, and she would certainly use it. The last paragraph was revealing. She had not mentioned the storm nor Captain Smith in her letter to him. He must have persuaded Helen to show him the letter she had received, in which she had mentioned both, or at least have questioned Helen about it. And that sly reference to behaving with propriety – most of the time! She believed he was far from indifferent to her, and tucked the letter away in her reticule to read again – several times!

By this time in October, she had gathered enough names from Lady Stanhope and others to call an Inaugural Meeting together. She also wanted to run a Christmas Bazaar to raise funds, and had a list of promises from people willing to contribute gifts and goods for sale. She had enrolled a few of her sister, Louisa's friends to make extra jams and jellies from the Autumn fruits, which would furnish one stall, and she set up a weekly sewing bee in her own house to start making soft toys and fripperies for another. She booked a hall, asked her Church congregation for helpers, and looked for success.

But first she had to visit Glasgow, and see if she could persuade the Colonial Committee to support her specific cause from their overall provision.

Chapter 9 - Winter

Isabella's visit to the Glasgow Colonial Society took place as October gave way to November, and the golden leaves were skittering from the trees in Scotland. She wondered about Autumn in Pictou. The colours of the deciduous trees, Alexander had said, were usually wonderful, especially the blaze of maples at Maple Tree Grove. It would be getting much colder there. In many areas of Cape Breton the trees were pines, conifers at any rate, and not likely to show much difference. She pictured the scenery as it might look with snow weighing down the branches, and she pitied the people as they entered upon another long winter.

She had secured a friend's hospitality in Glasgow, stressing that Joanna should share in the work of the household and learn from them, and looked forward to seeing many of her former social circle again. The Chairman of the Society, William Farquhar, had readily agreed to meet her to discuss 'a special project.' He had a lively appreciation of Isabella Liddel's organising qualities, for she had been instrumental in collecting 245 volumes of books to be sent to Merigomish, for lending on the same principles as the free circulating library had been operating in East Lothian for many years. The books, over-wrapped with heavy paper, affixed with a catalogue and a set of rules, were a judicious collection of ancient and modern histories, biographies and sermons, and were proving popular.

Mr. Farquhar's Committee was, of course, entirely composed of gentlemen, a mixture of Church people and those prominent in Glasgow society. William Liddel had been a Committee member until his death, as befitted a man with such extensive North American interests, but it had been his wife who had proved the one with the greater capacity for practical work. While it was traditional for the men to discuss the principles, it was equally accepted that it would be their wives and daughters who did much of the actual work – of fund-raising for instance.

The objects of the Colonial Society were to support the Scottish colonists throughout North America. It was typical of many philanthropic and missionary societies, which were springing up as the hedonism of the Georgian era began to be replaced by the moral ethic, which would reach its height in the Victorian age.

Mr. Farquhar greeted Isabella in an avuncular manner, and noted approvingly that the dove-grey silk was particularly becoming. He rang for coffee to be brought, while he and his visitor engaged in small talk about her new life in Edinburgh, and her Trans-Atlantic voyage. "Quite daring!" he had thought, when he first heard about it. Now she seemed to have benefited from her experience, judging from her air of assurance and her confident bearing.

"I have discovered a great need for our support," began Isabella, describing the virtually total lack of official Presbyterianism on the island of Cape Breton. "Nova Scotia is more advanced, and I believe Prince Edward Island is also," she went on, "but Cape Breton is largely settled by Gaelic speakers, and no Minister has ventured to set foot in it." She added conscientiously, "Except for two brothers, lay-preachers, who voluntarily make an annual expedition to some of the more remote communities. There are no Churches, so people cannot come together to worship, no baptisms, no teaching to encourage people to respect their God, and follow his Holy Commandments, little schooling for the children. It is a desert, Sir, which deserves to be watered by the fountain of our Faith."

Mr. Farquhar questioned her at length about the practical aspect of building Churches. She thought land could easily be made available. She would, from her own resources if necessary, provide some of the materials from which they could be furnished. She explained that some of the settlers were in the habit of providing goods in kind, particularly timber. But it was vital that a Missionary be sent and supported at least for an introductory period. It was a big island. Ideally they should send two Ministers on exploratory missions as soon as possible to assess and report.

While appreciating her enthusiasm and the need, Mr. Farquhar said the Society was already over-stretched. There were many more demands than their resources could possibly fulfil. He would put it to the Committee, but she was to have no firm expectations . . .

It was the reply Isabella had foreseen. "I believe I could raise additional money," she said, "through an auxiliary society in Edinburgh, with links northwards and eastwards to Dundee, Perth, Aberdeen, Inverness even. I already have a group of ladies who will raise money through a Bazaar; I can address meetings and seek collections; and I have a scheme for subscription appeals. I already have Lady Stanhope as President and Mrs. Tennant as Secretary. I really need your Committee's blessing for an Edinburgh Ladies' Association to be formed, as an offshoot of your established Society, and for it to be allowed to concentrate in the first instance on Cape Breton, without detracting from your resources, in any way."

Mr. Farquhar saw the benefit of this. It would extend the power and influence of his own Society if it had a subsidiary. He agreed to support the idea if Isabella would provide him with a memorandum outlining the concept, which he could present to his Committee, and to which he could speak.

Isabella returned to Edinburgh well pleased with her progress. She had taken the opportunity also to visit the Mortimers and acquaint Thomas and Agnes with details of her visit to Pictou, where his uncle had been such a prominent merchant. There was no need, of course, to refer to the debts, which had been recovered. Edward Mortimer's estate had been settled several years previously, and in any case William Liddel had bought out that business, but she did describe the bustling port as it was today, and the loading of the *Thetis* from the timber yard, and her journey home.

She had worshipped on Sunday at her old Church, seeing many friends, and had visited William's grave to lay fresh flowers and say a little prayer. She had apprised Mr. Goodrich of her partial success in tracking down the names on Mortimer's List. Joanna had enjoyed her experience in the larger household, and had helped at a dinner-party and learned from cook how to make light pastry. Now it was time for Isabella to plunge into the activities of the Edinburgh Ladies' Association.

* * *

Meanwhile, Alexander in Pictou had his own problems to unravel.

He spent a week hunting with a party of friends up MacLellan's Mountain, and returned, exhilarated by the strenuous exercise, the camaraderie of male companions, the challenges of making camp, and with spoils of venison, skins and an antler trophy.

The re-reading of Isabella's letter, however, produced another concern. Her description of Lady Stanhope's residence brought forcibly to mind the contrast between his own very meagre home and the well-appointed dwellings she would be accustomed to visit as she sought out donations and financial support for Cape Breton.

He wanted to expand his business interests and move into a higher league. There were opportunities in the timber trade, he knew, because of the collapse of Mortimer and Liddel. Isabella's first husband had been a timber merchant and that seemed a respectable enough operation. But, if possible, he wanted to aim higher.

He wanted to dispose of the store, which had been his life for so long and realise the capital it had built up. The grey overall of the shopkeeper was out-moded and had to go. He worked every night on his books and accounts to ascertain exactly what his business was worth. The total balance sheet, including the amounts of credit he had advanced, was a very substantial figure, quite enough, he thought, to launch into another venture. "Credit is money", Benjamin Franklin had said, and the sums he had advanced would be bringing their return in the years ahead.

To buy up land and re-sell it to immigrants was an opportunity he thought he could develop. The searching out of the right sort of emigrant from Scotland was another opening, which he saw as being neglected. He had mentioned this idea to Isabella. A plethora of impoverished immigrant crofters was one thing, but some educated leaders, some Ministers, schoolmasters, some clerks, some shopkeepers, some businessmen, some professional people were also badly needed to balance the new communities. He thought if the sea-passages were priced right, and the opportunities in North America described attractively, and assistance provided on landing, more immigrants of a more varied type could be encouraged. There would be profitable margins in this, and in the land re-sale or leasing. He felt, however, that Pictou might not be the best base. Upper Canada was where many people now wanted to go, or America of course, but he was not prepared to venture there. Some of the successful Pictou and Cape Breton people might even want to transfer to Upper Canada, if it was successfully opened up and marketed. He thought a better base might be Quebec.

All this took time to work out. Alexander established priorities in his own mind. First, he must find a purchaser or manager for the store. Secondly, he must assess the possibilities of assisted emigration from Scotland. Thirdly, he must assess the opportunities of land purchase from a base in Quebec.

He talked it through with his father during the Christmas festivities at Maple Tree Grove, William the Pioneer, saying, "Nay, lad, ye're putting t'cart before t' hoss! Get yr land first, and then ye'll have something t' offer the people."

Thus, despite the attraction of going to Scotland, where he could meet Isabella again, Alexander reluctantly determined that it would have to be Quebec next summer, and that priorities two and three would have to be reversed. He needed to dangle the carrot of land in Upper Canada before the potential immigrants from Scotland.

After Christmas, Alexander was dragooned by his sisters into supporting them at the dances they were organising. He played his part in these, but found no-one among the young ladies attending to hold a candle to Isabella. To him they appeared insipid. Admittedly they were younger and probably prettier, but her companionship had been stimulating and challenging, much more exciting.

Fortunately the store problem became capable of solution earlier than he had anticipated. One of the debtors on Mortimer's List came to see him, James Reid, who owed a comparatively small amount, but who had suffered an injury to his left arm when felling timber. Reid was looking for work in Pictou, for his disability was hampering him severely in running his property. He thought it would be better to sell up when he could find a purchaser, and move into a lighter job in the town. He was obviously an intelligent man, and Alexander asked him about his reading and writing abilities and his capacity for figure-work. The man had a Scottish primary and secondary school education, as Alexander had himself, and seemed an ideal candidate.

Alexander promised to look for a purchaser for Reid's farm if the man would be interested in taking over his store. Eventually they came to an agreement for a two-year contract as Manager and tenant of Alexander's apartment, while Reid learned the business, and assured himself that it was a feasible proposition. Alexander explained that he would be seeking new openings himself, and offered him an additional firm option to purchase at the end of two years if he wanted to do so.

* * *

Back in Edinburgh, Isabella's Bazaar had done well, and produced the princely sum of fifty pounds. The collections from Churches and other meetings she had addressed were also totalling fifty pounds or more, and a new subscription scheme had been launched.

This was sparked off by a visit she received from John Sutherland immediately after her return from Glasgow. Mr. Sutherland had been doing some serious thinking while she had been away. He certainly admired Isabella, and was in a position to please himself, should he wish to be leg-shackled to a wife. At the same time, he surmised her to have only a small independent income, and there would be no dowry to come his way, if he sought her hand in marriage. Money was always a consideration in these matters.   Would the expense of a wife justify the social value of having a hostess?   Would he find that a lady of strong religious beliefs would be a hindrance to his various activities?   He had a finger in many pies, not all of them wholly upright, and while ladies did not concern themselves with business, there might be the added bother of ensuring concealment if he embarked on a closer union.   To counter that argument, he saw the advantage of having a wife with impeccable connections, and a reputation for good works.   Her reputation could be a cloak for his.   Also she would have plenty to occupy her mind, and might thus not keep a jealous eye on him.

It was very difficult, and he had reached no firm conclusion, other than to keep the relationship progressing smoothly until he could make up his mind. Being of a confident, if not arrogant disposition, it did not occur to him that Isabella might not accept his obliging proposal.

"I, too, have been busy, dear lady," he said.

"In what way?"

"Well, I have a scheme for port improvements in Morayshire, which has involved my travelling back to my office in the North, but of more importance to you, I can offer you a Treasurer for your Ladies Association.   Sir Walter Young has told me that he would be willing to help you."

Isabella had reckoned that they would need a man to support them as Treasurer. Ladies were more likely to be educated in singing, water-colours and piano-playing than in mathematics, and there was also the likelihood that a prestigious male figure would be more successful in persuading business people to part with money.   She was extremely grateful to John Sutherland, and said so.

"I do what I can," he said, rather languidly, in response to her thanks. "You are so energetic, dear Mrs. Liddel, that you quite put me to shame, but I have useful contacts sometimes, and they are at your disposal. I shall look for my reward. Do you come to Choir on Tuesday?"

She said she would be there, and having extracted Sir Walter's direction, she resolved to wait upon him the very next day.

The meeting went well. Isabella gave her usual spiel about the need for Churches and Ministers in Cape Breton Island, and she was now able to add the support of the Glasgow Colonial Society for this endeavour. A scheme was agreed between them to be launched, whereby beautifully printed green booklets would be circulated to lists of prospects, headed with the name of at least one generous subscriber. There would be five guinea books, two guinea books and one guinea books, tooled in green leather, the colour of which was to denote the green shoots of a new society. Subscribers would be invited to inscribe their names, and return the books with their donations, which, if psychology was to be relied upon, would be at least as much as the lead donation, and possibly more if the recipient felt that he, or she, could outbid the lead amount. Sir Walter would persuade a printer friend of his to donate the books, he would provide a five guinea list of business people to be approached, while Isabella would provide lists for the lesser amounts from social and Church contacts she had made. She would draft the appeal letter, and he would provide the postage or messenger facility to get all the letters out.

It proved a happy scheme. She took Alexander's advice, and, as Christmas was approaching, they began the letters with a reference to the recipient's own

Christmas. How would they feel if there were no Church at which to celebrate our Lord's birth at Christmas time, and no Minister to lead the rejoicing, and no hymn books and no carols?   She went on to describe Cape Breton in graphic terms, and urge generosity at this time of Our Lord's birth.   The Appeal proved especially successful, and over 100 guineas had been received by January.

Over £200 was successfully raised and deposited in the British Linen Bank; and the Appeal continued into the future through the little green books, though with a differently drafted letter. With their collections at meetings continuing into the future, the Edinburgh Ladies Association was in a position by January 1827 to recruit their first Missionary.

Chapter 10 – Fruits of Success

To attract the right Missionary to the post was no easy task. The Edinburgh Ladies' Association drew up a description of the land of opportunities in Cape Breton, and circulated it through Church papers far and wide. They specified that the Minister must be Gaelic-speaking, but even so, received applications from some who were not. Those were discarded, as Isabella emphasised how very difficult it had been for her to communicate with the people without knowing their language and customs.

They fixed eventually on Patrick Stewart, a retired farmer from Stornoway, who was fluent in Gaelic, but not so fluent in sermonising, nor particularly erudite in his knowledge of the Scriptures.

The Glasgow Colonial Society raised strong objections to Edinburgh's choice. "Too socially inept and badly educated to ever get anything done," was their verdict. Isabella wrote back vehemently. "The Rev. Stewart comes from Stornoway in the Outer Hebrides, and has an island background not dissimilar to that of the Cape Breton people, some of whom I identified as coming from Lewis. He needs no social graces, for there is no society – as yet. In fact, some of the poverty is extreme, and he will need patience and an attitude of care to understand the dejection of these simple people, and lift their aspirations. A man who has worked for much of his life with dumb animals will have such patience and understanding."

"It matters not," she continued, "that he has no University degree. That he writes legibly and can read the Scriptures is acceptable. Philosophical dissertation will not form part of his duties. I could wish that he were a little more eloquent, but he has a practicality and true sincerity, and these will carry him through."

Grumbling, the Glasgow Colonial Society acquiesced, and the Rev. Stewart set sail for the Gut of Canso, bearing a letter of introduction to Nathaniel Thomson at Mabou, urging him to help the new Minister in any way he could.

She also wrote to Alexander, as part of a bumper bundle she had been compiling all winter.

"Here are your 'Scotsmen,'" she wrote. "I hope they will enliven your evenings – those you can spare from your Scottish dancing, I mean!   If you look at the top of Page 5 (19th January), you will see the piece which trumpets our successful raising of the first £200 of our Appeal, and our search for our first Missionary.   Sir Walter Young got the Editor to put this in.   He is our Hon. Treasurer and knows all the foremost businessmen in the City.   He was introduced by John Sutherland, who sings in the same Choir as I do – in fact he encouraged me to join it – and I shall be eternally grateful, for Sir Walter is a splendid asset, and so helpful.

"The Rev. Stewart will need any help you and Nathaniel can give him.   I have written to your brother, by the way, to introduce Mr. Stewart.   His task is to encourage the communities to come together where possible and build a Church in their most convenient location. He will service that Church while he also visits other communities for the same purpose.   He will go ashore at Canso and cover the Western part of the island, while we look for a second Minister to undertake the same function for the eastern part.   We shall have to raise more money before we can do that, but I am hopeful that we shall succeed before the end of the summer."

She then went on to describe their emissary in much the same way as she had described him to Mr. Farquhar, and Alexander felt she had probably made a good choice.

There was much more in the letter, which Alexander had rushed down to the Harbour to fetch, as soon as he heard the first ship was in. She had not disappointed him, and her bumper bundle was full of interesting anecdotes, and the energy of her personality shining through the letter warmed his very being. Only one sour note crept in. He did not care for the reference to John Sutherland, who seemed to be someone she met regularly. He felt a flicker of jealousy, but dismissed it firmly. He had no claim on Isabella. She could see whomsoever she wanted to see.

Alexander was pleased she had found a Minister so quickly. He had been worried that, if he went to Quebec this summer, he would let down Nathaniel by failing to accompany him on their annual preaching expedition to Cape Breton. He could hardly manage two periods away from Pictou and the store, even though James Reid's farm sale was under way, and he and his family would be moving in to learn the ropes of the store business some time before the Autumn. Now it seemed that Nathaniel would be able to team up with Minister Stewart instead of himself. To facilitate this he wrote to Nathaniel to tell him of his plans to go to Quebec, and made that suggestion.

Another letter among the pile of business correspondence from Scotland attracted his attention. He turned it over; there was no return address and he failed to recognise the writing. It was from his cousin, Robert Bell in Cromarty.

"We see the big timber ships from Aberdeen and Leith from the hilltop overlooking the Sutors," wrote Robert. "They sail right past us on their way to America, and some of them are half-empty. If only the ship-owners knew there are lots of us here who want to be collected to go to Quebec and Pictou. If you could write and tell us what we may expect there, it would strengthen that wish.

Things are very bad here and folks don't know which way to turn to scratch a living. The passage prices on the boats are getting steeper, particularly if we have to travel down to Aberdeen with all our chattels and wait for a ship."

This chimed in so perfectly with what Alexander hoped to achieve, that he wrote back instantly to his cousin, asking him to collect people who wanted to emigrate. He wrote also to Isabella telling her that he hoped to start a new scheme, arranging shipping services for people wishing to emigrate from Morayshire. It was some years since his father had dealt with ship-owners. Could Isabella help him locate any in Leith?

She put this problem to the invaluable John Sutherland, who had mentioned his port improvements in Morayshire, after all. He pursed his lips while he turned the matter over in his mind. Lacking Isabella's commitment to Cape Breton and the New World, he wondered what advantage might accrue to himself in such an arrangement.

"Leave it with me, dear lady," he said, and trusting him implicitly, she did.

The result was that a letter from someone called Charles Daniels, a shipping agent in Leith, reached Alexander in April, offering *The Lovelly Nelly* of Leith for a keen price to sail in the middle of June, calling at Cromarty en route for Pictou and Quebec to collect Canadian timber.

He clinched the deal to charter the ship on the outward journey, worked out a fair price to charge the emigrants, put Daniels and his cousin, Robert Bell, in touch with one another, and departed himself for Quebec.

* * *

Alexander's first call was on Archibald Buchanan, the Immigration Agent in Quebec. Buchanan was a high-ranking official, newly-appointed by the Colonial Office of the British Government in London. He was a knowledgeable gentleman, currently busy with the construction of a new Quarantine Hospital at Grosse Isle, where ships would call before they reached the City, for their passengers to be checked for illness and disease. Those who were sick would be taken off and lodged in the hospital. Those clear of disease could continue on their journey.

Alexander explained that he was looking to purchase land, which he could offer to a shipload of immigrants from Cromarty. He emphasised that he had a good reputation in Pictou for assisting immigration voluntarily, but people were now wishing to settle in Upper Canada, and he wanted to involve himself in that. He claimed relationship with William the Pioneer, and said some of the immigrants were likely to be cousins from Morayshire.

Archibald Buchanan was impressed. The two men liked one another on sight, and Buchanan sensed that this was not another speculator seeking to make a killing, but someone who had the interests of immigrants at heart. They arranged to meet again to go into matters more fully. Over a chop and a tankard of porter, Buchanan told Alexander about some of the past Scottish successes.

"There are emigrants from Sutherland flourishing at Zorra in Oxford County, and tenants from the Breadalbane estate in Perthshire who are doing very well in North and South Easthope, in Perth County. They were able to build a school and Church just three years after their arrival, and they keep talking enthusiastically about their current worldly comforts, compared to their lives back home. Then there are Baptist communities from Argyll who are now happily ensconced in Middlesex county."

Alexander described to Archibald Buchanan the work Isabella had undertaken to improve the lives of people in Cape Breton, by building Churches for them. "Do you think there is any chance of Government help?" he asked him.

"Not for Churches," was the reply. "For roads, maybe, but it would take special pleading, for Cape Breton is really a backwater compare with the rest of North America. If you want to buy land, the Canada Company has a million acres, known as the Huron Tract, coming on stream soon. They will be building some roads, and it is particularly fertile land. You could perhaps get in on that. The man to see is Stuart MacLellan. I think he's over here at the moment, rather than in London."

Alexander obtained the address of the Canada Company, and made a call on MacLellan. Another Scot, he proved helpful to a fellow countryman.

"Huron is not being released just yet," advised MacLellan. "But it will be available within the next two years. You could register an interest. However, if you've got people coming over soon, there's still some land at Zorra which might be suitable." Maps were spread over the table, and MacLellan explained what happened.

"Canada is not a free-for-all like the United States. The scramble for land there is quite unregulated. Squatters' rights, mainly, as the frontier stretches westward. Here the Government has learned something from the earliest settlements, and now releases areas at a time, so one place gets to be properly organised before another comes on stream. Our company has been formed to encourage settlement in the more remote, yet fertile areas in Western Upper Canada. You can buy cleared or wilderness land, the former more expensive, of course, and we provide a basic structure of roads and mills, and offer work to tradesmen and labourers. We have a million acres, and we offer easy terms."

Alexander asked what 30,000 acres would cost, and was pleasantly surprised at the figure. "But as I say," MacLellan went on, "it's not yet available. Put down a deposit as a registration fee, if you like, but if you want to buy for now, then this is the best spot," and he pointed to a tract somewhat nearer to Quebec. "We prefer to deal in larger packages; it saves trouble with the little man. It's your decision whether you use it yourself, or sell it on, or lease it, and it's then up to you to get your money back."

Alexander took a deep breath, bought 1,000 acres at Zorra, and took an option on 30,000 acres of the Huron Tract when it became available. He reckoned the first package would carve up into five or six farms, and a dozen or more small-holdings for the new arrivals. He asked a few more questions, then left, mentally exhausted by the speed of the transaction and the responsibility he had undertaken.

Chapter 11 - Disaster Strikes

Isabella had become so accustomed to events, which she organised, prospering, that she was mentally unprepared for one going wrong. She had been extremely pleased when Lady Stanhope had persuaded a fellow aristocrat from Haddington Hall, South of Edinburgh, to host a Cape Breton Appeal Garden Party in May while a minor Royal was staying with her.

Isabella had visited the site, met the hostess, organised publicity and gathered goods for both a further publicity stall and a couple of Sales Tables. Invitations were despatched and a happy and profitable day envisaged. Alas, many people felt the venue was too remote, and declined with regret; when the Garden Party took place, the heavens opened, and down came the rain. Although the event continued in the main hall of the big house, the atmosphere was ruined, some guests' gowns were dampened by the sudden onset of the heavy shower, and the minor Royal threw a tantrum.

Although Isabella's disappointment was slightly assuaged by the hostess's husband sending a fifty guinea draft on his bank, so that the funds should not suffer, she had been soaked herself, the dove-grey gown was ruined and she had caught a heavy cold. She kept to her bed for some days. She felt so languid afterwards that she had to postpone a speaking engagement, with more loss of potential funds.

Writing to Alexander, when she felt well enough to do so, and to recount this history of mishaps, she managed to look on the bright side: "I have had an enforced rest, which I probably needed, as I have been very much occupied since Christmas. I shall also have to take the time to commission some new clothes, for I have not had leisure to do that, and I have at last an opportunity to look through the fashion magazines and mark some styles I might like.

"I have embarked on Joanna's induction into catering for polite society," she wrote. We have acquired a recipe book, which she studies under my supervision, and then assembles the ingredients we need. I check that the method is understood and followed, and she then makes up the dish. Yesterday's was a syllabub – delicious!"

Their letters to one another had now fallen into a regular pattern. The time taken by the ship bearing the letter to reach the recipient and the time taken to carry back the reply meant an interval usually of two months or more. Consequently, the letters took on the quality of a diary, and two monologues, rather than a true exchange of news and opinions.

Nevertheless each tried to write each week, so that the other should not be bereft of news. Sometimes, due to the vagaries of shipping, two or three letters arrived together. Isabella marvelled that Alexander should keep up the correspondence so faithfully. Men were not notoriously good letter-writers, but he certainly was, and she rejoiced at the sight of the square black handwriting. No-one had told her that men in love tend to have different standards of correspondence from others of their sex!

* * *

Isabella's mishaps in May were as nothing compared with those, which befell Alexander in late July.

By this time James Reid had become established in the shop, and Alexander had moved out. He secured a couple of first floor rooms above a shop near the waterfront, and used one as an office, the other as a bedroom/living room. They would do temporarily, he thought, conscious of the need at some stage either to build or buy a house of his own – but now was not the time!

He became aware, early in July, that *The Lovelly Nelly* had not arrived on or about the date when he expected her. He knew that she had sailed, through correspondence from the Agent, via another ship, but enquiries at the harbour gave no indication that any other ships had even glimpsed her on the way over. It was very worrying.

The worry grew to deep anxiety. Normally June was a good month for Trans-Atlantic voyages. The ship could not have been lost. There had been no major storms reported. But the fishermen had seen no sign of her on the Newfoundland Banks. She was seriously overdue. A week's delay grew to a fortnight, and the fortnight to almost three weeks. Two letters arrived, via other ships, from people complaining that there had been poor organisation at the Cromarty boarding-point and they had missed the ship. Alexander expected his cousin and his family to be among the passengers, and he knew his father and mother, who knew Robert better than he did, were also very worried. For a ship to take seven weeks at this time of year was highly unusual.

He went down to the harbour daily to chat and enquire. Several ships, which had left different Scottish ports and Liverpool on dates after *The Lovelly Nelly*, came in. No Captain had seen her! Eventually, when the seven weeks were almost up, men from a fishing-boat reported that they thought they had seen her approaching the Banks, but the mist had closed in, and the men did not know what had happened after that.

At least they had a sighting, but Alexander was concerned for the passengers. Conditions after such a long voyage would have deteriorated, he knew, for though ships were provisioned to last for seven weeks, it was usually with the basic beef and biscuit ration. There would have been no fresh food. He thought there would be hunger and probably a shortage of water. He made provision for the ship to be re-supplied before it continued its journey to Quebec.

At last the ship reached the Gut of Canso, and the pilot boat went out to meet her. It guided her into Pictou Harbour and Alexander went on board. The crew looked exhausted and lackadaisical. To his astonishment the Captain turned out to be a black-bearded Dutchman named Kruger, who spoke little English!

Below decks, the foetid stench, worse than cow byres after a long winter or an overcrowded pig-sty, turned Alexander's stomach, and he had to come up again to vomit over the side. Recovering, and holding a handkerchief to his nose and mouth, he made his way down to find about fifty people lying more or less comatose, or staggering weakly about.

"We're in port!" he shouted. "Come up if you can." Two or three men followed him up the companion-way.

"It's been very bad," muttered one. "I never thought we'd live."

"I think the sickness is typhoid," said another. "There've been four deaths."

There was no time to be lost. Alexander realised that if it were typhoid, contact with the residents of Pictou must be avoided. He called on the Harbour-Master to set up barriers to separate those greeting the ship from the passengers. He obtained clean straw to lay on the quay, so that those who could be carried into the fresh air would have somewhere to lie. He provided a water-barrel, and set up a table with the food he had intended to use for the ship.

The two men who had come up with him fell upon it.

"The Lord bless you for a kind gentleman," said one.

The doctor from Pictou was called down to the emergency. Alexander made the crew carry up the sick passengers into the fresh air. There were children among them

"This one's dead," said the doctor, of a boy about eleven years old. Alexander shuddered. Five deaths! It was a devastating outcome.

He and two Pictou women who said they were not afraid of the disease, took cups of water to the victims, and urged them to try a little food. Some of the relatives who had come to meet the boat asked if they could take their kinsmen home. They certainly could not stay on the harbour-side, and the doctor gave permission where he could.

The Presbyterian Minister appeared to offer help, and Alexander commandeered the Church Hall as a refuge for the others, and sent to the store for all available bedding. They would have to stay for some days while he arranged for the ship to be cleaned and fumigated, and made fit to continue the journey to Quebec, for those who were travelling on.

When order had been restored outside, he stormed back to the ship, and demanded the log and the passenger list from the bemused Captain. "Where, in God's name, have you been?" he asked.

With the first mate as "interpreter" he pieced the story together. The real Captain had not been seen since Leith. Jon Kruger had been substituted as relief Captain at Leith Docks when the ship was almost ready to sail. The Dutchman had neither captained a ship before, nor had he more than one journey's experience, and that as a Mate, on the Atlantic run. He had steered a wrong course too far to the south, and they had had to beat up the American coast to make the correct landfall.

At Cromarty there had been fewer passengers to pick up than the first mate had expected, which was a mercy considering the ship had taken on no fresh water or food there. The water had been provided in Leith, and had been putrid now for some time. Food supplies had never been adequate, and while the crew was used to the basic ration, the supplies steerage passengers had brought with them went bad or ran out as the voyage lengthened and they were unaccustomed to the rations the ship provided. The cook had been drunk for most of the way, but would not let anyone into his galley to help, until he had been forcibly over-powered, in order that water could be boiled.

The Captain had laid down no regular routine for ventilating and cleaning the ship. At first the First Mate had done what he could to provide this, but the crew were getting weaker themselves because of the lack of proper meals. Moreover, the First Mate was himself overwhelmed by the need to shadow his "Captain's" work, provide proper look-outs, and supervise the crew to ensure the safety of the ship, with the result that the needs of the passengers were overlooked.

The log correctly recorded that four passengers had been buried at sea, but their names had not been removed from the passenger list. Alexander gave this list to the Presbyterian Minister, who was still hovering around, trying to be helpful, and asked him to identify the missing passengers and console their relatives.

Alexander also called the crew together. They could stay at the Seamen's Hostel overnight and the following night, while their quarters were cleaned, but he wanted them to report each morning for duties to prepare their ship for its onward journey. He would himself be travelling with the ship to Quebec.

At this point he hoped to find a reserve Captain, but none proved available. Navigation of the St. Lawrence was tricky, he knew, but pilots would be aboard for the last 250 miles, so he thought Kruger and the first mate would have to manage. He ensured they had the necessary charts. At Quebec he would surrender the responsibility for the ship he had chartered. It was not his concern to deal with the return trip.

After three days the ship was cleaned, re-victualled and watered, and left Pictou Harbour, Alexander occupying one of the cabins. Two families had to be left behind at Pictou, too weak to continue, but the doctor thought they would recover, and could follow on a later ship. Alexander was devastated by what had happened, and during the remaining voyage discovered more of the story from his cousin, Robert Bell.

"It was a living hell," said Robert, considerably restored by three days at Maple Tree Grove. "To start with, some of the people who told me they wanted to emigrate, cried off, saying it was too quick, and they'd make arrangements to go next year. Then when we were assembled at Cromarty, there were another two families missing – lost the meeting-point or something—I don't know. We were fifty in the end."

Alexander thought the two angry letters he had received were probably from the families missing at

Cromarty – but there was no point in arguing over it with poor Robert.

"I hadn't met the Captain before," went on Robert, "although the Agent said it would be someone called Kirk. But this fellow, Kruger, was in charge. I couldn't understand him, and he couldn't understand me, so I couldn't check whether he knew what he was doing. He seemed surprised there were passengers, though he knew he had to call at Cromarty. Perhaps he thought it was cargo, but he seemed to think he'd been booked to take an empty ship to Canada, and bring timber back. He certainly never took any notice of how we were going on. I went up to see him several times to complain, but he used to shrug his shoulders."

"None of you will be charged for this voyage," said Alexander. "I will refund the passage money, and I'm going to get to the bottom of what happened, if it's the last thing I do. I suspect some sort of trickery somewhere."

During the voyage he was able to discuss with the men whether they wanted to take up the offer of land at Zorra. He said it was an extension of land partly worked by men from Sutherland, and they might find it congenial. All but one family, who knew other settlers elsewhere, accepted the offer, and contracts were made, discounting the cost of the disastrous voyage.

* * *

On arrival in Quebec, Alexander sought out the Immigration Agent he had met earlier that summer, Archibald Buchanan.

"We've had typhoid on *The Lovelly Nelly*," he confessed. "She's been disinfected, cleaned and re-victualled, but five of the passengers died, and some are still ill."

"Five!" said Archibald. "Well, you got off lightly. There were sixty deaths on a Liverpool ship last year, Irish and severely over-crowded. There will be an enquiry."

"Enquiry?" queried Alexander, a new nightmare rearing its head.

"There's not enough control at the embarkation points," decreed Buchanan. "Your ship wasn't overcrowded, so you can't be blamed for that. I think they're setting up a Parliamentary Committee in London to look into deaths on emigration ships."

"I do blame myself," said Alexander. "It seemed all too easy. I just put the people and the ship together. I'm going over to Scotland to find out what went wrong at that end."

"Very wise," said Archibald Buchanan. "I suggest that, if they do add *The Lovelly Nelly* to the Enquiry, which they may do, as I'm in duty bound to make a report, you need to find out all you can, and be prepared to bring witnesses in your own defence. It may never come to that, but it is as well to be prepared."

Alexander spent a day or so at the Quebec shops in mid-August, spotting items which James might stock. There was a little beauty of a camping stove, and a clasp knife, which he bought to show him. He also obtained some clothes for his visit to Scotland. Anything would do for Leith docks, but a Parliamentary Enquiry sounded like a need for something formal.

He wrote to Isabella to tell her he was coming.

"I am absolutely mortified and disgusted with myself," he wrote. "It is fundamentally my fault for approaching this business too casually. I assumed my cousin could find passengers. I trusted an Agent I did not know. I am coming to Scotland to find out for myself why the original Captain did not command the ship. I feel I have the deaths of five people on my conscience for a disaster of a voyage."

"I will come and see you as soon as I can," he continued, "but first I have to understand what went wrong, in case I have to face an enquiry, which Archibald Buchanan thought possible, though not necessarily certain. Then, as I am certain that there is a market for a scheme of this kind, I must put in place fool-proof arrangements for the future. I could never let something like this happen again."

Chapter 12 - Dirty Work

Alexander caught the first boat he could for Scotland, which left in mid-August, having visited the Creightons to ask Helen if she had any message for Isabella, should he happen to see her while in Edinburgh. "Tell her she will always be welcome whenever she can come back," said Helen, "and the children are well, and the eldest is learning the piano."

His parents seemed to have no doubt but that he would see Isabella. "Tell her there have been two more payments from Mortimer's List," said his father. "And tell her that Gertrude's wedding will be July next year," said his mother, "if she can get over for it."

By chance the ship he caught was the *Thetis* bound for Glasgow. She was going only to the nearer port with the intention of making a quick turn-around, and getting in another voyage before the winter. It didn't matter. Alexander could get a coach across to Edinburgh, and would probably be there before a ship having to sail around the North of Scotland.

Captain John Smith was pleased to welcome him aboard. "We'll have some talk over a noggin," he promised. There was only one other passenger on the homeward trip, a farmer going to his ancestral home to sort out an inheritance, a pleasant enough dinner companion, but not a great conversationalist.

So much had happened this summer. Alexander was not averse to a few quiet days to put all the developments in perspective. Last summer he had met Isabella. This summer had seen him divest himself of the store, establish himself as a land-owner of currently a small, and potentially a very large, acreage of Upper Canada, and finally come to grief with the disastrous voyage of "*The Lovelly Nelly*", which might well put paid to any ideas he had of developing immigration from Scotland to Canada, should the Enquiry go against him.

He had only the vaguest idea as to what a Parliamentary Committee holding an Enquiry would consist of, or how it would conduct its business, and a top priority must be to find out what he might have to face. He must also find witnesses to what had happened to the voyage in the beginning, as Archibald Buchanan seemed to think might be necessary.

He discussed some of these issues with Captain Smith, who approved of Buchanan. "He's tightening up the procedures at Quebec," he said, "and that's all to the good." He also thought the enquiry might be a follow-on to the Select Committee, which sat in 1826. "The Colonial Office has been badgered by a number of MPs, who have had constituents complaining to them about standards on emigrant ships. Of course, they never say anything about the dozens of voyages that go well. I've never had any real trouble, but then I don't over-load, and I make sure we've got food and water in hand. You never quite know when you might have to alter course, and give some poor beggar assistance if they've got into trouble, and that can put days on the trip, apart from bad weather, of course. Your captain must have been an absolute fool to be three weeks late!"

"He wasn't a proper Captain at all," explained Alexander. "Just someone who had been substituted at the last moment. I want to find out why."

"Dirty work, somewhere," suggested John Smith. "You'd be surprised at what some of these so-called agents get up to. It's not too bad with regular contracting, but for a single journey they pay as little as they can get away with, and charge the customer as much as they can get away with. Kruger would probably come cheap, compared with a regular Captain. Was the crew foreign labour?"

"No, Scots all, I believe. Only the Captain was Dutch. And the cook seemed to be Chinese."

"They all are!" agreed Smith. "Ships' cook is not a popular occupation. Luckily mine has been with me for years. Mind you, I pay him well to keep him. Ours is a miserable job if you don't get good dinners. Changing the subject, that was a nice lady I took back with me last year about this time. Friend of yours?"

"I only met her last year," replied Alexander. "But yes, I would count her a friend. She is working to raise money to provide Cape Breton with Churches and Ministers. Did she tell you about it?"

"She talked of little else," said Smith. "No, that's not true. She was widely read and she sketched and painted, and Creighton is an entertaining chap to have on board. But I did get the impression the lady was devoted to this mission of hers."

"She's having great success already," divulged Alexander. "She has raised over £200 – enough to employ their first Minister, who came over in May, I believe, and they're well on their way to employ a second. I'm personally very grateful, for if they get established, it will relieve my brother and I of a considerable responsibility."

Capt. Smith noted that his companion seemed singularly well-informed about Mrs. Liddel's activities. "How about a game of crib?" he suggested. "It goes well with the Scotch."

* * *

The voyage came to an end at last with the reduced sail progress up the Clyde. They had made good time across the ocean with the prevailing westerly winds behind them for much of the way. After weeks of seascape, it was pleasing to observe the green, wooded Kilpatrick Hills, rising above the melee of wharves and warehouses. They passed one timber yard on the left bank still bearing the name LIDDEL in large letters, but tied up half an hour later at another. It was a busy river, with small ships scurrying hither and thither, hooters sounding, sirens wailing, klaxons honking, as they worked their way up to the wharf.

Alexander wished John Smith a successful return voyage as he and the farmer disembarked. They shared a hansom cab to an area where the industrial chaos began to give way to a commercial area – some shops and offices, inns and coffee-houses. Here they parted company, the farmer taking the cab on further, while Alexander refreshed himself at an 'ordinary', and enquired where he could board a coach for Edinburgh.

It seemed there was a coaching terminus half a mile further on, and Alexander trudged this distance with his bag, eventually finding "The Falcon." Here he planned to spend the night, having booked a place on the stage for 8 o'clock the following morning.

That arrangement gave him a few evening hours in which to explore on foot the more fashionable parts of the City and its civic centre. He was astonished at what he saw, and amazed by the massive stone buildings and imposing Churches. He was aware that Glasgow had first grown rich on the tobacco trade. The "Tobacco Lords", as the wealthy importers were called, had constructed many fine buildings. The development had continued as "King Cotton" became important, and the City was now well into the next phase of the industrial revolution.

The "Merchant City", or New Town, had been
developed in the period 1786 to 1790, and he saw these
dates on some of the buildings. Walking slowly down
Ingram Street, he was overwhelmed by the stately beauty
of the Assembly Rooms, designed by Robert Adam, and
impressed by Hutcheson's Hall.

He felt some sense of awe comparing it with little
Pictou. Isabella had been until two years ago a part of
this impressive scene. He asked directions to Charlotte
Street, where he knew she once lived.   Built from 1779
onwards, it proved to be a street of elegant, mercantile
mansions, each with its own coach house, closed off from
Glasgow Green by a private gate.   From the chandelier
lights displayed in many houses, it appeared that most
houses had their principal rooms on the first floor. He
could imagine her entertaining parties of guests in those
stately apartments.

Returning to the inn, he passed a disturbed night,
not uncommon in coaching inns, as hooves clattered over
cobble-stones, ostlers shouted, passengers demanded
rooms and refreshment.   The timbers in his room
creaked; he surmised there were mice behind the
wainscoting, but eventually he slept.   Renewed activity
about six o'clock prompted him to get up, eat a hearty
breakfast, pay his bill and find his coach.

Its team of four horses was being assembled when
he went out to the yard. The coachman was being critical
of one beast, which was rejected. He was simultaneously
checking over his passengers, whom he couldn't reject,
disposing their weight fittingly inside and on the roof.
Alexander climbed up to his outside seat.   If the weather
held, it would be a pleasing novelty of a journey. His
fellow-passengers seemed more at home with the
procedure, and discussed the places where they were
likely to change the teams, and what refreshment would
be available there. They were curious about him too, and

discovering he came from Nova Scotia, wanted to know about the land and its prospects.

Alexander found their diction somewhat difficult to comprehend. Although his father retained quite a strong burr of the Scottish way of speaking, Alexander's own Scots accent, in common with many fellow-settlers, was already slipping away in favour of a more relaxed style. In any case, this was Glasgow, where the gutteral pronunciation was stronger than on the East coast.

The coach passed through Rutherglen, changed horses at Bothwell, passed through Motherwell, and changed again at Wishaw. Here they also changed coachmen, as the Glasgow driver would wait for the stage travelling in the opposite direction, while the Edinburgh coachman would take their coach on over the Pentland Hills to his base in Edinburgh. It might be a long wait, Alexander surmised, and took the opportunity of ordering a well-cooked meal. Only a small village, and only a country inn, it could nevertheless rely on regular custom for its stables and tap-room, and trade was brisk.

Another coaching inn in Edinburgh led to another disturbed night. Alexander had wondered whether to try and find Forth Street where Isabella lived. It would be foolish, he decided. There was no guarantee she had yet received his letter telling her that he intended to visit Scotland. There was no guarantee she would even be at home. She might have visitors if she was. He did not want to give her a sudden shock. He compromised by writing a note, careful to include both the day and date.

"September 14th, and I am in Edinburgh," he wrote. "Tomorrow I intend to go to Leith Docks and make enquiries about the circumstances surrounding *The Lovelly Nelly*. After that I shall go to Morayshire to investigate possibilities of resuming the emigration organisation which I have in mind. If I am able to complete the business in time, I shall want to try for a return ship before the winter, as there is so much for me to do back home. It is my earnest desire to see you before I go. I will keep you informed of my direction, and pray your engagements will not prevent our meeting on my return."

He mailed the letter and set forth for Leith Docks the next morning. Unsure of whether he would return to that inn, he perforce took his luggage with him, although he had some qualms about this, as he was likely to be in a rough, tough area. He did not fancy being robbed. He dressed therefore in his homespun clothes, adding a neckerchief and cap.

Leith Docks was a smaller and less frenetic version of Glasgow. He picked his way round the detritus of the dockside until he found the Harbour-Master's office, and enquired for Captain Robert Kirk, who had been due to captain *The Lovelly Nelly* on that fateful day in June. He half-expected the Captain might be at sea, but the Harbour-Master's assistant thought not, and when he explained that he was enquiring into a failure to sail, provided him with Captain Kirk's home address.

Another trudge, another lunch, a walk up a steep hill and he reached the Captain's abode, a substantial cottage or small house, with a colourful front garden, a spyglass mounted on a tripod over-looking the port approaches, and the Captain himself, with his eye to the glass. He looked up as he heard footsteps approaching, and Alexander introduced himself.

Sitting on a garden bench in tranquil surroundings, Captain Kirk took his mind back to early June.

"I was having a drink, it is true," he acknowledged, "but I hadn't taken too much, I swear. I was due to sail *The Lovelly Nelly* the next day, and I'd worked hard all that day preparing her, and I was just wetting my whistle at the dockside tavern, when I went out like a light! I may have hit my head when I fell, I don't know. There was a bit of a bruise next day, but I didn't notice anything at the time, so I'm sure I wasn't hit. The barman and a drayman put me in a back room, they tell me, and they know where I live, so after closing time they carted me home. Very good it was of them. I slept for a good eighteen hours before I began to come to, and by then *The Lovelly Nelly* had gone. It's my belief someone put something into my drink, and I was drugged."

"Did you try and find out who could have done such a thing?" asked Alexander.

"Well, I found out they'd put a relief Captain on to the ship in my place, and it was Jon Kruger. The man is incompetent. Whoever appointed him to captain the ship must have been plain stupid, or had evil intent. I wouldn't have him as a First Mate. But he would come cheap, no doubt, and the ship was all ready. He only had to walk on board."

"Who would have installed him, and instructed the ship to sail?" Alexander inquired.

"Why, Charles Daniels. I went round and accused him of it, complained of losing my berth and my eight weeks or more wages. It didn't do me a ha'porth of good. He just said I wasn't on board and on duty when I should have been, and he'd had to make other arrangements. Are you the man who chartered her?"

"Indeed I am," replied Alexander. "She was due to pick up passengers in Cromarty and take them to Pictou and Quebec. Costs were all arranged for the ship and for the fares."

"Well, it's my belief someone wanted me out of the way, but why, I don't know – unless it was to be sure the voyage went wrong with that fool, Kruger, in charge."

"It did go wrong," said Alexander. "He steered too far to the south, whether accidentally or deliberately, I don't know. The crossing lasted seven weeks, all but a day, and they were short of food and the water was putrid. When I met the ship in Pictou, it was in a dreadful state, with typhoid rampant. Five died, including a child of eleven. Now I hear an Enquiry may be likely before a Parliamentary Select Committee."

"Phew!" whistled Kirk. "You've caught a packet of trouble. I don't wonder you want to sort it out. But why was it done? It wasn't particularly to damage me – and it didn't – because I was in command of another ship the very next week. In fact I've only just come back from that journey."

"Then it must have been done to damage me," said Alexander. "Should I go and see Daniels, do you think?"

"Well, you could, but I don't think I would! Daniels has a reputation as a bit of a sharp operator. The Agent you really want, if you intend to do this again, is William Allan, who is straight. Who recommended you to Daniels?"

Alexander thought for a moment. "A lawyer, John Sutherland, through a friend of mine. He contacted Daniels, and Daniels wrote to me, with a proposition, which I accepted."

"Don't know Sutherland," said Kirk. "But he'd expect a back-hander, no doubt, for the introduction and probably Daniels found the money by swapping Kruger's wages for mine.   But it still doesn't seem worth it.   Could this Sutherland have an extra motive?"

They had to suspend discussion of the problem over tea and scones, kindly provided by Mrs. Kirk. The lady was a noted housewife, hailing originally from Yorkshire.   Her husband was welcome to be the Master of his ship, she was fond of saying, but in her house, she was the Mistress. And in the absence of the Captain for months at a time, she had indeed to be independent. Thus, while she fed the men lavishly, she would not countenance business discussions over the tea-cups, and it was not until they repaired to the garden again that the vexed question was again addressed.

"Sutherland, Sutherland," mused Kirk.   "Any connection with the Duke?"

"A distant cousin only, I believe, though I think," he added, remembering a remark in one of Isabella's letters, "he's put some money into some Morayshire port development.   I can enquire when I go up there, I expect."

"You'd better dig into it," recommended Robert Kirk. "Mebbe they're thinking of cornering the emigrant trade themselves, and don't want you muscling in."

"I can't believe anyone would be so wicked as deliberately to set up an unsafe voyage."   Alexander was scandalised. "There were five deaths. It may have to go to an Enquiry."

"There you are then!" replied Kirk, triumphant at having his theory reinforced.   "Discredit you, and they can set up an emigration service themselves, charge high prices for filling an otherwise empty ship, and they're in clover."

Alexander was still reluctant to believe the possibility of such a plot, but Kirk urged, "Go and see William Allan. He's a prominent and respected shipping broker, and he may tell you what he thinks of Daniels. And if you're going up to Morayshire, you could at least enquire around."

It was good advice, and after a convivial evening, and the offer of a bed for the night, Alexander felt he had found a good friend, whom he would be happy to entertain in Pictou, whenever Captain Kirk made that particular crossing. In the morning, he checked that Robert would be willing to act as a witness, or at least make an affidavit, and set off to see William Allan.

* * *

WILLIAM ALLAN, Shipping Agent, was painted in gold letters on the glass half-door of the office Alexander visited next morning. The Agent was busy until after lunch, but his clerk booked a meeting with Alexander for the afternoon.

Sitting on the harbour wall in the sunshine, Alexander, who had exchanged the homespun for his new Quebec suit of clothes, in honour of his role as a potential well-to-do customer, turned over in his mind an alternative theory.

Just as he had been momentarily jealous of John Sutherland, perhaps John Sutherland was jealous of him. True, he had no knowledge of whether Isabella had mentioned him to Sutherland, or in what terms, but it was just possible that Sutherland wanted to fix his interest with Isabella, and saw Alexander as a rival. He would keep an open mind until after his next interview and his visit to Morayshire. Whatever the reason, those five deaths had to be avenged.

As he shook hands with William Allan, Alexander felt that this was a man he could do business with. The Shipping Agent was calm, matter-of-fact, business-like and efficient – rather like himself, in fact.

Alexander succinctly described his plan to encourage emigrants from Cromarty to come to Upper Canada. He stressed that he wanted to attract a variety of talents among immigrants to the colony. He had land to offer them, good quality land, where it would be comparatively easy to make a start. He explained that he had failed with his first venture, *The Lovelly Nelly*, because of a rogue Captain, and insufficient preparation in the North.

The Lovelly Nelly debacle had obviously already reached the ears of William Allan. He sympathised. "Did you charter through Daniels?" he asked, snorting when the answer was in the affirmative.

"Well, I can do charter work, or I can operate the ships and give you a commission on each passenger," he offered. "The latter way I take more of the risk – you may prefer it. I run three or four ships a year to Pictou and Quebec of varying capacities, cabin and steerage. You already know it is in our interest to find passengers, as otherwise the ships would be empty one way."

Alexander had envisaged working on charter rather than commission, but when they discussed figures, either seemed feasible. Alexander said he would need to find a good recruiting agent in Morayshire, as his cousin had now emigrated, and was not available.

"I can give you an introduction to Richard Gordon," suggested William Allan. "He's a retired Naval man. I came across him when he was stationed here. Lives at Fearn, near Tain. He may know someone."

Alexander thanked him, and mentioned his suspicion that there might be more behind *The Lovelly Nelly* incident than just a rogue Captain. "It has been suggested to me that someone actively wants to stop me developing an emigration agency because they want the trade for themselves."

"That could be," responded William Allan cautiously. "Clearances are certainly anticipated up North. They want more land for the Big Sheep, I gather, and there are moves to evict the crofters. Quite a neat fiddle – to move them off the land, and then charge them high prices for their passage to the New World!"

Alexander was again horrified, and exclaimed that he did not think people could be so wicked.

"Well, sometimes the lairds will pay; sometimes there are charities to put up some money. Talk to Richard Gordon," urged William Allan. "He'll know what's what in Morayshire and northwards, I don't doubt. If anyone knows who was behind that miserable sea crossing you got landed with, it could be him!"

While at the docks, Alexander enquired about local ships, and booked his passage on *The Pride of Scotland*, sailing north the very next day. He then spent a glorious hour stocking up on newspapers and books in preparation for the voyage and his later travels. He had the hunger for knowledge natural to a man whose intellect had been frustrated by the limitations of his daily existence.

Chapter 13 – Tain

Isabella, still in ignorance of these developments, had undertakings of her own to occupy her mind. Although there had been only one letter back from Patrick Stewart, her first Missionary, she had found it so encouraging that she was determined to press ahead with the appointment of a second. She knew this would put a strain on their funds, but she thought that, should the second Missionary reach Cape Breton this Autumn, he could meet up with Patrick Stewart. They could then share the planning and preparation that would be needed in order to use Cape Breton's relatively short summer next year to best advantage in commencing to build the Churches. To make a start seemed to her of great importance. It is always easier to raise money if you can point to positive achievement rather than pious hopes.

The Committee interviewed again, and this time did find someone who also met with the approval of the Glasgow Colonial Society. James McLeod was an Edinburgh cleric, a man of some erudition, who had been enthused, since the early days, with what Isabella and her ladies were doing. Indeed, he had joined in with it, offering his Church for some of the fund-raising, and supporting the concert, which Isabella had organised. He had, moreover, been acquiring a library of religious works, which he wished to send to Cape Breton, badgering his fellow clergy for Bibles and catechisms, which he thought they would need. It was probably not his original intention to go himself, but he claimed to have received a "call" to do so. This so impressed the Interviewing Committee that they could hardly refuse. Isabella had her reservations as to whether he would be able to cope with the cold and the poverty, but allowed herself to be swept along with the majority. She was not a dictator, after all, and she might be wrong. Thus James McLeod and his packing cases of books were despatched to Greenock to catch a late boat to Cape Breton.

To support the salaries of two Ministers was a major undertaking. Isabella redoubled her efforts. While Edinburgh remained their primary source of funds, she saw the need, as she had discussed with the Chairman of the Glasgow Colonial Society, to expand the organisation into other towns. She felt like a Missionary herself as she made plans for a tour, taking in Falkirk, Stirling, Perth, Dundee, Aberdeen and Inverness, and even penetrating as far North as Tain, at the earnest request of the Churchmen there.

She let Joanna make the promised visit to her family, shut up her house, and took Mrs. Tennant with her, as between them the two ladies could count on hospitality from friends and relations in many of the places to be visited. They planned to travel by road, at least on the outward journey, though it might be possible to come back by sea. Isabella would speak to meetings and congregations, while Mrs. Tennant would look after the pamphlets and descriptive tracts they would take with them, and gather names of new contacts. They hoped to form groups who would continue the good work after they had left the area.

It was to be a three-week journey, and Isabella had in fact left her little house before Alexander's letter describing the disaster to *The Lovelly Nelly* had arrived. She certainly did not know that he intended to come to Scotland. For the same reason – slowness of the mail – her letter describing her plans for the journey had not arrived before he left.

* * *

Alexander, thus spared the disappointment of not finding Isabella at home in Edinburgh, since he had voluntarily denied himself the pleasure of calling on her while he was in the city, enjoyed his coastal voyage.

There was much to see, they called at various ports, and he had his newspapers, with which to acquaint himself with current information.

The ship eventually rounded the headland at Tarbat Ness, where one of his fellow passengers said they had plans to build a new lighthouse, and proceeded westward along the south side of the Dornoch Firth, passing Portmahomack before arriving at the tiny port of Tain. Alexander went to check in at the Balnagowan Inn where, if William Allen's message had produced the desired result, he hoped to meet with Richard Gordon.

The former Naval Officer was in the lounge bar, and identified the stranger quite easily. A tall, upright man, he excused himself from his party of friends and came across to greet the newcomer with a firm handshake.

"Mr. Thomson?   William Allan sent you?" he enquired.

Alexander had thought it important to prepare his approach with some care.

"I have relatives in Morayshire," he explained, when they had sat down and ordered a drink, "who have told me that there are many in this part of Scotland who would like to emigrate to Upper Canada. I want to try and set up an organisation, which will help them. Have you time to listen to a strange story about my first attempt?"

Richard nodded, and Alexander recounted the history of his investigations at Leith, after the disaster of *The Lovelly Nelly's* voyage, and how he was determined to get to the bottom of the problem before he would feel confident enough to set up his agency.

Richard Gordon asked a question or two as the account progressed, but when Alexander reached the suppositions of William Allan and Robert Kirk from Leith as to what might be behind the discredited voyage, he drew in his breath sharply, and made a contribution of his own:

"This John Sutherland," he said, "I think we know him up here from what has happened – or not happened – over the harbour.   Your boat called at the very small pier here, which, four years ago, was scheduled for enlargement – new breakwater, deepening, new pier, that sort of thing.   The Town Council wanted the work done but could not find enough money for an undertaking on that scale.   They could find some money – to prime the pump, as it were.   A local businessman brought in this John Sutherland, who has a local office, but also seemed to have all sorts of contacts in Edinburgh, whom he swore would put up the capital. A lot of us here said we would take shares if the capital could be raised.   We got a prospectus and an invitation to subscribe, but after that, nothing!   The Town Council is furious, because their money paid for the prospectus, and now they've been left high and dry, with no further sign of a harbour."

"Did people part with their money?" asked Alexander.

"I believe some did, which would make it fraud. I'm not accusing him of that – yet!   I'm accusing him of lifting everyone's hopes and dashing them down again. If he couldn't raise the money, he should have said so . . . ." his voice trailed off, as he realised his companion was not listening.

Alexander had been suddenly transfixed by the sight of Isabella walking into the lounge with three other people.   He could not believe his eyes.   He got up to rush across and greet her. Then sat down again. She was registering at the hotel desk.

"It's someone I know," he explained to Richard Gordon. "I had thought she would be in Edinburgh. I must speak with her."

"Don't mind me," said the Naval Officer. "I think we must talk more about this anyway. My wife says I should invite you to lunch with us tomorrow."

Alexander expressed his thanks, but by now had caught Isabella's eye. She was similarly turned to stone, as she recognised someone who should have been in Pictou.

"I'll come back," said Alexander. "Excuse me for a moment."

He walked quickly to where Isabella was standing, and seized her hand.

"What are you doing here?" she asked.

"What an unexpected surprise!" They spoke simultaneously. They both laughed.

"I must introduce you to Mrs. Tennant, who is travelling with me," said Isabella, "and to Mr. and Mrs. Lechie who have invited us to Tain Church to appeal for Cape Breton. This is Mr. Alexander Thomson, whom I last saw in Pictou," she explained to her companions. "I had no idea he was coming to Scotland, which is why I am so surprised to see him!"

Alexander greeted Mrs. Tennant and the Lechies as was proper. "I have had to come over on a serious business matter," he explained. "But certainly I never expected to meet Mrs. Liddel in a small place like Tain, when she is almost the only person I know in the whole of Scotland!"

The others tactfully drew away a little.

"I am due to speak after the Church Service," said Isabella. "It starts in about half an hour, and I must wash and change. Can we meet later?"

"For supper?"

"If they still serve it. If not, for whatever you can get. Alexander, what has happened?"

"Did you not get my letters? No, you couldn't have done ...Never mind, we'll talk about it later. It is so wonderful to see you!"

She smiled and re-joined her party, while Alexander returned to Richard Gordon.

"A very elegant lady," observed Richard. "Is she a special friend?"

"Very special," Alexander admitted. "But I should tell you about her. She is a widow who came to Pictou last year to try and re-claim some debts due to her late husband's estate. While she was there, my father insisted I escort her to Cape Breton Island. I went with some reluctance, because it is very primitive in most places, but I had plans to preach there in any case. My brother and I are virtually the only people who represent the Presbyterian Church on the island, and that only once or twice a year as we are lay people. Mrs. Liddel was so dismayed at the sad lack of Churches or Ministers that she has set herself the task of raising funds to supply them. She works incredibly hard to achieve that, and I now see she is bringing the message to Tain."

"All power to her elbow!" said Richard. "I am sure my wife would like to meet her. We don't see many interesting visitors here. Bring her to lunch, too, tomorrow, if she can be persuaded to come. Twelve noon or thereabouts."

Alexander obtained directions to their house in Fearn, warned Richard Gordon that John Sutherland was known to Isabella, and they parted company.

To say that Alexander was overjoyed at the turn events had taken would be an under-statement. To have deliberately deprived himself of the opportunity to visit her in Edinburgh, only to be pitch-forked into an encounter with Isabella here, was extraordinary. He wanted to hear her speak, but did not wish to embarrass her. Perhaps if he crept into the back row once the service had started, he might be able to do so.

It was now six o'clock. He judged a service starting at six-thirty, followed by a talk, would mean a meal at eight. He embarked on a protracted negotiation with Mine Host and his good lady to secure this concession, and went to his own room to change.

From the window, which overlooked the cobbled square, he could see the Church to the left of the hotel. People were already assembling. He watched Richard Gordon, now joined by a lady he presumed to be his wife, meeting and talking with other worthy citizens. Eventually, the church clock struck the half-hour and the congregation went in.

* * *

For her part, Isabella also was disconcerted, but her long training in social etiquette stood her in good stead. It was impossible to give way to the emotions she felt, while she had, first, a speech to deliver, and secondly, had a close companion observing her every move. As she brushed her hair carefully, she studied her face in the mirror.

She was not vain, and she was prepared to be critical. No longer girlish, her skin was still smooth and clear, her hair glossy, her lips firm, her eyes bright. She assumed a new lilac dress, banished that secret smile which was playing round her mouth, and went downstairs, composed and serious, to perform.

That it was, by now, a performance, was inevitable. She had done this speech so many times that she had got it to a fine art.

First, she had to make a delicate reference to the generosity of the Church in allowing herself, a mere woman, to speak in these sacred precincts. Then she had to describe the outline of her journey to Cape Breton. Then she needed to create a picture of the sheer poverty of some villages; then to describe the way the more self-sufficient were triumphing over adversity. Then to ask how her audience would feel if they were deprived of the comfort and solace of their Church in times of death and despair, at times of joy, or in times of temptation; how would they feel if the well-ordered structure of their society suddenly ceased to exist, because there were no rules or commandments any more? She said the Edinburgh Ladies Association was launched to right these wrongs in Cape Breton, to provide that structure, to convey the generosity of the comfortable to the acute needs of the pioneers, to enable Scotland to assist its own people. She wanted them to give generously tonight, but also to continue the crusade for the benefit of the whole island until it was in a position to stand on its own feet.

She spoke without a note. Her voice was clear, well-modulated, using pauses to good effect, her words telling, her commitment and feeling shining through. Alexander, a speaker himself, thought how brilliantly she gave her address. He had kept his head bowed at the rear of the Church, so as not to catch her eye and distract her. He understood why she was in such demand, and how she had achieved success so quickly. He felt quite humble, quite unworthy, even to try to take this admirable woman away from her self-appointed mission —and at the same time determined to do so, if he could!

* * *

The meal proved a disappointment, which tested Alexander's good manners to the limit. He should have foreseen that Mrs. Tennant would be impossible to shake off, and would make an unwelcome third at the table. She was undoubtedly a very good woman, but obsessed by the trivial. The collection had amounted to £18.6s 8d, which was a welcome addition to their funds, but was it worth coming all this way for, Mrs. Tennant complained. In vain, Isabella said it was not only the collection, but also the good-will and the prospect of forming an off-shoot of the Edinburgh Ladies' Association, which was important.

Alexander, at Isabella's prompting, started to tell the story of *The Lovelly Nelly's* disastrous voyage and his subsequent investigations. Here again, a distinct problem arose. Isabella was seemingly impervious to implied suggestions that John Sutherland could have had any deliberate part in the ship's misfortunes. She pooh-poohed the idea and put it all down to "tittle-tattle."

He had every reason to know that she was an intensely loyal woman, and he honoured her for that. In order not to raise her antagonism, he suppressed his misgivings, despite being more than ever convinced of the case, since he had heard Richard Gordon's own doubts about Sutherland's integrity.

Isabella was more encouraging over his plans to continue the emigration venture, but with more reliable agents, and enquired whether he hoped Richard Gordon would take the job on himself. She would happily accept the invitation to lunch tomorrow if he thought she could help to persuade him.

"You won't mind, will you, Mildred?" she asked Mrs. Tennant. "I don't think we can inflict tthree extra guests on poor Mrs. Gordon."

"Indeed not, dear Isabella," twittered Mrs. Tennant. "I shall wander round this delightful little town, and go and have tea with the Lechies, if they are available, and check up on some of our contacts."

With that Alexander had to be content. He would have Isabella to himself for at least part of tomorrow. Judging from the skill with which she had disposed of her companion, he hoped that was what she wanted too.

Chapter 14 - Partnerships

At about eleven the next morning Isabella joined Alexander on the steps of the inn. Alexander had arranged with a nearby stable to hire a pony and trap for the day, and they set out on the road south from Tain. On the left they had a fine view of the hilly terrain of Sutherland, stretching northward into the distance along the East coast of Scotland. The clear air made it possible to see great distances. It was a mild, September day, but as always, there was an edge to the wind.

"I'm sorry this is such a simple equipage," said Alexander. "It is so long since I've driven a pair, I think I would get the ribbons mixed up."

"You will do better than me. I never learned to drive, even when I lived at home in the country."

"Used you to ride, Isabella?"

"A little. Gentle exercise, rather than hunting. But I didn't even do that in Glasgow."

"I walked round the central square when I was there last week. I thought it very grand. Did you live nearby?"

"We lived in Charlotte Street. . . a big house with principal rooms on the first floor, and separated from Glasgow Green by a private gate. We had a mews for the horses, and a dozen servants. I can't think why we wanted them all. I'm much happier in my little house in Edinburgh. Will you have time to come and see it?"

"I hope so," he answered. "Depending on the ships, and whether the Parliamentary Enquiry is to be this year or next."

"Parliamentary Enquiry?   Is that on account of *The Lovelly Nelly?*"

"Yes, I did not want to say too much last night, with your friend present, but there were <u>five deaths,</u> Isabella.   I am very conscience-stricken about that. Moreover, it will have a detrimental effect on confidence in this part of Scotland.   Archibald Buchanan, (you may remember from my letters he is the Immigration Agent in Quebec) thinks they may tack *The Lovelly Nelly* on to the end of an Enquiry which is to be held in Parliament to examine the conditions on emigrant ships.   There have been some very serious cases. Buchanan has to put in a report. I must find out when the Enquiry is likely to be. It might be at a time when I couldn't travel from Pictou because of the ice."

"I know some Members of Parliament," offered Isabella. "Perhaps I could discover that for you."   She felt great sympathy for him, and they fell silent, reflecting on the disaster.

After a few minutes the road veered left towards Nigg and they saw the hill of Fearn coming into view on the right hand side.   Alexander turned the pony to the right up a sheltered drive leading to a substantial stone house with mullioned windows, and tall chimneys. Two large, happy dogs appeared and ran round the trap, as it drew to a halt in front of the heavy wooden door.

Standing in front of the door was a distinguished-looking figure.   Richard Gordon was a retired Vice-admiral.   An Englishman, who had completed a successful career in the Royal Navy, he had retired to Fearn only recently to live with his Scottish wife in her ancestral home. Although he had made many contacts in the area, he was still at something of a loose end. He was looking forward to the further contact with Alexander, as he sensed there was a possibility of a new project in which he himself might become involved. There were few of those in this part of Scotland, with its deteriorating economy. His eyes had the clear look of one accustomed to a position of command. He greeted his guests, helped Isabella down from the trap, and introduced his wife, Jane, who appeared at the door to welcome the guests inside. A manservant took the bridle to lead the pony round to the stables.

They went into a spacious, well-appointed drawing-room, and sat down. Alexander and Richard exchanged pleasantries, and talked of their mutual acquaintance, William Allan. It also transpired that Richard had visited Halifax, Pictou and the St. Lawrence ports several times during his naval career, so there were reminiscences to be mulled over. Isabella soon discovered Jane was a staunch Presbyterian. They had attended last night's service, and Jane warmly congratulated Isabella on her appeal. She said she was inspired and prepared to help behind the scenes to raise money for the work in Cape Breton.

A maid came to announce lunch, and they withdrew to the dining-room. After grace, conversation moved on to the question of emigration to the Maritimes and how it could be promoted. They discussed the way in which potential emigrants might be made aware of ships leaving for Pictou and Upper Canada.

Alexander described the land he had already acquired, and the further land, which he hoped would become available. He stressed that it was his own desire, and he understood also the policy of the Immigration Officer, Archibald Buchanan, to encourage viable communities, which could work together as one, and better endure the harsh conditions and isolation of life on the frontier.

"This is not a particularly new policy," he added. "My father, William the Pioneer, was recruited by Lord Selkirk in 1803, as an experienced farmer, to give guidance to other immigrants who might not have acquired the more modern skills. The land I shall buy will be good land," he added. "Those coming over will face nothing like the same hardships as the first settlers did. But we need a balanced community. While farmers will be the mainstay of it, they will need teachers for their schools, Ministers of Religion, shop-keepers, skilled craftsmen of many kinds. I want to encourage people who may not even have thought about emigrating to see and seize the opportunities. I would like to start in 1828 with three or four ships, then build up in 1829 and 1830, when my bigger land purchase goes through, to double that number. But I need someone over here to advise and promote the scheme, a respected figure, to make sure the ships are not over-crowded, and organise the scheme at this end."

From Richard's point of view, this seemed an attractive opportunity. He had an extensive range of contacts in the area, from the Black Isle in the south, to Sutherland and Caithness in the north, and he described some of these. Furthermore, he had used his time since retirement to find out the economic facts of life in Northern Scotland, and he concurred with Alexander that it would be in the best interests of many to seek to emigrate. He wanted to assist in this process, while at the same time he could see that there was money to be made from that assistance.

Richard was impressed by what he saw in Alexander. They had discussed some facts about *The Lovelly Nelly* at their first meeting the previous day, but he felt he needed to probe further. What exactly had gone wrong?

"I must accept the blame," said Alexander. "I relied upon people I did not know, and I arranged it all without the checks that were necessary. Nevertheless, I suspect the worst. Fact One: the Captain I had hired, Robert Kirk, was definitely drugged. Who ordered that? Fact Two: the replacement, Jon Kruger, was totally unsuited to captain any vessel, let alone one carrying my passengers to Pictou. Who appointed him? The disaster that resulted was an inevitable consequence of him gaining command of the ship, whether or not he was ordered to steer too far south. I hate to say this in Isabella's presence, but I fear there was a plot to discredit me and my operation. I suspect John Sutherland may have been at the heart of it."

Isabella coloured at the mention of John Sutherland. "Vice-Admiral, I must tell you that Mr. Thomson and I do not agree about this," she interposed. "I have known John Sutherland for some time, and cannot believe he would have acted in such an underhand way."

The atmosphere became tense.

"Mrs. Liddel," began Richard Gordon heavily, "you might well have been misled. Let me tell you of Fact three: John Sutherland has been behind a shady and so far abortive scheme to raise money for harbour improvements here in Tain and in the Moray Firth. None of these schemes has come to fruition after four years, although prospectuses have been issued, and money subscribed. There could well be a reason for his trying to get the port of Tain expanded if he intended to profit from forced emigration from the Sutherland and other estates. There are already burnings of crofts and clearance of villages. The people live in fear. It is my impression that John Sutherland is a smooth-talking rogue, and could well have taken the opportunity to try and dispose of an unwelcome business rival, who would set up an honourable emigration agency, instead of a situation where he exercised sole rights."

Isabella subsided. She could not take on the two men together in argument, nor was it fitting to argue with her host.

Richard continued: "Mr. Thomson was right to suspect Sutherland. I would certainly not do business with him, and I would certainly not do business with you, Thomson, if you had allowed yourself to be hood-winked. But you have not. You may never be able to prove it, but the result of that piece of trickery has been manslaughter, if not murder. However, as we see eye to eye over Sutherland, I believe I can help you overcome the difficulties caused by *The Lovelly Nelly* incident, even an Enquiry, should it come to that. If you have finished, let us adjourn and talk terms, while the ladies have their coffee."

Isabella's confusion increased. Five deaths as a result of incompetence were one thing, but five deaths, as a result of possible knavery, was different – and unforgivable.

She and her hostess walked round the extensive gardens in the afternoon, enjoying conversation far removed from emigration and death. Her observation and delight in the garden provided a safe topic of conversation as she and Alexander drove back into Tain later in the afternoon. She described the arbours, where seats were placed from which to enjoy the view, the lily pond, the copse of trees which provided a wind break and shelter. She enthused over the fruit cages, where raspberry canes had provided luscious fruit, and where the stems were now brown and withered, with the new shoots green and full of promise at their feet. But the shadow of the argument over John Sutherland still lay between them, too fundamental to be broached in case it led to further disagreement.

What they did establish was that both had booked passage on *The Pride of Scotland*, returning to Leith the following day. "I hate being jolted over rough roads," said Isabella, a trifle mendaciously. "So I persuaded Mildred that we would do better by sea."

Alexander could not remember whether he had mentioned his own plans the previous evening, but whether by accident or design, it was a happy outcome!

* * *

As the little coastal ship pulled away from the pier next day, leaving the Tolbooth with its conical towers, and the ruins of St. Duthac's chapel behind, Alexander, Isabella and Mildred Tennant were leaning over the rail, and waving to the send-off parties on shore. Isabella retailed the story of St. Duthac, as she had learned it from her hosts. James 1V of Scotland had visited the shrine of St. Duthac each year from 1492 to 1513, conferring royal approval on the little town.

Eventually, as the ship reached more open water, Mildred Tennant and many other passengers went below to escape the chill wind, while Isabella and Alexander moved imperceptibly closer to each other. Alexander planted his right hand over hers.

"There's something about sunlight on water, and ships, small and large, that have a magic for us, isn't there?" he said quietly.

Her mind flew back to the first day off Cape Breton Island. She did not pretend to misunderstand him. In fact at Alexander's touch she felt again that physical magnetism that he had excited in her on Cape Breton. "I know . . ." she whispered softly. He held her gaze for a moment, then deliberately looked away again at the sea.

"If I were to ask you to marry me, would you consider the possibility?" he asked in a level voice. Her heart skipped a beat. She had not expected such a quick declaration, although she knew their lives had developed a close and common interest. She understood him so much better through their long Trans-Atlantic correspondence. She was not in doubt that he was very important to her.

"Yes, I would consider it," she replied, trying to keep her voice equally matter-of-fact. The hand, strong, dependable, hardened by physical effort, tightened on hers. He glanced quickly around to see if they were observed. Satisfied they were not, he kissed her lightly.

"But you've not actually asked me?" she queried, when their lips parted.

"Not yet. I do not know how this matter of *The Lovelly Nelly* will develop. It could be very damaging to my reputation, and injurious to my business. I don't want to drag you into that."

"Not even if I were willing?" Her response was becoming even more positive.

"No, I must not. It would not be fair. And there's more to it than that. I have a rival, I know."

"John Sutherland can no longer be a friend of mine," Isabella replied with firm emphasis. She had thought long and hard about that relationship the previous evening, and had concluded that the presumption of evil intent was too strong for her to ignore.

"I am thankful about that," said Alexander. "But I wasn't referring to another man. No, this is more fundamental. My real rival is your Faith."

"You could not ask me to give that up?" she questioned, disbelieving that she had heard aright.

"Of course not," Alexander reassured her hastily. "But you have a mission you are determined to fulfil. That is my rival in your mind and your loyalties. I believe that it will be possible for your fundraising and organisation to stand firm and continue, whether you are here in Scotland or not. It might be time to move on. If we were living in Pictou, you could see the results of your work in Cape Breton, and help to organise the receipt of the aid. But you need to be sure that that would satisfy you. So, when I ask you again, and I will, I want you to be sure that you would be content with that."

Isabella was a little mollified, but still not totally clear about his meaning. "But, Alexander, you have the Faith too;" she said. "How can it be your rival?"

"Indeed, I have. We share the same beliefs. But with me, it is a part of my life and not the whole. You have been seeking to make your Faith the whole of your life, my love, and I want to be sure there's a piece left for me!"
"Then I promise I will think it through."

"A conditional proposal and a conditional response! But I do love you, Isabella, and I do want us to be together, if that is what you truly want, too."

He produced a small pouch from his pocket. "I want you to have a keepsake. Tain is famed for its silversmiths, so I thought this might suit."

She drew a silver scarf-ring in the shape of a flying bird from the pouch.

"It is quite delightful," she said, touched by his thoughtfulness and the symbolism of the gift.

This time the lady initiated the kiss, and the gentleman converted it to one of passion.

Chapter 15 - The Select Committee

The gavel thudded down on the oak desk. The black-coated usher closed the double doors and stood with his back against them to deny further entry.

Alexander and Archibald Buchanan had secured places in the middle of the long side of the panelled room, having received formal notice to attend. From their position they could observe both the Chairman and his semi-circle of Committee members, and the point opposite to the Chairman, to which witnesses would be called to give evidence. The Chairman, Sir Impney Bigby, was a formidable Member of Parliament, large in stature and of considerable independence of mind. He usually employed a single eye-glass as a weapon of interrogation, fixing his gaze upon a mesmerised victim until he received a satisfactory answer.

The Parliamentary Select Committee enquiring into conditions on emigrant ships was about to begin, in late April 1828, having been postponed from the previous year.

Alexander, who had left Scotland for Nova Scotia on almost the last ship of 1827, had returned on the first ship of 1828 to attend the hearing.

Among the Whig, Tory and cross-bench Members of Parliament were some who had served on the 1826/7 Select Committee which had considered the use of public money to promote emigration to the colonies, and had rejected it. The Committee had concluded that emigration should be self-financing, but retained an on-going remit to consider emigrant issues of grave public concern. There had been four shipping disasters the previous year, all involving loss of life on emigrant ships; two from Liverpool, one from Glasgow and one from

Cromarty.   Attempts to bring criminal charges had failed in each case because of insufficient evidence.

Consequently the MPs for the areas affected, who had campaigned strenuously for a public enquiry, had been referred instead to the Select Committee, and were now representing their constituents' anxieties over lost relatives.   The Committee was to hear evidence from them, and a great many witnesses, -- ship owners, sea captains, crew members, emigration agents and customs officers. Each would have their turn, as the Committee sought to get the bottom of the shipping disasters and make suitable recommendations.

The Lovelly Nelly would be the last case to be heard, and was unlike the others.   The death toll had been very small, compared with the 60 lost on one of the Liverpool ships.   Moreover, the suffering and deaths on the other ships had mainly been brought about by severe over-crowding, not the case with *The Lovelly Nelly*.

The clerk told Alexander that all attempts to locate Jon Kruger, the relief captain on *The Lovelly Nelly* had failed, but that Robert Kirk, the original Captain, and Daniels, the shipping agent, had been subpoenaed to attend. He understood that Charles Daniels was bringing a witness.

The proceedings ground on each morning. Archibald Buchanan was to be called in all cases since he and his department had been at the receiving-end of the various voyages.   He therefore could not leave, but Alexander, who only wanted to ensure that he understood the procedure, on some days left the hearing early, and enjoyed the Spring sunshine in London.   He went to a bespoke tailor and ordered two more suits of clothes and other garments, wanting to ensure that his appearance matched that of the many well-dressed and fashionable men with whom he was to come into contact.

The small hotel in which he and Buchanan were staying made no demands on style, but in the evenings the two men sometimes visited West End establishments, or special sites of interest in the Metropolis. Archibald knew the city well from his years as a colonial civil servant. He and Alexander had become firm friends. Both shared a burning desire to see emigration to Upper Canada and the Maritimes succeed. Both knew that haphazard schemes were likely to fail, often at serious cost, not only in the loss of life which was currently under investigation, but because the reception of immigrants in North America left much to be desired. The Canada Company would go some way to redress that balance, in providing emigrants with job and land opportunities in settlements which had a basic infrastructure of roads, houses and in some cases schools and churches, but the transit of immigrants to the promised lands had also had its disasters.

Archibald had made contact with a wonderful lady in Quebec called Mary Talbot who was about to set up a Quebec Immigrants Society to raise funds to help the destitute on their further journey. Alexander expressed a wish to meet her. He had also been concerned with this problem. Although, in his conversations with Richard Gordon, he had stressed the need for emigrants to be well-briefed before their departure to ensure that they knew what to expect on arrival, he also knew that there would be families, desperate to leave Scotland and bereft of resources, who would make the journey regardless of advice, and need help, both monetary and practical, when they got there.

Alexander discussed with Archibald the need for a balanced intake of immigrants. He would be prepared, from his own resources of land, he said, and mindful of the Cape Breton experience, to make parcels of land available at no cost for the provision of churches and schools. He would be prepared to employ diviners to find water, and sink wells. He would want to set up and operate the first stores in each developing area, since, from his own experience, he knew what was needed, and he would find purchasers or managers.

Archibald was delighted. To work with such a man, who had both vision, and much practical knowledge, would be a pleasure. He must ensure that *The Lovelly Nelly* incident could be put behind them, so that the good work could begin.

* * *

The investigation turned at length to the subject of *The Lovelly Nelly* and her ill-fated voyage.

"Call Charles Daniels," the usher intoned.

Charles Daniels moved to sit in the appointed seat, glancing to left and right uncertainly, and was questioned about his name, experience and expertise.

"Do you own *The Lovelly Nelly*, a ship registered at Leith?" asked the Chairman.

"Yes, well, part-own," said Daniels.

"Part-own?" queried another member of the Committee. "Explain who are the other owners."

"It's like a company, sir," explained Daniels. "I have the biggest share, and operate the ship. Others have some shares in her in varying proportions."

"How long have you operated this ship?"

"Five years, Sir. Mostly on the North Atlantic run. But I also deal with other ships. I am a shipping agent."

"Can you name the other shareholders?" asked a Committee member from the opposite side. "How many are there?"

"Four, Sir. I have a list here. But the shareholders have no day-to-day control. I book the captains, pay the wages, arrange provisions, and the job the ship has to do."

"Describe what happened with the booking of that particular voyage."

"I received an indication that there was a man in Pictou wanting to find a ship to pick up emigrants from Cromarty. I wrote to him to offer terms."

"Do you see this man in the room today?"

"I would not recognise him, Sir. I never met him. His name was Alexander Thomson."

"We shall be questioning Mr. Thomson," intervened the Chairman. "Who did you tell Mr. Thomson would be the Captain?"

"I told Mr. Thomson that the Captain would be Robert Kirk, who had captained the ship many times before and was experienced, and knew what was wanted. I have a copy of the letter, Sir. I quoted a price which Mr. Thomson accepted."

"We shall be questioning Robert Kirk," said the Chairman. "Was he actually in command of *The Lovelly Nelly*" during this voyage?"

"No, Sir. He arrived to prepare the ship, and provision it. Then on the morning of the voyage, he did not turn up."

"Did you enquire where he was, or send out a search party?"

"No, Sir, there was no time."

"What did you do?"

"Well, there was a Captain I knew, who had asked me for a berth, and I had not been able to offer him one. He was actually in the office at the time. I asked if he would be willing to sail the ship, as the booked Captain was missing. That was Mr. Kruger."

"Mr. Jon Kruger is not available," said the Chairman, disapprovingly. "Efforts have been made to trace him, but it seems he may not be in this country. Apparently he is of Dutch nationality."

"What steps did you take to ensure that Mr. Kruger was qualified?" asked another Member of Committee.

"He showed me a Certificate. He said he'd been on a North Atlantic run before."

"A North Atlantic run?" pounced another Committee member.

"Well, yes, but they're all much the same. And it wasn't as if it was a difficult time of year. There would be no ice, nor expectation of bad weather. And the ship was ready, Sir."

"So, instead of waiting a day to contact the experienced Captain, you sent an inexperienced man out in his place?"

"I suppose it amounts to that," agreed Daniels, sullenly. "But there were people waiting in Cromarty to be collected. Waiting a day would not please them."

"Waiting a day would not please you, I suggest," interjected another Committee member. "You would have to pay the crew another day's wages, would you not?"

"Yes." The reluctant acquiescence came grudgingly.

"I think that is all for the moment," said the Chairman, after a prolonged eye-glass-assisted stare at Daniels. "You may stand down, but please do not leave the room, in case we need you again. Call Robert Kirk."

Robert Kirk, who had fulfilled his promise to Alexander that he would be willing to testify, then took the appointed chair. After the usual preliminaries, when he confirmed his name, that he was a Ship's Captain on the North Atlantic run, and that he had fifteen years' experience, he asked to make a statement.

"You are not likely to ask me this, Sir," he said, "and so I'll need to tell you. I was appointed Captain; I did provision the ship for an expected 70 people in addition to the crew, and hired my usual sailors, though I had to take a substitute cook, and I was all ready to go to sea, when it is my belief someone drugged me to prevent me taking the ship out."

"Drugged?" The Committee was startled, and all looked up at the Captain. There was a perceptible rustle of surprise among the audience.

"Describe what happened, please."

"I went into the local tavern to have a pint after a hard day's work.   I'd drunk a little, when I suddenly crashed out, and hit my head on the floor."

"Had anything like this ever happened before?"

"No, Sir. I can hold my liquor, and in any case I'd only had a few swallows. I can't tell you who did it, or how they did it exactly, but I know the effect. I was dead to the world, and the barman and the drayman said afterwards they carried me into a back room till closing time, and then they carted me home.   I didn't come round for eighteen hours."

"Could you have been suffering from ill-health?"

"No, Sir. I had a thick head for an hour or two, but I was as right as rain afterwards, and I've never had anything like it from that day to this, though I've drunk my usual pints often enough."

"Why do you think anyone would want to drug you?"
   "To stop me sailing."

"But why stop you sailing?"

"There are two possibilities," said Kirk. "The first one is to damage me, and I don't know why anyone would want to do that, and I've had no trouble since. The second is that someone wanted to damage Mr. Thomson, to stop him setting up an operation, Sir, to discredit him."

"Have you any proof of such an allegation?"

"No, Sir, and you can't get hold of Mr. Kruger for his evidence, but I understand that he sailed the ship on a wrong course to the south. Whether he did that through sheer ignorance, or whether he was instructed by someone to do so, to delay the ship and make Mr. Thomson look ineffective or unreliable, I can't tell."

There was some conferring among members of the Committee. The Chairman allowed the discussion for a few moments and then called them to order.

"Are you accusing Mr. Daniels of this?" asked one.

"Well, he sent the ship off, post haste, didn't he, but whether there was anyone behind him or not, I can't tell. I've worked for Mr. Daniels off and on for five years, and he's never done such a thing to me before, so it's my guess there was someone else behind it, mebbe someone who's got a hold over Daniels."

"Any more questions?" the Chairman asked of his Committee. "Well, it's possible there will be, after we have taken further evidence, so please don't leave, Captain Kirk. Call Mr. Alexander Thomson."

Alexander was nervous and in awe of his surroundings as he took the witness chair. His throat was dry and constricted, and the palms of his hands were damp with sweat. There was water in a carafe, and he took a glass from which to sip. So much depended on the outcome of this enquiry – not only his reputation and the future of his developing business, but by his own decision, the development of his romance with Isabella. He had spent much of the intervening six months since he had seen her in Scotland, pondering over their future. He had made plans to build a house in Pictou, interviewed builders, and located an ideal piece of land. But the fulfilment of this dream depended on the decisions made by this British Committee.

He was pleased at the Kirk testimony, but, although they had rehearsed the questions he was likely to be asked, and the replies, which he would give, there was always the unexpected. He confirmed his name, his occupation as a merchant, and his expertise in the field of immigration as voluntary only. He was asked to expand on that.

"Sir, my father is William Thomson, known as William the Pioneer," he replied, "who went from Morayshire to Prince Edward Island and Nova Scotia at Lord Selkirk's instigation in 1803, when I was sixteen. My father and I have worked in Pictou to help immigrants to settle. I ran, until recently, a store at which Scottish immigrants could purchase necessary implements on credit, and I used to meet most ships at the harbour to ensure people had somewhere to go. I am also a lay preacher."

"Why did you seek to charter *The Lovelly Nelly*?"

"I mentioned that my family originally came from Morayshire. I have cousins there still, and they wrote to tell me how many people wanted to emigrate, but that few ships called at Cromarty. I sought to help them by chartering a ship. One of my cousins actually travelled out on *The Lovelly Nelly.*"

"Was this your first venture?"

"Sir, I accept full responsibility for not checking on the ship, and for not making sure that my cousin was able to muster a full load of passengers. To that extent, I realise that much tighter arrangements must be made, and I have put them in place for the future. But, yes, it was the first venture in what was intended to be a continuing process."

"When did you discover the substitution of the Captain?"

"Only when *The Lovelly Nelly* arrived in Pictou. I had been waiting for her arrival for nearly three weeks, and I was horrified at the condition I found her in when she did arrive. I tackled the Captain immediately I had helped the passengers off the ship. He is Dutch, I am told, and spoke hardly any English and so I questioned the First Mate at length also."

"What conclusion did you reach?"

"Well, first I had to get the passengers treated for their illness. I concluded that the typhoid had been caused by lack of a cleanliness regime, and through foul drinking water. It was vital for me to get the ship cleaned, re-victualled and watered. We had to leave two families behind in Pictou to recover, but then I went on with the rest to Quebec, and questioned the passengers on the way. As soon as I returned, I hurried over to Scotland to find out the facts."

"Have you formed any theory as to what might have happened?"

"I have established these facts: Fact one: the voyage lasted seven weeks, and the ship was inadequately watered for that length of time. But for the fact that only 50 people embarked at Cromarty instead of the expected 70, the hunger and water shortage would have been much worse. I have established that fresh water was not taken on at Cromarty, as it should have been. Fact two: the bad state of the ship was exacerbated by poor hygiene, and that was the responsibility of the Captain who sailed her and his crew. The passengers were put through an unnecessary and dreadful ordeal."

"The suggestion has been made by Captain Kirk that this could have been an exercise to damage you. Have you any comment?"

"I have naturally thought about it a good deal," replied Alexander, who was beginning to feel more at ease. "Obviously the passengers who suffered would tell their friends about their dreadful experience. That would deter others from emigrating; it would also damage my reputation and scupper my chances of running a successful agency."

"Did you make a profit?" One of the Committee shot out the sudden question.

"No, Sir. I refunded all passenger money. In fact, I made a substantial loss."

"Did you pay Daniels?"

"Yes. I had already paid half the cost in advance. The rest I intended to retain until I had investigated all the circumstances. However, it would seem difficult to find proof for a court of law, and the cost of legal fees would probably swallow up more than the outstanding amount. Besides, I didn't want to meet him. I was afraid I might half kill him for putting my passengers through that hellish experience."

The Chairman intervened. "Mr. Thomson, it would seem that we have to look into these circumstances more thoroughly, and there may not be time to conclude that examination today. I suggest that we now adjourn. You will be required again tomorrow morning, as will Mr. Kirk and Mr. Daniels."

The Enquiry broke up, and Archibald and Alexander walked through the vaulting, impressive historic lobby of the Palace of Westminster.

"Will you drop Sutherland into the equation tomorrow?" asked Archibald.

"I think so, yes. I believe his name may have been among the owners' list, which Daniels gave to the Chairman. Can we find out?"

Any answer was suspended by the totally unexpected sight of Isabella, attired in blue, walking through the lobby towards them.

* * *

"I don't believe it," said Alexander. "What brings you to London?"

"I always planned to come if I could," she replied, taking his outstretched hand. He introduced Archibald Buchanan to her, and they turned to walk out of the House together. "If you can come all the way from Pictou for the Enquiry," she went on, "surely I can make the relatively short journey from Edinburgh!"

"It is good to see you, and I know we intended to meet some time, but I would have travelled to Edinburgh, as soon as I was free," Alexander said.

"I found an urgent need to see a Member of Parliament," replied Isabella. "William Wallace of Ross and Cromarty. I want to put on a big function in Inverness and I need his support."

"He's in the Enquiry, I believe," said Archibald.

"Then I'll wait till it's over. Have you given your evidence yet?" she asked him.

"I've reported on the other three cases. Not on The Lovelly Nelly as yet. I think Alexander has made a good impression, however."

They continued talking over lunch, walked on the Embankment afterwards, and spent the evening together as a threesome, until Isabella returned to her hostess's house in Kensington.

"Where did you find such a lovely lady?" asked Archibald with some degree of envy.

Alexander laughed. "I think she found me. She turned up at my store in Pictou accusing me of owing money to her husband's estate. We had a furious row. But that is long ago. Since then, we have become very good friends."

"More than that, I suspect," probed Archibald.

"Perhaps," admitted Alexander. "It cannot be more until I have cleared my name of this shoddy business."

"You were convincing today, I feel," comforted Archibald. "We'll have to see what tomorrow brings."

* * *

Things got rather out of hand the following day. Alexander took the stand first. He requested sight of the list of owners of *The Lovelly Nelly*. Sure enough, John Sutherland's name was one of the four.

Isabella had entered the room shortly before the proceedings started, the only woman present, her blue outfit standing out in the gloomy room among the funereal black of most men there.

"We have established," began the Chairman, "and you will remember that those testifying are on oath, that there is a suspicion of evil intent on the part of some of the people Mr. Thomson dealt with when hiring *The Lovelly Nelly* for his voyage. Mr. Thomson, what is it you suspect?"

"Sir, I believe from further enquiries I made in Morayshire that Mr. John Sutherland, who is one of the part-owners of *The Lovelly Nelly*, may have instructed Mr. Daniels to sabotage the voyage."

Again the Committee members looked up in surprise at the turn events were taking. There was an audible intake of breath, and someone dropped a book, creating a noise, which reverberated in the sudden silence.

"Why would he do that?" asked the Chairman.

"You will need to ask him, Sir. With respect, he is not likely to tell me. He has port interests in Morayshire, I believe."

"Is Mr. Sutherland present?"

The answer was given in the affirmative. The Chairman conferred with his colleagues. "You may stand down, Mr. Thomson. I think we will re-call Mr. Daniels first."

Charles Daniels looked extremely uncomfortable, and tried to bluster.

"I don't know what all the fuss is about," he said. "I booked Robert Kirk as Captain, and it's not my fault if the silly man got drunk."

"The fuss," said the Chairman with strong emphasis, "is because five people died on this ill-fated voyage. It could become a manslaughter charge at the least. I suggest you re-consider your position, Mr. Daniels. Did Mr. Sutherland or anyone else instruct you to sabotage the voyage?"

"Of course not." The answer came pat, and with all the conviction Daniels could give it. But it committed John Sutherland to support it, at the risk of perjury.

"Call Mr. John Sutherland." The tall lawyer lounged to the witness point, gave his name to the Committee, his profession as lawyer. He had already observed Isabella's presence in the room, and frowned, wondering why she was there. She should have been in Edinburgh, busying herself with bazaars or begging letters for her charity. He had not seen her in the last six months, for she had avoided the Choir to concentrate on her fund-raising. Ladies had no place in the world of shipping contracts and business. Alexander had turned round to look at Isabella, and John Sutherland intercepted the glance between them. His jaw tightened. She seemed mighty friendly with this colonial fellow. He hoped she would not be spreading it around Edinburgh that he himself had been involved with this case.

The Chairman leaned forward. "Mr. Sutherland, you have heard it suggested that you may have had an interest in the voyage of *The Lovelly Nelly*. You are on oath, remember. Did you have any conversation with Mr. Daniels on this subject?"

"Yes. A lady of my acquaintance asked me if I knew any shipping agents, and I mentioned the matter to Mr. Daniels. I see the lady is here, and she could corroborate that."

"What was the context of this discussion? Did you at any time suggest that it would be best if the voyage was unsuccessful?"

"Certainly not. I was a part-owner of the ship and it was in my interest that the voyage should be successful."

The same man who had asked Alexander about his profit again intervened.

"Did you receive any reward for putting Mr. Daniels in the way of receiving extra business?"

John Sutherland hesitated. Daniels might well tell the truth if he didn't.

"Yes, there was a small commission," he said. "10%, I think."

Mr. William Wallace, MP for Ross and Cromarty, and hitherto a silent member of the Committee, then sought the Chairman's permission to question Mr. Sutherland.

"Did you at one time issue prospectuses for an expansion of the port at Tain?" he asked.

"I did, yes."

"Was this four years ago?"

"About that, yes."

"Did people subscribe to the enterprise?"

"Very few actually subscribed. Most people just expressed interest."

"What was your objective in expanding the port?"

"Well, communications are bad in that part of Scotland. I thought it would be helpful to the community, and the Town Council agreed."

"Tain is a small community, Mr. Sutherland. Would there have been enough traffic to justify the new port facilities?"

"Not if you take Tain only; but it has quite a large hinterland."

"Did you envisage that emigrant ships might use the new facilities?"

"Possibly."

"I put it to you, Mr. Sutherland, that you included this possibility as a probability in your prospectus?"

Alexander thought Richard Gordon had probably been busy on his behalf. Mr. Wallace was certainly waving a copy of the prospectus, and was now handing it to the Chairman. Sir Impney received the document gingerly, as if it was a red-hot coal, which figuratively it was.
"I may have done," Sutherland replied.

"Then you would not welcome an interloper developing a trade with Cromarty instead?"

John Sutherland's temper was obviously beginning to fray. He turned to the Chairman for protection. "This matter has nothing to do with the subject of your enquiry," he stated. "I had nothing to do with *The Lovelly Nelly*, and I think Mr. Thomson's accusations are slanderous."

"I think we will be the judge of that," said the Chairman. "There is no question of slander. We are here to establish the truth, and Mr. Thomson's remarks have the protection of privilege, having been made to a Parliamentary Committee. I see from this document that you did write that there was a probability of developing the emigrant trade. Are you connected with the Sutherland estates?"

"I have a distant link with the Sutherland family."

"You have a legal practice in the area, I believe."

"Yes, my father founded it, and I have kept it on."

"You would know the situation in the area. You would be able to obtain knowledge of planned clearances in Scotland?"

"I know of nothing currently planned."

"That is not what I asked," said Sir Impney severely. "I asked whether you, with your family connections and your practice in the area, would be able to obtain advance knowledge of planned clearances in North-East Scotland?"

"I could probably anticipate them from hearsay. But I resent the implication that my business affairs would be based upon them." Witness and Chairman glared fiercely at each other.

"My Committee must make up its own mind on that issue," said the Chairman. "You may stand down. Call Archibald Buchanan."

A shorthand writer took the opportunity to scurry away, his papers of precious evidence shuffled together, and there was a pause as a new clerk entered and joined his fellow at the writing bench. Sir Impney polished the lens of his eye-glass on the edge of a white handkerchief, and swung it to and fro reflectively by its fine golden chain. Alexander had time to look at Isabella. She nodded her head and smiled in approval.

Buchanan's testimony, knowledgeable and gentle as it was, was like a breath of fresh air after the charged acrimony of the last hour. He said that *The Lovelly Nelly* was in an acceptable state of fitness when Alexander had brought her into Quebec, though he understood that had not been the case at Pictou. Mr. Thomson had immediately told him that they had had typhoid on board. He had detained two families in case they developed symptoms. He had made his report on the four deaths, which had occurred on the voyage, and the fifth, that of a child, discovered at Pictou. In his opinion emigrants needed more protection at the port of embarkation if they were to have reliable and safe crossings. He recommended that more customs officers should be employed at Scottish ports to enforce the minimum standards of food and space, which were already covered by legislation.

"I would add," he said, "that if any Captain takes a ship out to sea before a customs officer has come on board to make an inspection and give clearance, he should be apprehended on arrival, and taken to jail to await trial."

"With regard to food," queried a Committee Member, "do you consider the current requirements sufficient?"

"I consider the quantity sufficient, but not the type of provisioning. The food the emigrants like and which they will take with them are potatoes, oatmeal, bacon, eggs, butter and molasses. The basic provisioning is beef and biscuit, which they don't like. The main trouble with hunger on this voyage was that it lasted so long that the stores the emigrants had with them became exhausted, and they then had to fall back on ship's rations. In their weakened state through illness, this was unsuitable."

"Would a more varied provision prove more expensive?"

"Not at all. I could victual emigrants in a way they would like for thirty-five to forty shillings per head."

"You mentioned illness," queried another Member. "Would you advise that there should be medical assistance always on board?"

"If due attention is paid to cleanliness, it is not necessary. Emigrants should normally feel and look a great deal better on arrival than when they went on board. That is, if the ship is well-run, they have fresh air and exercise, good food and clean water."

"So your conclusion in this case," summed up the Chairman, "is that basic hygiene was disregarded by the relief Captain?"

"That and the extension of the voyage, due to incompetence or evil designs," agreed Archibald.

The room was silent, as the audience reflected on the evidence given. The Chairman, as he had done when each ship's case had been considered, asked those present to remember the victims of the voyage and those who had been bereaved. The Committee would now consider its conclusions in private. The current proceedings ended with a prayer.

Chapter 16 - Revenge

Isabella joined William Wallace by appointment later in the day for tea at the House of Commons. She took Alexander with her, and he expressed gratitude for the M.P.'s intervention in the enquiry, which had established a possible motive for John Sutherland's actions.

"Yes," the MP replied. "Richard Gordon supplied me with a copy of the prospectus, but you probably know that many people are angry over the promises made and delays in any action over the proposed port expansion at Tain. I have a duty to inquire into that on their behalf. Probably nothing is capable of proof, but I think the implications were clear and relevant. I shall be releasing a transcript of the proceedings with some comments to the local press when the Report comes to hand."

"Do you think Alexander will be cleared? asked Isabella.

"I should not discuss the case, but it seems likely. It is obvious he had no knowledge of the machinations at this end of the journey, for he was in Pictou. However, we shall have to wait for the report's publication before we can be sure. It will take two or three months at least."

"Will you be able to get a copy of the Report for me please?" requested Isabella.

"Certainly. Mr. Thomson will be sent one, of course, as a material witness. Now, you wanted to see me, I think, about a function in Inverness?"

Alexander, sensitive to the proprieties, realised that it might not be appropriate for the MP, as a Member of the Select Committee, to be seen in close conversation with one of its key witnesses. He excused himself, and withdrew a little way from the other two. First, he gazed from the window over the view of the murky Thames, with several little boats bobbing about on its waters. He marvelled at his very presence here in the capital city of the Empire. If indeed the MP was right and he was exonerated from blame in the matter of *The Lovelly Nelly*, it was all he could hope for, and his way would be cleared to pursue the dearest wish of his life.

He turned to enjoy the nearer vision of Isabella in her deep blue hat and lighter blue summery dress keenly discussing her project with the MP. She spoke animatedly, although he was not near enough to hear what she said. She also seemed wholly comfortable in that masculine place, self-assured as she had been at Tain. In some ways she was beyond his touch, a genteel, high-born lady. Yet they were friends, sharing ambitions to improve the condition of immigrants and settlers in the New World. He thought she really ought to be marrying a politician or someone in the public eye, rather than a rough colonial like himself. And yet she had fitted in so well with his family in Pictou! And she had promised to consider marrying him!

Isabella had meanwhile launched into her description of Cape Breton's sad lack of churches and Ministers. She referred this time to the incident of the little children, processing down to the river to fetch water for their mother's flower garden. "It is just the same with the Scriptures," she added. "Unless the seedlings of faith are watered with the words of the Gospel, they will not grow to bear flowers and fruit. I have set myself the task of raising funds to provide Ministers who have the Gaelic tongue, and to build churches for their worship."

"You have set yourself a huge task," the MP replied. "I have no doubt of its worthiness, but is it not too much for one woman?"

"Precisely. I am learning to share out the tasks. I have a committee in Edinburgh, and I seek to promote committees elsewhere in Scotland. I have found that often a big function will attract attention and bring people together, from which I can provide the motivation, and meet some local people who will form groups to continue the good work. I now have enough groups formed in different towns to make it worthwhile to establish a Newsletter to keep news flowing between them. Ideas of what one group has found to work well will be an inspiration to the others. I also hope to include reports from our two Ministers already in Cape Breton. Would you or Mrs. Wallace be able to provide me with names of contacts in Inverness, people prominent socially or active in the Presbyterian Church, and could you perhaps suggest a location where we could hold a function?"

They talked further. She was so charming in her appeal, that he found it difficult, indeed impossible, to refuse. Brodie Castle was suggested as a venue, and Mr. Wallace promised his attendance, provided the function took place in the recess.

As they rose, Alexander rejoined them, and seized the opportunity to outline to the MP how he and Richard Gordon hoped to develop the emigration agency. He pledged the highest standards of assistance to emigrants, detailing the openings he would offer in Upper Canada.

* * *

Leaving the cool gloom of the House of Commons, Alexander and Isabella walked companionably together along the Embankment by the side of the Thames. The water was at high tide, and the view pleasing.

"What would you like to do this evening?" asked Alexander. Isabella reflected: "Isn't there a place called Vauxhall Gardens we might visit?"

"There is a place called Vauxhall Gardens, but I don't think you would care for it," he answered, with a sudden recollection of the noise and bawdiness they had found when he and Archibald had sampled it the other evening.

In the event, they alternately walked arm-in-arm, or sat on park benches, absorbed in each other's company. As neither was known in London, nor likely to be recognised, a gaiety born of freedom from convention captured Isabella.

"I am perfectly and utterly happy," she declared.

"I hope I can always ensure your happiness," said Alexander, with more seriousness. He suspected that she had a mercurial temperament, capable of the heights of enthusiasm, but equally of deep despair.

"If you were to renew your proposal, and if I were to accept, where would we live?" she asked.

It was a problem, which had concerned him throughout the winter. "I have plans to build a house," he said. "Somewhere in the hills above Pictou, I suggest, with a wonderful view, and all the latest in comfort that we can find in London and ship out there."

"Could we have a log cabin on Cape Breton, too, for the summers?"

"We could, but you might find it rather primitive, still."
"It is too primitive, and I shall try and persuade this lazy Government to give us some roads. But will you not have to be in Upper Canada part of the time?"

"Some of the time, perhaps. That is why it would be better for you to be in Pictou where you can develop a circle of friends, starting with Helen, of course. I could take you with me to Quebec, which I think you would like. It is a lively, growing city, and Archibald is there."

"When does your ship sail back to Nova Scotia?"

"The day after tomorrow from London Docks. Archibald Buchanan and I have booked cabins."

"It is so short a time – after a whole six months."

"I know. I will come to Edinburgh with you if you wish, and sail from there."

She hesitated. "I should not keep you from your work. And it would be more companionable for you to return with Archibald. Shall we be able to come back to Scotland sometimes?"

"Isabella, you are making me feel bad about this. I shall be taking you away from all you know, and planting you in the New World. But I think I have to be there. It is where our income will come from; it is where the future lies."

"I have a little money of my own, too. Not enough, but an independence."

"Your money is your own," he insisted. "I hope to provide more than enough for two. We shall be quite rich eventually, if all my plans succeed. But you must think very carefully about this as well. Yours would be the greater sacrifice. I can only say that, having found you, it would turn my life to dust and ashes if you decided 'no'."

Isabella knew then that she had gone too far to draw back, even if she wanted to. This was no light flirtation, nor yet a marriage of mutual convenience. Though the Atlantic Ocean might lie between them, their destiny was surely to be together, though it could not be just yet. She tried to lighten the mood.

"Well, let's enjoy today at all events. And what shall we do tomorrow?"

He suggested Greenwich by river. "Boats, again," she teased, but agreed.

* * *

The only disagreement on the trip to Greenwich, which both admired, both for its spacious lawns and its classical buildings, was over Isabella's return journey to Edinburgh. Alexander was horrified to hear that she had come to London on the mail-coach. "But I brought Joanna with me," she protested. "It is quite acceptable to travel with one's maid."

"I am not talking about it being acceptable. I am concerned about danger. There are highwaymen and footpads frequently abroad. Besides, you would be jolted to death in a fast coach, which has to keep up to time. Why not go back by sea?"

"We can wave one another off, then. To please you, I will. Alexander, if I come to Nova Scotia, when do you think that should be?"

"I would like it to be next Spring, if possible."

"And that's a whole twelve months away," she sighed.

"We can write," he consoled. "And there is much for me to do if I'm to keep you in the style to which you are accustomed!"

She laughed, happy in the prospect of a relatively early climax to their unusual romance. They walked up the hill after visiting the Painted Hall, and viewed the river from another angle. The wharves were busy on the commercial side of the river, as the docks were occupied with their daily business. The river was very wide at this point, and Alexander was reminded of the St. Lawrence estuary. In time he imagined that would become just as busy as this hub of commerce, and he conveyed this thought to Isabella.

"I think it is very exciting to be in at the beginning of a new country," she said. "I hope that it will be possible to avoid some of the mistakes of the old, for Scotland is a sad case now, I fear. Perhaps not in the cities, but certainly in the northern countryside."

"Times change," he replied, "And it is cause for concern that human beings don't always embrace change very readily. I truly believe that most of the people who seek their fortune in the New World will find that their lives will be freer and better. However, the change needs to be managed better."

By March, 1929, however, things had taken several turns for the worse.

Isabella had been troubled over the autumn months by some falling-off in the enthusiasm of the Edinburgh Group. Their Treasurer, Sir Walter Young, had unexpectedly resigned for "business reasons", and she felt an indefinable cold-shouldering on the part of some of the older matrons, who had been supportive in the beginning. She was avoiding the choir meetings, because she would have come across John Sutherland there, and thus she did not at first appreciate that a whispering campaign was operating against her. Also income for the cause was falling.

The faithful Mrs. Tennant, who had been listening to the gossip, was the first to enlighten her. "There's a feeling, dear Isabella, that you are spending too much time in the other cities, and not enough here," she said, adding mysteriously. "And Mr. Sutherland is putting it about that you are entangled with this man who was responsible for the deaths of the Cromarty emigrants on *The Lovelly Nelly*.

"Entangled!" exclaimed Isabella.

"Well, too friendly, then! Mr. Sutherland says you went down to London to support Mr. Thomson in the House of Commons Enquiry, and that Mr. Thomson subjected him to a slanderous attack. I can't quite believe that, Isabella. Mr. Thomson seemed a very nice man, when I met him in Tain, but you know what gossip is like!"

Gossip appeared to be rife, and Isabella did not know how to contain it. She longed for the publication of the Enquiry Report, which would surely scotch the rumours by its factual conclusions, but Mr. Wallace told her that it had been delayed over the Recess, and was unlikely to appear until October. She hoped that the Report would exonerate Alexander. However, it would not exonerate her. She felt wretched that she had been the one to ask John Sutherland to recommend a shipping agent, and in her highly charged emotional state, she blamed herself for starting the train of events, which had led to the deaths on board the ship.

"Mr. Thomson was not responsible for the deaths on the ship," declared Isabella vehemently to her friend. "It is expected he will be completely cleared. If anything, it is likely that Mr. Sutherland bears the real responsibility, because he may have interfered with the planned journey."

Mrs. Tennant accepted the explanation with relief, and promised to tell other committee members that the truth was very different. Isabella, now that she was apprised of the problem, assumed that John Sutherland was also behind Sir Walter's resignation. She considered tackling her Treasurer directly, but came to the view that it would be an embarrassing and difficult encounter, without any assurance of a satisfactory outcome. She wrote a civil note of thanks instead, for all his past support.

Into this deteriorating situation, Patrick Stewart's first report arrived from Cape Breton. The Missionary detailed his itinerary:

"The first Protestant settlement which I visited is called Grand River, about 35 miles from the Gut of Canso where I first went ashore. It is inhabited exclusively by Scottish Highlanders, numbering about forty-three families. Very few people are able to read and write. Some of them have been settled here for fourteen years, and during that time, the only ordained Minister they had seen was myself. I preached to them on the Sabbath and on the following Monday, both in Gaelic, and baptised about twenty children.. The settlers are in general very poor, and without efficient aid from some outside quarter, there is but a faint prospect of such a Ministry taking place . . .

The next place I visited was the entrance of St. George's Channel, or the North-West arm of Bras d'Or Lake, distant from Grand River about eighteen miles. My route lay along this lake, which is sixty miles long and from six to ten miles across. Around this bay there are no less than one hundred and fifty Protestant families without a Minister, schoolmaster or catechist.

On the north side of Bras d'Or Lake are the settlements of Merigonish, Denny Lake and River Denny, consisting of upwards of two hundred families scattered over a surface of some twenty to thirty miles, much indented by water, and consequently difficult of access. These three settlements could be joined under one Minister. . . I then continued to Margaree and preached to about sixty people . . . I then proceeded to Lake Ainsley, where the settlers, and those near Broad Cove would be sufficient charge for one clergyman . . ."

The Rev. Stewart went on to say that he had wintered in Middle River, having been offered hospitality by an elderly resident, and that the settlers had made a start on building a Church there. He had undertaken to make it his winter base, while ranging further afield to preach in the summer months.

Isabella was thrilled with this. To have achieved a survey and a first Missionary, and a first Church within three years, she thought very satisfactory, and would read well in her Newsletter, and could be proclaimed at her meetings. She was not so pleased, however, with the Rev. McLeod's first letter, which complained about the cold and the difficulty of getting about. There were no horses and no hay with which to feed them. There were streams and deep rivers to cross, and he was exhausted with walking or getting people to row him about. He was also pressing for funds to pay the wages of school teachers, expressing the view that it was imperative that the new Churches should also be used for educational purposes.

The Autumn meeting of the Edinburgh Ladies Association received both the Report and the letter, and agreed that fund-raising should proceed immediately and with renewed intensity. They agreed to target the wealthier church congregations in Glasgow, Edinburgh and Dundee, and to renew pressure for public funds.

Isabella could see no chance with all this activity needed, that she would be able to leave Edinburgh in the Spring of 1829. She concluded that she would have to stay at least another year.

* * *

The rumours which Mrs. Tennant had identified had also reached Isabella's sister, Louisa, who wrote that she intended to come in to Edinburgh on a shopping expedition, and hoped to stay a night or two with Isabella.

When Louisa arrived, however, and Joanna opened the door to her, Isabella had not returned from one of her meetings. It was not "done" to question the servants, but Louisa could not miss the opportunity. When Joanna brought in a tray of tea, she said, "So my sister has a new admirer, I believe . . ."

Joanna twisted her apron in her hands. "I don't know what you mean, Ma'am."

"Didn't you both go down to London to meet a gentleman from Nova Scotia?"

"Oh, yes, Ma'am. Mr. Thomson had come to Parliament to give evidence."

"What is this Mr. Thomson like, Joanna?"

"He had a store in Pictou, Ma'am. He's a friend of Mrs. Creighton. I think he's very nice, Ma'am. My mistress went to Cape Breton with the two Mr. Thomsons, as I expect she told you, ma'am, and that is how she got so wishful to help the people there. They write to each other, Ma'am."

Isabella fortunately came in at this juncture, shaking the rain-drops off her umbrella, and apologising that she must change her skirt first, where it had been splashed by the puddles, but she was delighted to see her sister, and they would have a comfortable chat over the teacups. Before long, however, the comfortable chat had become distinctly critical.

"What's this I hear about you gallivanting off to London?" asked Louisa.

"Yes, I did go. I needed to see William Wallace, the MP, about a function in Inverness."

"Doing it too brown, Sis! I'm told you went to see this Mr. Thomson who was over here from Nova Scotia."

Isabella was nonplussed, but thought honesty the best policy. She conjured up a laugh. "Well, yes. Perhaps I killed two birds with one stone. There was this Parliamentary Enquiry, which was a great worry to Mr. Thomson, and I wanted to show that I supported him.

"You supported him against that well-bred and eligible John Sutherland I introduced you to."

"John Sutherland has turned out to be a schemer in whom I can put no trust," replied her sister. She added a few details about the Enquiry. "I have to say that I admire and like Mr. Thomson. In fact, I am considering whether to accept his offer of marriage, if the Enquiry clears him of blame over *The Lovelly Nelly.*"

"A colonial!" exclaimed Louisa. "What are you thinking of? With your birth and breeding, you could look much higher, Isabella! You have become quite obsessed with this Cape Breton adventure. If they are all so poor over there, how are you going to have a life of culture such as you are used to?"

"I expect I'll miss some things," responded Isabella. "But not everyone is poor. Alexander's father has a prosperous farm, and Alexander himself has land and property and is building a house."

"Henry is bound to disapprove," said Louisa, bringing her husband into the argument. "He'll say that, even if this man can provide for you, you'll be totally alone, in a strange land, without family or friends, and very vulnerable."

"Pictou is a pleasant, small town," replied Isabella, "and I already know the Creightons, and have met friends of theirs. In fact I felt very much at home. Society is not so formal, you know, and I enjoyed that. Many of the settlers were born in Scotland, or their fathers were."

"This man keeps a store, I believe."

"He used to, but he has many other interests. He is a good man, who does a great deal for the Scots going out to settle in Nova Scotia and Cape Breton. I've met his family and they were very helpful to me. Don't forget, William, my first husband, had a profitable business in Pictou. I don't think the situation is so very different."

"William was a leading light in Glasgow Society. It is <u>quite</u> different!" declared Louisa, not to be pacified.

Isabella felt she could not continue to argue. She had taken the decision not to go out to Pictou next Spring, and she hoped that time, her enemy in one respect, would be her ally in another, and she could gradually win over her family's support.

One thing the argument had proved. Life would prove dust and ashes for her too, if she never saw Alexander again.

* * *

In October, the Enquiry Report was published. It completely exonerated Alexander Thomson of any blame in connection with the deaths on *The Lovelly Nelly*, but criticised Charles Daniels for sending a ship to sea with an inexperienced captain. It found that there were unexplained circumstances surrounding the incapacity of the Captain who had been booked for the ship, but there was insufficient evidence to blame any other person for the debacle.

It made no reference by name in the Report to John Sutherland, but included a transcript of all evidence in its Appendix. With regard to the other cases of deaths at sea, the report was much more severe, recommending Parliament to consider legislation for customs officers to have additional powers at ports of embarkation. It set out and made a number of recommendations on food provision, it being argued that ship's rations currently on offer were not suited to emigrants' dietary habits, and were therefore frequently rejected by them.

Isabella wrote to Alexander, as soon as she had read the report, although she was not very sure that her letter would reach him before the winter.

"I am so delighted that the Report has cleared you completely. It must be a great weight off your mind, for I know how concerned you have been that your name would be besmirched by the affair. I hope the detail of the Report has reached you directly, for I feel scarcely competent to rehearse all that it says, except that Archibald's recommendations seem to have been accepted.

I have had some trouble this autumn as rumours have been circulating starting, I understand, with John Sutherland. As a consequence, some of my ladies have been difficult with me, and my Treasurer, who was introduced by John Sutherland, has resigned. I must bend my mind to replacing him, as soon as possible, or our fund-raising will go sharply into decline.

We have had a full report from Rev. Patrick Stewart and a letter from Rev. James McLeod, both of whom have made progress on Cape Breton, and Patrick Stewart in particular has a Church started at Middle River. I am so pleased about this, but the Rev. McLeod has asked for funds to start schools as well. I am not inclined to pursue this myself, but have been over-ruled by the committee, who want a major fund-raising campaign, and approaches made to Government. I feel that I am the only person currently involved, who can co-ordinate these successfully. I cannot leave the Edinburgh Ladies' Association yet awhile, which I fear, puts my journey to Pictou in the Spring in jeopardy.

With two Ministers to fund, and a new campaign to be launched, and no Treasurer, you will appreciate that I am indispensable.

I remain, dear Alexander,
Your loving friend,
Isabella."

Chapter 17 - The Search for Funds

Isabella tossed and turned for most of the night after she had sent her letter to Alexander, in October 1828. She suffered through the knowledge that he would be acutely disappointed. She also found herself at a loss to know what her next steps should be. It was obvious that more money was needed before the Churches could be built, but what seemed obvious from the letters of Patrick Stewart and James McLeod were the problems of access in Cape Breton.

From her own visit she knew that boats and paths, sometimes rocky and steep, were all they had. It seemed, from what Alexander Buchanan had said, that the Government would not provide any money for Churches, considering, probably rightly, that that was the responsibility of the Churches themselves. Nevertheless, basic roads were seen as needful by the Canada Company, which was acting as a Government agency in Upper Canada. It might be possible to persuade the Government to provide roads for Cape Breton. They ought to provide schools, too, but she felt that also would be seen as a church responsibility, as indeed it was in Britain.

If a road, or roads, were provided, it would be possible to bring materials to Cape Breton with which to build the Churches. She resolved to tackle the problem from this angle, and began to search mentally through her considerable list of contacts to find the right approach. The Tory Government might not last much longer, she understood, and that was where most of her contacts lay. Viscount Goderich had been Prime Minister for a short time the previous year, and was now Secretary of State for the Colonies. He would surely be able to act. Should she approach directly or ask Lord Stanhope, husband of her President, for an introduction, perhaps? Time was of the essence, and she thought she would ask Lord

Stanhope for a letter to back up her case, and then go down to London, and sit on the doorstep if necessary until Lord Goderich agreed to see her.

Mercifully, this last desperate measure was not necessary. Lord Goderich did remember her from the days when her husband had been a powerful force in Glasgow politics, and an appointment was readily granted.

Isabella was a little nervous as she turned from Whitehall into Downing Street in November. The houses occupied by both the Foreign Office and Colonial Office had seen better days. Indeed British world-wide interests were causing severe overcrowding as papers overflowed into corridors, and staff were squeezed into inadequate and unsuitable rooms. However, the room into which she was ushered was spacious enough.

Isabella had prepared her case carefully. She had copied out in her neat script some of the relevant material from Patrick Stewart's Report, and from James McLeod's letter. These she intended to leave with The Secretary of State. She added material from the Edinburgh Ladies' Association Minutes in which she was instructed to seek Government aid, and a brief history of the successful fund-raising which the Association had employed to achieve their church-building objectives. She added a memorandum detailing her own experiences when visiting Pictou by boat.

Viscount Goderich was pleased to see her and greeted her warmly. He had only recently been succeeded as Prime Minister, having held the post from 1827 to 1828, by the Duke of Wellington. It made a welcome change to have a visit from an attractive lady. All MPs of course were men, as were all the dignitaries, High Commissioners and others whose requests formed most of his current daily correspondence and interviews. There were plenty of wives and widows, debutantes even, at the various receptions and soirees he was required to attend, but an intelligent lady seeking an audience was a novelty.

His secretary ushered her to a seat, and Isabella began to present her case. She spoke clearly, cogently and persuasively as she handed the Secretary of State her documents, and begged his special consideration for the cause she had made her own.

"This is a poor little island, is it not?" queried the Secretary of State, looking patrician and formidable with his high shirt points and flowing cravat.

"Very poor indeed. Most of the present settlers speak Gaelic only, which is why I have had to find Ministers who are Gaelic-speaking if they are to be any use. But they are Scots people, Sir, from the Highlands and Islands, who have been forced by poverty to escape from Scotland, and I think we have a duty to them."

"The New World is expanding very rapidly," said his Lordship, "and we have responsibilities, not only to North America, of which Cape Breton is but a small part, but to India, and probably Africa too, as it begins to be opened up."

"Africa is for the future, I suggest," said Isabella. "Cape Breton's need is now; it is almost the nearest part of North America to Great Britain and yet it is overlooked. A road across the island would give access to the communities. There is a beautiful lake in the middle, some sixty miles long, which would mean that most of the road, if it ran from west to east, would be along reasonably flat land. There would be some need for bridges over some of the other streams, but a central road, whether it went to north or south of the lake as your surveyors advise, would enable horse-drawn transport to operate. And if you cut down the trees, I could always use the timber for my Churches, " she added.

Lord Goderich reflected. "I'll see what I can do," would be the standard answer, followed by masterly inaction. However, the Tory Government might not last much longer. It seemed a sensible scheme from a sensible lady. He could commit a part of next year's budget, which they were just consulting on now. Really, her visit was quite opportune.

Isabella was speaking again: "I don't want to press you, my Lord, " she said, "but it is a fact that when Governments come to consider these matters, the big schemes are much to the fore, and the desperate needs of smaller communities get elbowed out of the way. I represent the still, small voice of conscience that says we should look after the least of our brethren."

He made up his mind. "Then, yes, subject to feasibility, I'll put it in hand."

Isabella's breath was quite taken away. "Thank you, Sir," she uttered. "You will never regret that generous decision."

He thought, as he shook her hand, that he might not be in his Office to regret it, but instructed the secretary when he came back into the room, after escorting Isabella out:

"They want a road from west to east in Cape Breton. See to it, Rooker. Next year's budget!"

* * *

Isabella wrote to Alexander again from London, recording her triumph. She hoped that he might be able to tell Nathaniel the good news, and perhaps they could have some thoughts as to where the new road might go. She also wanted him to see whether the saw-mill owner in Pictou, Mr. Galbraith, might set up a similar operation in Cape Breton, so that the trees cut down for the new road might be prepared for use, by her Church Ministers among others.

Her next letters were to Rev. Stewart and Rev. McLeod, telling them also what she hoped would happen, and urging them to take the new road into their planning for the new Churches. She added a somewhat sharp comment to the Rev. McLeod to confine his new schooling to religious matters only, but softened the rebuke by saying that her Ladies' Committee was enthusiastically endeavouring to raise the necessary funds.

In fact, by the Spring of 1829, the Committee had indeed achieved a sudden rush of funds. The Inverness event, organised by Isabella, had been a notable success, and the appeal to the congregations of specially selected Churches had shown a pleasing response. The Dundee Branch had submitted a report for the Newsletter, together with a remittance, congratulating themselves on a successful Book Fair. Following the publication by the MP, William Wallace, of the transcript of the House of Commons Report and its Appendix, giving verbatim the unconvincing evidence of John Sutherland, criticism of herself seemed to have died down, and when she returned from her successful lobbying of Lord Goderich, she was warmly congratulated.

Last but not least, the Committee at its Spring Meeting co-opted the Rev. Michael Johnson, a retired clergyman, who was to run the Green Book appeal scheme. Mr. Johnson was a supporter of the use of the Cape Breton Churches for general schooling, and Isabella took the view that she would not waste her breath opposing this, as it was obviously the view of most of the committee. Obviously, if he raised the money, he had a right to say how it was to be spent.

The one big question outstanding was whether or not she should accept Alexander's proposal and leave Scotland for Pictou.   The conflict between duty and personal happiness remained acute.   Her imagination pictured a happy home life in a new country, with a husband immensely congenial in outlook and faith.   That Alexander adored her, she knew, and the intimacy of marriage would be satisfying and fulfilling in a way her first marriage had been lacking; he also respected her and treated her as an equal and not a 'mere woman.'   They were too old to found a family, but they would be partners in life's adventures.

Before she met him, however, she had sworn to devote her life to the Church.   After their meeting, she had in particular identified the mission she would fulfil. Was it not a dereliction of faith and duty to abandon it so soon? While she was popular and active, her mission was very satisfying, but what would happen later?   Her physical and financial resources would dwindle and she could become ever more lonely.   She would need to pray for guidance.

* * *

The first ship to arrive in Pictou in Spring 1829 bore dozens of letters for Alexander.   In addition to the bundle from Isabella, there were some from Richard Gordon, there was his copy of the House of Commons Report, together with a letter from William Wallace, congratulating him on the outcome, and there were offers of ships from his new agent in Leith, William Allan.

He opened Isabella's letters first.   The initial one caused him great concern, but some of the later ones seemed more cheerful.   The House of Commons Report was all he could have hoped for, and both Richard Gordon and William Allan had been busy, and had both ships and customers for the current summer sailings. He forced himself to deal with the business matters first, as decisions were needed, and he needed to despatch replies as soon as possible.

In the evening, perusing Isabella's letters again, he concentrated on two sentences in particular. "I have had some trouble this Autumn with rumours which have been circulating," she had written. He felt deeply angered by this. John Sutherland, he had no doubt, had been seeking revenge for his exposure at the Enquiry, by blaming Isabella and spitefully seeking to damage her Ladies' Association. He wondered exactly what the rumours were. They probably concerned him also. He knew that their meetings in London had been conducted with all propriety, but it would have been easy to infer otherwise. Damn the man. It seemed to have upset Isabella, and that was unforgivable.

"You will appreciate that I am indispensable," wounded him even more. If she meant, as the letter stated, that she could not fulfil their provisional plan to come out to Pictou this Spring, then he understood. Indeed the delay in the publication of the Enquiry Report had already put it out of the question, but if she meant that she was permanently indispensable . . ? He feared that this had been in her mind when she wrote. There had been no mention of an alternative date.

He looked at the later letters. There was still no mention of an alternative date. She had obviously been elated by her success with Lord Goderich, and her account of the Edinburgh Ladies Spring meeting was cheerful, and pleased at their success, but there was no hint of leaving them now things were going well.

He was literally terrified that, when he put his proposal in writing, she would refuse it. He contemplated rushing over to Scotland to see her. He knew that he could persuade her, if only they were together. He could probably even bring her back with him! He also tossed and turned for most of the night, as he tried to decide what to do.

In the end, he decided to write. To force her into a decision would be grossly unfair. Yet his letter would have to offer her a way out of problems, which seemed to her insurmountable. He accepted with the utmost reluctance that this year was not an option. Could he even achieve 1830? He did not doubt her affection, but he feared that her love was not yet as strong as his, and it might even weaken with time. He had himself said that his rival was her Faith and her commitment, those invisible chains, which bound her to a cause she had adopted. He discounted the claims of Scotland and the society she knew. He thought those would not dissuade her if the commitment link could be weakened.

He had thought it through, and now wrote without hesitation.

April 1829

My dearest Isabella,

Your bundle of letters arrived yesterday, as did the Enquiry Report. I was dismayed by the thought that you had been the target of rumour and gossip, probably instigated by John Sutherland. I should have foreseen that possibility, but I am pleased to hear from your later letter than the problem seems to have died away. There was a nice letter from William Wallace, also, commenting on the Report. It is certainly good to know that no blame attaches to me for *The Lovelly Nelly* disaster. Nor should any attach to you for asking Sutherland to recommend a shipping agent. We were neither of us to know that he would turn out to be so base, and indeed cruel. Spreading rumours about you could only cause you distress and harm – and do him no good since it was too late to improve his own situation.

My darling, I said that I would ask you to marry me, when my name had been cleared, and I now want to do just that. You know that I love you very deeply, and want us to be together always. We have shared many happy hours, at Cape Breton, on the ship coming back from Tain, and in London. We have even discussed where we might live if we married and made a home together.

You have not, however, given me your answer, and I have not asked you for one, knowing that you have a life of your own, which would have to be sacrificed. I was indeed extremely unhappy to hear that you thought your role in Edinburgh "indispensable". That it was so at the time you wrote, I do not doubt. I hope that it may be less so now, and perhaps if I were to offer a solution, you might find that you could leave with a clear conscience. That you are quite indispensable to me I know for certain.

Cape Breton has been launched on a forward path, thanks to you, my love. You have built up, through ingenuity and energy, a strong organisation of support in Scotland. Your first Ministers are in place. The road, which will mean so much to the populace, has been promised. The first Church has been founded, and others will surely follow.

I propose that you should call back Rev. McLeod to take your place in Scotland. You have given the inspiration and the knowledge, but he could now offer even more up-to-date knowledge, and because he is a splendid orator, and knows the Edinburgh scene very well, he would be a fresh inspiration to the cause you have established. I happen to know that he feels out of place among the simple folk on Cape Breton. The Rev. Stewart is much more at home (he was an excellent choice), and now that he is ordained can take on more supervision of new clergy.

Will you think about it, dearest, and let me know whether you think this would release you to come out to me? I also think that places such as Halifax and Quebec, which are well established, should bear some of the responsibility of looking after Cape Breton, and your talents need not be wasted if you . . ."

The sound of a klaxon from the harbour interrupted Alexander's thoughts. The ship was leaving and he had been so engrossed that he had forgotten the time. No matter, the business letters were done, and this was too important to rush.

. . . consider the possibility of raising funds there also. Cape Breton itself, and your Ministers, could well prosper even more with your support and backing here.

It may be that the re-organisation this would involve would take us even beyond next year and into 1831. If so, so be it. I would wait almost for ever if I thought I could have you as my wife.

The klaxon has sounded, and I have missed the boat. Never mind, there will be another ship. What I think will not come again, if we miss this opportunity, is a lifetime of happiness together.

Your devoted
Alexander

* * *

In May a strongly optimistic letter arrived from Richard Gordon.

"I have set in place a network of informants," he wrote. "This is in no sinister sense, but I have made it known to tradesmen, innkeepers, harbour officials and others, covering almost every village in North-East

Scotland, that I will assist anyone wanting to emigrate. The ships will call at Thurso as well as Cromarty, and I intend to meet the ships at Cromarty, and ensure that everything is well-organised. I may then travel on with the ship to Thurso, to ensure that the second party boards without trouble. The following are the dates of departure and approximate arrival at Pictou and Quebec." He then gave estimated dates in June, July and August. "I am going to suggest that you should meet the ships in Pictou. Whether you decide to accompany the parties on to Quebec is entirely up to you. What I want to ensure is that there is the opportunity for emigrants to send back good reports of their experiences, in order that others may be encouraged to join them.

On the June ship will be five families from Rogart, a village in Sutherland. There are ten adults and sixteen children, and there is an equal or greater number planning to leave next year, if the reports are good. Next year's party from that village is likely to include an innkeeper, and a schoolmaster, which will be helpful, I think. There is no shortage of people to fill the berths on the ship, but William Allan and I are determined that we will not exceed, even by one or two, the limit that is set. A couple of families from Thurso will be disembarking at Pictou, intending to settle in Nova Scotia, but, as you surmised, the chief demand now is for Upper Canada. Do you know yet how much land you may have available there, and whether it is cleared, for example?"

Alexander determined that he would go, probably on the first ship, to Quebec, and there follow up his potential purchase of 30,000 acres of the Huron Tract. It would also give him an opportunity to meet again with Archibald Buchanan, the Immigration Agent. Archibald would tell him if there was anything further he should be doing to ensure that his passengers passed through immigration, and he would make some enquiries about their onward transportation. If he went to Quebec this year, it would leave him free, if necessary, to go to Scotland in 1830. But first he must await Isabella's reply.

When it came, it was all that he could have hoped for. Isabella wrote that she was feeling much calmer now, that she was thrilled with his proposed solution of her dilemma, and that she believed it would work well.

"I must tell you, as I told your father when we met him, that he has a very clever son. Your solution will not only release me, but will enable me to work with even more of a determination to recruit more Ministers to replace James McLeod. My first duty must be to ascertain that James is a willing party to this arrangement, and then I must prepare the ground with my committee.

For that reason I think that 1830 (next year) must be ruled out for my joining you, but I shall hope to book a passage on the very first boat in 1831. That is only two more winters and one more summer, dear Alexander, before we can be together, for always.

To be formal, I should thank you, dear Sir, for your most obliging proposal, which I have much pleasure in accepting. Now you will be able to go ahead with your house. I know you will keep me informed of your plans, and I shall haunt the shops over here looking for bargains, which will help us furnish it neatly! You will see, I shall need a ship to myself before I have finished.

I hope all is going well with your Emigration Agency. Richard Gordon has written that he and Jane are to visit Edinburgh this autumn, and will call to see me. That will be something to look forward to, especially as Jane is now very active with our Tain group.

My regards to your parents, Nathaniel and Minette, and my love to you,
Isabella.

Alexander heaved a sigh of relief. He would try and go over to Scotland next year, for the sheer pleasure of seeing her, but he was no longer feared losing her. What Isabella promised, she carried out.

Chapter 18 - The Vision Lives on

Alexander's world was shattered suddenly in March, by the death of his father, William the Pioneer. The old man had seemed good for many years, but succumbed to a heavy cold turning to pneumonia, and finally his heart gave way. The family relied heavily on Alexander to arrange the funeral and his burial at Antigonish. Nathaniel, of course, made the difficult sledge journey across the ice from Cape Breton, and a family conference agreed that Maple Tree Grove should continue to function through the work of the younger sons, providing a home still for the widow and one daughter remaining unmarried.

Alexander was glad that he had had the opportunity to discuss with the old man not only his own business plans, but also his future with Isabella. He knew of his parents' liking for her. He wrote, of course, to tell her what had happened. Her return letter was a great comfort.

"We have lost a wonderful person," she wrote. "Your father had that breadth of vision which inspired so many people, combined with an earthy practicality that made things happen. I shall never forget the "boys' boots" he made me buy, and of course, if he hadn't urged you to take me to Cape Breton, so much of our later lives would simply never have happened. He triumphed over adversity himself, and he tried always to imbue others with the same courage, but lending his helping hand."

In May 1830 no fewer than three ships contracted by Alexander and Richard Gordon lined up to collect emigrants at Cromarty and Thurso. They were top quality ships with experienced Captains, insisted upon by Alexander. Richard Gordon inspected them all on arrival. As a retired Naval man he knew everything needful about provisioning and preparing vessels for a sea crossing. Moreover, he was able to prepare villagers, who might never have ventured more than twenty miles from their homes, for what they should expect from the voyage. His aim was that every passenger, however poor and downtrodden their state, should feel fitter and rested from their voyage, and able to face their new life in North America, strengthened by that experience.

Alexander met the ships at Pictou, but already fewer passengers were disembarking there, most intending to travel on to Upper Canada, where Alexander's land deal had enabled him to offer good packages of fertile property to those who wanted it, and most did. Among the passengers this time were two families from among the wealthier farmers in the area, who saw the chance of buying in the Huron Tract five times as much land as they already farmed, and at a very reasonable price. Since they were able to pay cash, Alexander's speculative purchase began to show a profitable return. There were also cabin passengers on business trips, who had heard that these ships were fast, safe, reliable, and provided an embarkation point closer to their homes than Dundee or Leith.

Alexander had his own reasons for joining the first ship and visiting Quebec again. He wanted to establish contact with Mrs. Mary Talbot, who was organising the Quebec Immigration Society to raise funds to set up rest centres along routes taken by immigrants. He thought he should not abandon his immigrants entirely to their own devices, having to find transport for journeys, which could extend for hundreds of miles to their eventual destination.

He called first on Archibald Buchanan to discover where he might find Mary Talbot, and was shocked to discover that his friend was ill. Coughing, Archibald refused even to shake hands for fear of transmitting his illness.

"How did this happen?" asked Alexander.

Archibald thought that his close contact with the Quarantine Hospital might have led to his contracting a disease. He would work as long as he could, but the doctor held out little hope of a full recovery.

"Should you, in fact, continue working?" asked Alexander. "Would it not benefit you to rest, perhaps by the sea, and give yourself a better chance of recovery?"

Archibald fretted that he still had much that he wanted to do. The Immigration Agent was more than a faceless bureaucrat. He was responsible for the immigrants when they arrived, and had to be certain that their just grievances were investigated and acted upon. When they came with insufficient funds to proceed to their destination they had to be helped.

He was particularly furious today because Major Fitzpatrick, the medical officer in charge, had opposed his latest scheme for succouring immigrants.

A ship had lately arrived from North Uist in the Outer Hebrides with a particularly under-nourished and penurious set of immigrants, cleared from their holdings by a peculiarly heartless landlord. Most were in rags and some were naked. One or two men had a lady's petticoat as their only garment, and most of the children had no shoes. Archibald, appalled by their appearance, insisted that the Quebec Ladies find some way of clothing them, and an urgent appeal for clothes and blankets was published in the Quebec Mercury. Mary Talbot's women volunteers set to work making clothes out of any material, even sackcloth, which they could find.

Major Fitzpatrick had been obstructive, however, reminding Buchanan of the hospital regulations, which set out strict time-limits for keeping immigrants. Archibald Buchanan had flown into a rage at this heartlessness. As the Chief he could and did pull rank on his subordinate, and insisted that the group should be kept longer until they could be kitted out and their onward journey organised. Fitzpatrick tightened his lips in disapproval. When he was the Immigration Agent, he would have none of this loose behaviour. He did not even approve of the voluntary efforts being made. His own wife would not demean her position by making clothes for peasants, and he did not see why Mrs. Talbot should do so.

By contrast, when Buchanan inspected Alexander's ship, he was able to give it a clean bill of health immediately. Alexander's passengers were well turned out, had their papers in order, knew where they were going and why. He approved very much of the organisation Alexander had set up, and gladly introduced him to Mary Talbot so that he could discuss with her their onward journey.

An idea suddenly struck Archibald after Alexander had gone. He was conscious that his illness might prove fatal, and he had been very worried about his successor. Such a person had to care deeply for his fellow men, and had to have vision and commitment, all of which Alexander had shown.

His presumed successor was this same Major Fitzpatrick, who had just displayed such a cold preference for regulations over common humanity, and who wanted the job, he knew. Fitzpatrick was ambitious, had come from Army Life into the Colonial Service, and was undoubtedly efficient, but this was not the first instance when he had demonstrated his rigid approach. He would be adequate as a successor, but was not good with people.

While he did not have Fitzpatrick's knowledge and contacts, Alexander Thomson had the commitment, intelligence and inner strength to do the job really well. Archibald thought he should, as the present incumbent, try to ensure that the best man to do the job was appointed.

He drew pen and paper towards him, and commenced a letter to Lord Goderich at the Colonial Office.

* * *

Meanwhile Alexander was making friends with Mrs. Mary Talbot. While his present immigrants did not need her services financially, nevertheless he would be glad to make use of her rest centres. It was his intention to travel with this party, to see his new acres for himself, and to ascertain the problems people were likely to come across as they toiled towards their promised land.

Mrs. Talbot was impressed by this commitment alone. She knew of no other emigrant contractor who cared a toss what happened to new arrivals. They were only concerned with getting their hands on the cash. When she heard that some of the immigrants were buying plots outright, while others would rent from Alexander, or buy on credit terms, she was also amazed. And when Alexander happened to mention that he was the son of William the Pioneer, whose fame had even spread to Quebec and whose funeral notice had appeared in the Quebec newspapers, she approved even more of the man she was meeting.

Mary Talbot was also mad with Major Fitzpatrick. She was in the midst of organising the provision of clothing for the poor Highlanders, and greeted Alexander with her arms full of jumpers and cast-off trews she had begged from her helpers.

"That man!" she fumed. "I can get them all clothed if he gives me a fortnight to gather it all together, but he wanted to turn them out yesterday, just because no-one had an infectious disease. He'd rather keep his beds empty than let the poor people use them."

Alexander sympathised, relieved her of her burden, and helped sort the garments into men's, women's and children's piles.

"I have very little with me," he said, "but I will certainly collect what I can from friends, so that you can build something of a store in case you have a future need."

Mary Talbot also knew of Isabella Liddel. The activities of the Edinburgh Ladies' Association in raising funds for Cape Breton were known in voluntary circles. She asked Alexander if he was acquainted with her. "Archibald Buchanan has been singing her praises, and saying that if our Quebec Immigrants Society does half as well, he will be very pleased."

"I know her very well," Alexander responded. "She has been tireless in travelling around Scotland forming groups of people who will help to raise funds to build Churches. She is a brilliant speaker, and has a charm and enthusiasm, which make people respond to her. She has established a Newsletter, recruited Ministers, and lobbied the Government. Archibald met her with me in London, and I hope very much that she will come out to Pictou next year, and that we shall be married. I am planning a house for her."

"In Pictou?"

"Why, yes. That is where my business is based."

"You should bring her to Quebec. We should welcome her very warmly."

"I would like to introduce her to you. No doubt we will visit Quebec sometimes, and I will find an opportunity." They went on to talk of mundane matters, like the hire of horses and wagons, and stopping-places on the journey.

The one hundred and eighty miles from Quebec to Montreal was accomplished by steam-boat, on which fares had, of course, to be paid. Then there was the 120 mile journey to Prescott. Some went by open Durham boats while others, including Alexander's party, went by land, avoiding a particularly awkward stretch of the St. Lawrence which could not be navigated by steam boats.

The land journey westward was a slow trek, but already Mary Talbot's practical work had eased their travelling. Usually there was a cluster of homes where a welcome awaited. Once they used a school-room; another time the stables attached to a humble tavern. If there was no village, the wagons drew up in a circle round a camp-fire. The Scots would wrap themselves in their plaids, and found their own entertainment with a tambourine and a sword-dance, or singing their homeland songs. Alexander had his hunting-kit, a moose-skin sleeping-bag, and his hunting rifle at the ready in the unlikely event that it might be needed.

He drew out their story from several families. All spoke highly of the advice given by Richard Gordon, and contrasted it with some of the over-flattering sales pitches offered by employees of the Canada Company. Few of this group had been evicted, but all had stories to tell of friends and relatives who lived in fear of this happening.

Moreover, the Scottish economy was so depressed that they could not get good prices for their produce or their services. Some had been encouraged by former emigrants to come out and share in the opportunities in Upper Canada, some relatives had sent money to encourage them to come, while others had sold their few possessions to find the passage money. Still others boasted that they had kept their money hidden, and claimed to be destitute in order to obtain money from a charity. "Ye mun nair flash yr siller about," said one stalwart man, "But keep it by ye for a rainy day!"

It was not cold, and tucked up in the sleeping-bag in the shelter of a rock, and gazing at the stars, Alexander's mind drifted back to their trip to Cape Breton. Isabella would soon be coming to him at Pictou. While his Highland companions fixed their sights on land and farming, his own vision was of the house on the hill, now roofed and almost finished, where they would make their home.

Sometimes, and indeed more often than not, there was a shelter assigned to the travellers, and some refreshment offered by Mrs. Talbot's women. Fresh bannocks and a dish of tea were warmly appreciated. Alexander thought that to build on the rudimentary facilities would not be difficult. He could offer stores along the way, find water and fix up wells where there were no washing or drinking facilities and no village nearby, and ensure supplies of fodder.

When they reached Prescott, they embarked on a steam-boat for York, later to be called Toronto, on the next stage of the journey, and the wagons were left to return for the next immigrant group. The vastness of Lake Ontario soon came into view. Virtually an inland sea, the land around it looked good and fertile. He was no expert, but he could tell that it would be much easier to cultivate than Cape Breton, and his purchase seemed to promise a good return on his investment.

It had been a brilliant day, the sun sparkling over the lake, turning its waves to beaten silver. Now it had sunk below the horizon, leaving the specks of cloud in the azure sky as bright white or dark grey flecks where the last light briefly caught them, or left them in shadow. On the horizon the dark grey cloud-bank had an ochre strip above it, lightening to pale yellow for a few moments until night descended gloomily and darkness crept over the whole scene.

It was a two hundred and fifty miles distance from Prescott to York, and from York, still travelling westward, it was another one hundred and ninety-five miles by land, to the settlements at Zorra in Oxford County, and still another seventy miles further to Williams Township on Lake Huron. They had covered a distance of five hundred and fifty miles just in getting from Quebec to York. Many of the immigrants, and indeed Alexander himself, had not visualised that the Huron Tract would be so far inland. But inspection of the area he had purchased proved the wisdom of the deal, for it was fair and fertile and more than met the expectations of the weary travellers.

* * *

Back in Pictou, after his trek and return, Alexander prepared a cogently argued missive to the Colonial Office, urging more Government support for the really poor, who wished to emigrate. His conversations with those who had come over had convinced him that many more would have come, if they could have been advanced a loan towards the trip. He also knew, from his own experience, that loans would be paid back by Scots.

For prospective emigrants there was the cost of the voyage, both the passage money and their keep on board, and preparing and transporting the equipment they would need to start their new lives. Then they also faced that very long journey if they were proceeding to Upper Canada, where most of them now wanted to go, much further than if they had settled in the Maritimes.

He knew that the 1826 Committee had set its face against assisted passages, but while a grant was possibly not justified, a loan would be a mere fleabite to the Exchequer, but would make every difference to those barely able to scrape a living. The difference in farming potential between the Huron Tract and the neglected Maritimes was substantial. In Upper Canada, in ten years' time, or even five, most settlers would not only be self-sufficient, but producing for profit.

Yet in order to prosper in the New World, he felt those who came needed to be aware of the differences in climatic conditions, and to know what jobs might be available. What the Canada Company did, in providing basic amenities like roads and encouraging schools and Churches was an important first step, but factual Government information, on which prospective emigrants could rely, was an even earlier pre-requisite. The Government could best attract those emigrants with farming experience and special skills if it held out the hope of an even better life than they had back home.

He gave one or two brief histories of emigrants he had met to support his case, and praised Mary Talbot with her volunteer army of helpers. He also praised the work, which Archibald Buchanan had been doing as extremely enlightened, but was concerned that more staff might be afforded him to ease the burden of an ever-growing responsibility.

At roughly the same time, Mary Talbot, urged on by Archibald, and emboldened by her discussion with Alexander, wrote to Isabella Liddel.

"You will forgive my writing to you, I trust," she wrote. "I have just met your affianced husband, Alexander Thomson, for the first time. I have admired your voluntary work on behalf of Cape Breton, and I am trying to do similar voluntary work in raising funds to assist immigrants on their journeys after they arrive in North America.

I feel quite convinced that the vision Alexander Thomson has for bringing people to Upper Canada, and establishing them, with support, in their new homeland, is just what we need.

Sadly, our present Immigration Agent, Archibald Buchanan, whom you know, is very sick. He does not believe he will be able to carry on much longer. He has been wise and active in his work here, and we are very anxious that his successor should continue in the same vein. The possible successor is a Major Fitzpatrick, who I believe does not have the vision of either Archibald Buchanan or Alexander Thomson, for he is very much a stickler for regulations and lacks humanity in his dealings with some very poor and ignorant people.

You are, I believe, acquainted with Lord Goderich, the Colonial Secretary, who makes this appointment. I venture to ask whether you could write to, or speak with him, to urge the unusual step of appointing Mr.Thomson, someone outside the Colonial Service, but who has so many of the right qualities to recommend him."

Isabella was surprised to receive the letter, and unsure of Alexander's views on the matter. There was by now no means of asking him. She thought very carefully, and came to the conclusion that he always put the principle of helping immigrants above any profit he might make on his enterprises, and that in all probability he would view such an appointment as an opportunity for more good work. What would William the Pioneer have advised?

William, she concluded, would have advised Alexander to take such a post, if offered. He had been confined in a debtors' prison himself in his earlier life through not having assistance offered to him when it was needed. He would probably see the prestigious and highly influential occupation of Immigration Agent as just perfect for his son's many talents.

Isabella accordingly wrote to the Colonial Secretary, recalling their meeting eighteen months ago about Cape Breton, and recommending Alexander Thomson if the Immigration Agent's job should become vacant. She was in a dilemma on two points: should she disclose her own connection with Alexander, and should she mention the incident of *The Lovelly Nelly*? She decided to include both. It could lead to an adverse outcome if the connections were made later, or indeed now, and her motives became suspect. She added to the letter, therefore, "I must tell you, Sir, that I have recently become affianced to Mr. Thomson. However, I assure you that my intervention is made not on my own account, but as a result of urgent representation by Mrs. Mary Talbot of the Quebec Immigrants' Society, who is a volunteer organiser working in a similar capacity to myself. Furthermore, you may wish to assure yourself, by reference to the Parliamentary Enquiry into the voyage of *The Lovelly Nelly* (April 1828), that Mr. Thomson was fully exonerated of any fault in connection with that voyage."

* * *

Lord Goderich, having been notified of Archibald Buchanan's death in August, was presented with a file, and the intimation that a successor must be appointed. On the top of the file, neatly presented, were the biographical details of Major Fitzpatrick, obviously the Civil Service choice. Below it were papers relating to

Alexander Thomson - a budget consisting of Archibald Buchanan's letter of recommendation, Alexander's biographical details, Isabella's letter, a letter of support from Mary Talbot, Alexander's own letter proposing loans for poorer immigrants, and the appended Report of the Parliamentary Enquiry, marked with the relevant passages about *The Lovelly Nelly*.

Lord Goderich flicked through them. Isabella's reference to Cape Breton's proposed road caught his eye.

"What's happened about that Cape Breton road, Rooker?" he growled.

"I believe it's still at the planning stage, Minister," was the Civil Servant's reply.

"Well, better get a move on. Eighteen months and no action! Give me a full report next week."

"Certainly, my Lord."

Lord Goderich felt a momentary irritation at the slowness of the Service. These private enterprise merchants got things done a damn sight quicker. That little woman who came to see him, now, she had moved mountains with her Churches. So she was going to get married again, was she? How long since her husband died? Five, six years, he thought. Oh well, there had been a decent interval.

He gazed from the window at the narrow confines of Downing Street, and a contrasting vision of a vast expanse of lakes and forests floated before him. North America was so huge in its potential. His own background was Harrow, Cambridge and the Bar, but he had fished and shot in Scotland, tramping miles over the moorland. Yet the whole of Scotland could be lost in the one small corner of North America. He had known Lord

Selkirk, who was an enthusiastic proponent of Scottish emigration, believing their rough, tough characters would make them good settlers in a rough, tough country. One needed courage, energy and action to tackle the problems of the New World.

Who would be best to help the settlers? The practical store-owner, whose family had been settlers themselves, or the ex-Army medical Major with the titled wife? An enormous intellectual and constitutional gap separated the North Americans from the English ruling class, he knew. It had been part of the breakdown, which had led to the War of American Independence. He made a swift decision.

"Appoint Thomson," he said. "I'll sign the letter."

* * *

While Isabella had written immediately to apprise Alexander of what she had done, her letter, travelling by ordinary mail, took longer than the official Government document.

In Mid-September, Alexander, who had returned sadly to Pictou, after attending Archibald Buchanan's recent funeral, noticed the *Thetis* in the distance. The Glasgow-based ship, a regular arrival in Pictou, was being guided in by a small boat along the estuary to the waterfront, and preparations were in hand to off-load passengers and cargo. As always, Alexander walked to the harbour to get a closer look, have a chat with his friend, John Smith, and perhaps collect any mail. To his surprise, Captain Smith rushed over to him with a letter.

"I was told this was urgent, and very important, and I was to hand it to you in person," said Captain Smith. Alexander tore open the official-looking envelope. He could scarcely believe its contents. He, of all people, was being offered the appointment to take Archibald Buchanan's place as Immigration Agent in Quebec, and the letter, inviting him to take up the new post immediately, was signed by the Colonial Secretary, Lord Goderich, himself.

Chapter 19 - Ordeal by Ice

Alexander was honoured and excited by this sudden change in his fortunes. He wasted no time in writing his acceptance letter, and sent another to Isabella asking her now to book passage for Quebec instead of Pictou, and to write to him in Quebec to let him know by which ship she would travel.. Captain Smith was due to sail back to Glasgow in a couple of days with his final timber cargo of the season. Alexander confided his news to him, and explained how vital it was that the letters should reach their destinations safely.

He himself set sail for Quebec the following week, having asked the builder to try and sell his half-built house in Pictou. He would have no need of it now, for there was a Government house in Quebec, which Archibald had occupied, and which would now be available.

At the house a letter from Isabella awaited him. She knew about his appointment, and assumed that he would want her to come to Quebec. She and Joanna, and a mountain of luggage, would come on the first available ship, which she understood would be the *Albion*, out of Glasgow. "I am told it is the best ship available, and that her Captain, Bryce Allen, has the highest of reputations," she wrote. "It has been a busy summer, as you will have gathered from my letters, and I still have more to do. I must greet James McLeod when he returns from Cape Breton, and tell him all about our plans for him here. I must make all tidy in my little house before I leave it, to stay a while with my sister, Louisa, as it will be a long time before I see her again. I must also buy such furnishings for our new home as will make us comfortable. It will be a joy to see you again, my dearest, for it has been such a long parting. May God watch over us both and keep us safe until then."

While the prospect of Isabella's arrival was cheering, there were still problems to be faced with the new appointment. Naturally, perhaps, Major Fitzpatrick was furious at being passed over for a total newcomer to the service. During the winter, there was less activity at Grosse Isle, where Fitzpatrick was based, and he and his wife, Lady Penelope, returned to their house in Quebec, and were participants in all the winter social activities. In the office Major Fitzpatrick did his best to make life difficult by questioning every decision, and failing to refer to Alexander such problems as would naturally have formed part of a joint decision. Alexander, deep in perusal of all the Regulations and Acts of Parliament which formed the basis of his powers and responsibilities, found it impossible to know immediately when Fitzpatrick was wrong or right, or even partially right, but determined to confuse. A stickler for the rules, and showing little capacity to bend or interpret them in particular circumstances, Fitzpatrick caused unnecessary dissension with some ship Captains and the harbour authorities.

At the Governor's Ball, Lady Penelope Fitzpatrick deployed her fan to good advantage, whispering behind it to other ladies, and commenting adversely on Alexander's manners and appearance. Since she knew everyone, and was herself the daughter of a Duke and high up the social ladder, her strictures were attended to.

"Upstart," "Goodness knows what Lord Goderich was thinking of," "A poor substitute for dear Archibald Buchanan", "Short and undistinguished," "He does not dance, I see." "I see no reason to invite him to my dinner party," "A shopkeeper in Pictou" were some of the comments bandied about.

He had not wanted to go, but an invitation was tantamount to a royal command, and could not be declined. He had sought Mary Talbot's advice and was relieved that at least she and her husband were present, and were able to perform some introductions to the people he met. He became aware that, while the men were friendly enough, many of the ladies greeted his bow with chilly hauteur. How different it would have been, if Isabella could have accompanied him! The Governor himself was gracious and drew out details of his past experience and his plans to build on Archibald Buchanan's record of success.

* * *

The ship-owners had long been irked by the long winter delays to shipping between the British ports and North America. From December onwards the St. Lawrence would be frozen solid, and it could be May before it was clear, depending on the weather on that side of the Atlantic, which they had no means of knowing or forecasting. Some, having had the benefit of one or two milder winters, were beginning to offer sailings from Britain at the end of March, to arrive in April, and trust to luck that they could get through. This would enable them to get in three rather than two round trips during the summer season, which would be highly profitable. True, some of the Captains complained, but so far no ships had come to grief, although some had been delayed because of pack ice, and unable to reach port, or had to linger in a Nova Scotian port like Halifax before proceeding to their final destination.

In 1831, therefore, not only the *Albion,* but also the *Erromanga,* left Glasgow, the latter packed with 280 emigrants from the Western Isles. The ships saw little of one another for three weeks, for the *Erromanga* was about two days ahead, until on April 10th the *Albion's* look-out from the crow's nest, spotted a ship in the distance. He also shouted "Ice Ahead," and Captain Allen realised that the *Albion* was heading, after a sudden veering of several points in wind direction, straight for a gigantic sheet of ice, in which the *Erromanga* was embedded.

Captain Allen had been heartily sick of the blinding storms of sleet and gales, which had shown no sign of ending, but now there was real and immediate danger. His ship was at the edge of the ice pack still, but the law of the sea demands that all ships help one another in difficulty, and the *Erromanga* was stuck fast. She might be there for days, or even weeks. His cabin passengers, including the Rev. Peter Bruce, a Free Church Minister, and Isabella came on deck.

"We can't just leave them without offering help," said Isabella. "Will they have enough food, do you think?"

Loud-hailing and signals established that the *Erromanga* needed food and Allen offered 200 lbs. of beef, if they could traverse the ice to fetch it.

"Is it very dangerous to walk across the ice?" asked Isabella.

"Dangerous enough. We will knock up a sledge of sorts with rope for a handle, and they can tow that behind them. They should be able to manage if they don't come across any fissures. I must say this lot looks all too solid. It must be six feet thick in places."

The beef was prepared, and Isabella saw that the Rev. Bruce also seemed to be making plans to leave the ship. Isabella questioned him, and he said, "My place is with these people. We can bring God's love and comfort to them." Isabella was greatly impressed. Should she also go with the same intent? She knew that Captain Allen would never let her leave the ship. Subterfuge would be needed. An extra spur was given to her half-formed resolve when a letter from the *Erromanga's* Captain, carried by the two sailors sent for the beef, revealed that the *Erromanga* was carrying an unusual number of female passengers, who were "screaming and carrying-on alarming."

"I could certainly help with the women," Isabella said, and the Rev. Bruce agreed. Together they planned to bribe the sailors to take her with them. The sledge was lowered over the side, followed by the packs of beef, and while all attention was focussed on that operation, Isabella and the Minister clambered over the rail on the opposite side of the ship, and precariously descended the rope ladder. Once on the ice, Isabella wrapped her feet and shoes in wool to protect them from the cold and to get a better grip. She had a heavy cloak with a hood, which disguised her effectively. They shuffled along under the lee of the ship until they could see the two sailors. Beckoning one across, money changed hands, and they were able to walk some yards ahead, disguised from view by the bulk of the sailors' backs, and the mounds of beef.

"How far?" asked Isabella, already almost blue with cold. "Half a mile about," answered the sailor, "but what you want to come for, beats me!"

It beat the Captain too. He had had his long glass trained on the *Erromanga*, when suddenly he was nudged by the Mate. "Who is that with the sailors?" he asked.

"The Reverend, I expect. He insisted he wanted to go. I can't stop him."

"No, there's someone else. Much smaller."

The spy-glass swivelled to the small party, now a hundred yards away, and the Captain twisted it sharply to change the focus. "No, it can't be! I think it is! The religious lady! How in heaven's name did she get there? Come back!" he yelled through the loud-hailer. "Come back!"

Captain Allen contemplated sending a sailor to fetch Isabella back by force, but he could suddenly feel a breeze stirring. All his attention had to be on his ship. If they could get only a little wind in the sails, he could perhaps get his ship free. The main sail was raised, and Isabella was forgotten as the *Albion* moved slightly and some clear water came into view. "Axes!" instructed the Captain; some of the crew clambered overboard, hacking at the ice. The ship creaked alarmingly, but aided by the breeze, the sail and the ice-axes, the *Albion* broke free.

"We have to leave them now," said the Captain. "What a stupid thing to do! If I've got a chance I'm going to steer for that channel that looks clear, and stand further off the coast. Re-board!" he shouted to the men, who were now scrambling up the rope-ladders before the ship could make off without them.

Buffeted by the same breeze, which had scuds of snow in it, the small land party made its way to the *Erromanga*. There was no way out for her. Half a mile nearer the shore, she was stuck fast. Her Captain, Mr. Oliphant, was furious to see two further passengers. He shouted to Allen through the loud-hailer that they should be made to return to the *Albion*, but already he could see that it was useless. The *Albion* had moved away. Lucky devils!

Isabella was half-carried up the ladder. Her face and fingers were white with cold. She now had to face the Captain's wrath, and when he had calmed down a little, and she had thawed out a little, discuss what she could do to help.

* * *

Captain Oliphant soon came to learn that the lady whose arrival he had cursed was in fact his greatest asset. He became aware that the screeching and wailing had died away. At first occupied by greeting their new sister in distress, and then comforted by the fact that, if she had come out to them, they were hardly going to die immediately, the women became calmer. Isabella talked to them and soothed them, taking time to say a little prayer, that was personal to each of them, and the afternoon passed peacefully away.

"Well, you've had a remarkable effect," said the Captain, somewhat grudgingly as Isabella eventually came back on deck.

"They were frightened," she explained. "No-one had told them what to expect, and they assumed the worst was going to happen."

"God knows where you're going to sleep. The ship is as full as she'll hold."

"One of the cabin passengers has a double bunk. She says I can share with her."

"Allen's had a lucky escape!" observed the Captain. "We look like being here for days, if not weeks. Are you prepared for that?"

"I am, Sir, and I was thinking that perhaps you would like me to organise some activities to keep everyone's mind off their troubles."

"I was going to let some of the gentlemen go shooting tomorrow. They think they can bag some ducks, which would be a welcome addition and variety to our food."

"Then I will fix a duck-plucking competition, if I can. I expect some of the passengers in steerage have plenty of experience! May I make one other suggestion?" she added. "The Rev. Peter Bruce could conduct a short daily service; nothing too formal, but so that those who wish could join in.   Then if you, Sir, could give a daily bulletin after the service, on how you see our situation developing, I think the passengers would become more reconciled to their plight."

"A good idea!" he said.   "It's important to keep up the spirits in times of danger. If you can help me with that, I shall be more than grateful."

Isabella knew, from her conversations with Captain Smith on the *Thetis*, how much responsibility devolved upon the Captain of a sailing ship, pitted against the elements, and how little help and support he had. A Captain's own morale needed to be sustained as well, so that he remained convinced of an eventual safe outcome.

"What exactly is the danger?" she asked.

"Three possibilities, mainly - two bad, one good. One, the ice will drift, with us imprisoned and helpless in it. It may be six or eight feet thick, but the ship's draught is greater than that, and if we drift on to rocks we could easily be holed.   Second, the pack ice will collide with more pack ice, and the ship could be crushed between the two.   Thirdly, of course, the ice will begin to melt as warmer weather comes, and a breeze will spring up, and we'll escape as the *Albion* did.   The first is the greater danger, I think, as we are fairly close into the shore.   In fact, I intend the First Mate to take a party up that hill we can see, to try and spy out where there is some clear water to aim for."

"Then we will pray for a breeze, and some sunshine!"

He laughed.   "While you are at it, ask the Lord for a South-West breeze, will you? Easterly would kill our chances."

Isabella went below.   The *Erromanga* had been able to take so many passengers because it had been roughly fitted out by its own carpenter, with shelves of un-planed wood in three tiers, on which the passengers could sleep. It also had a doctor on board. She searched out the Rev. Peter Bruce and told him that the Captain would like to have a short service conducted daily for the support of those passengers who wished to attend. Although the cabins opening off the main stateroom in the first-class accommodation were small, there was a magnificent mahogany table around which the passengers dined, served by their own steward. In other circumstances than this it would have been an excellent ship on which to travel.

She herself had found a willing lieutenant in the Governess whose cabin she shared, and who was going out to a position with a wealthy family in Quebec. Together they planned to hold a concert, much as Isabella had experienced on the first ship on which she had travelled. They would rehearse the women in songs and sketches, which would keep them occupied, and they would entertain the men and the crew. She went below to see what talent she could muster for her competition and her entertainment.

* * *

Meanwhile Alexander's excitement at the prospect of seeing Isabella again was mounting. He had arranged that Mary Talbot would offer her hospitality until they could be married, an arrangement which delighted Mrs. Talbot, since she had the liveliest admiration for Isabella Liddel.

He had been worried about the ice and storms in the North Atlantic which might hamper a voyage as early as this, but his anxieties were dispelled by the news that the *Albion* had been spotted just off Ile d'Anticosti. It would not be long now, before he could greet Isabella and demonstrate just how much he had missed her.

Assisted by the pilots of the St. Lawrence seaway, the *Albion* gradually approached Grosse Isle, site of the proposed new Quarantine hospital. Alexander looked for Isabella on deck, but there was such a sea of faces, he could not distinguish hers. She would be there, somewhere, he was sure. He prepared his papers, ready to go on board from the small boat ready to go out to her.

As he climbed aboard the *Albion*, he became aware of an agitated young woman pushing to the front. The woman screamed out, and clutched frantically at him. It was Joanna, Isabella's maid. "Oh, Sir," she cried. "We've lost my mistress!"

"Lost?" he gasped, a deep dread seizing his heart and mind.

"She went to help the other ship," sobbed Joanna. "We didn't know she was going, so we couldn't stop her."

Alexander put the girl aside, "Don't cry," he said automatically. "We'll find her."

But Captain Bryce Allen could offer little comfort. "She slipped off behind my back," he said, "and went over the ice to the *Erromanga*. They were stuck in the pack ice half a mile away. We sent food, and your lady must have bribed the men to take her too. My colleague, Oliphant, said he had women on board who were distressed, and I think she must have gone to comfort them. I had to leave her, because a wind came up just then, and I saw a chance to get my ship out of trouble, and steered clear of the ice. They'll be there for some time, I think."

Alexander's deep disappointment had to be controlled – for the time being. He had a ship to inspect and clear, which he did competently, thoroughly justifying the time spent during the whole long winter poring over those instruction books, manuals and Acts of Parliament, for the implementation of which he and his staff were responsible.

He knew the dangers of ice on the Atlantic run. From icebergs to pack ice, or fog on the Banks, there were always Spring problems. In the meantime there was Joanna and Isabella's mountain of luggage to be off-loaded and conveyed to his house.

He saw Bryce Allen once more before he left the ship, after issuing its clearance certificate.

"What's your estimate of the time it will take for the *Erromanga* to get clear?"

"If she gets clear," was the depressing response. "Oliphant was a fool to take his ship so close inshore. He's very little sea-room, and it's a rocky coast. I wouldn't like to be in his shoes. It's a particularly unoccupied piece of coastline, so there's virtually no chance of a land rescue, I would think. Better to stick it out, hope for the best and a change in the wind. I hope it changes soon, for his sake. He's got 280 on board, he said, and he'll be short of food if this bitter weather goes on too long."

Alexander's first reaction to the situation was one of anger. He thought Isabella's action in going over to the other ship foolhardy, although he knew it was typical of her generosity to people in distress. It would not help the other ship to have an extra mouth to feed. He was angry with the *Erromanga's* Captain, too, risking his ship and passengers by going in too close to the shore, presumably to buy extra time as he rounded the headland. It was a mess!

By the time the *Erromanga* had been overdue for ten days, his anger had rapidly given way to acute anxiety. He was reminded of *The Lovelly Nelly*, overdue for three weeks, and the disastrous state she had been in, when she finally crept into Pictou. He could not bear that Isabella should be confined to such a hell-hole, and he worried that she might fall ill if she was trying to tend people who were sick.

The news, that a Scottish lady was coming to Quebec to be married to the new Immigration Agent, had filtered out. "The Quebec Times" elicited from Captain Allen a few graphic words, describing how Isabella Liddel had deserted his ship to go and help the poor people stranded on the *Erromanga*.

By the time *Erromanga* had been overdue for three weeks, Alexander's anxiety had deepened to despair. His imagination told him the ship must have foundered. Isabella would never be his. She would have died a horrible death, either from starvation, or her body crushed, as the ship would be crushed, by the pack ice grinding it to smithereens.

In vain, as long night succeeded long night, did he try to banish these fears. During the day, he could conquer them, for the work he had to do demanded concentration, and there were people to offer some cheer. He lost count of the stories, which were told by harbour Methuselahs about ships which had come home after four weeks or even five. But not knowing what had happened, and frustration at having no means of finding out or taking action, plunged him back again into the depths of despondency.

The hostility that had been almost tangible at the Governor's Ball had already begun to subside. True, Lady Penelope Fitzpatrick asked him waspishly why it had been necessary for his bride to travel so early in the season, but most people were deeply sympathetic and only embarrassed to know what to say in condolence.

Alexander haunted the harbour. Captains of other ships reported gradually clearer water, with ice only lingering round the fringes of the estuary, and no trouble on the crossing. But no-one had seen the *Erromanga*. There was simply no news. She had effectively disappeared.

Chapter 20 - The Miracle

Meanwhile on the stranded *Erromanga*, things went on quite merrily for the first fourteen days. The moving ice pack had pushed the *Erromanga* into an almost perfect natural harbour. She was able to anchor, her sails furled, and the ice was so thin here that the passengers were able to go fishing, returning with basketfuls of sea-trout. Isabella then organised a trout-filleting competition, with a prize for the woman filleting the most trout in an hour. There was great merriment when the prize was presented, and the fish, packed in ice (of which there was naturally no shortage) lasted for three days. A land party despatched to the shore was able to find fresh water, and six casks at a time were filled and ferried back to the ship.

However, the First Mate's look-out party, clambering on to the headland, had no good news for Captain Oliphant. The sea looked solidly frozen as far as they could see, and it was only this sheltered deep-water patch of sea, which was lightly covered. The Captain considered what he had to do. He was already a fortnight late. He could ride with relative safety here, or he could make a push, as soon as there was a favourable wind, to break through the ice. He had had to cut rations for himself and the crew, and despite the fresh water and fish, he had to make the provisions last for another six hundred miles until he reached Quebec.

The decision was largely taken out of his hands by more unfavourable weather. The wind sat in the wrong quarter. It was gusting to gale force at times, and it began to pour with rain, which lasted a full 24 hours. They set out every available container to collect the water for their use. He hoped the rain, instead of the eternal snow, would at least soften the ice, and the look-out reported that he thought he could see clear water about a mile ahead. With a light offshore wind, he thought he would make the attempt, ramming the ice with the bows and adding a party of the crew, with axes, to try and break it ahead of the bows.

They struggled all day to get clear, but as dusk fell the wind veered onshore again, the ice-party were exhausted and making little impression, and he had to give up the attempt.

Two days later there was again a little cheer; a small sailing schooner, which had come from Cape Breton, and which was steering in clear water alongside the pack ice, reported that the Gulf of St. Lawrence was clear. "If only we can escape from this vice-like piece of ice," Capt. Oliphant reported in his daily Bulletin to the passengers and crew, " we shall be in Quebec in no time."

It was the last day of April. They could hardly believe that the ice had trapped them so late in the year. Captain Oliphant wrote in his diary: "Tomorrow be the 1st of May, a day of enjoyment to many thousands in Scotland. God grant that it may be a day of enjoyment to me, but if we are still in the ice I am afraid there will be very little to remind me of May Day."

His pessimism was justified. In his Bulletin of May 3rd. he said, "Since I last addressed you, we have been dragged down a long shore, still fast in the ice, and have no prospect of any change." His words were greeted with groans, but the Minister, Peter Bruce, somewhat restored the situation with a spirited assertion that God had looked after them so far, and if they all prayed together, he was sure their prayers would be answered again.

To Isabella, the Captain was more forthcoming. "Every day we are being pushed nearer and nearer to land, and I am very much afraid that if the wind does not change soon, we must be driven ashore upon an uninhabited coast."

Mercifully the wind did veer again. The drift was halted before the passengers were aware that the Captain had ordered the ship's boats to be provisioned and made ready in case they struck a submerged rock.

Ten days later the food allowance to the sailors was cut to a quarter of a pound of biscuit a man, in addition to their ration of salt beef.

The Captain confided to Isabella, "I am heartily tired of the North American trade. Here we have a perfectly nice, fine day, with the ocean a beautiful bluish-green in the distance, and you are all sunbathing on deck, but we still have this pestilential ice six feet thick we can do nothing about. I am extremely hungry on the crew's rations as you all must be. What it must be like for the Irish and Highlanders below, I dread to think."

Isabella had been below, and she knew that many people were weak from hunger. There had been two deaths already. However, the Captain and crew had been rigorous in keeping the ship clean, and the doctor reported no sign of disease. She pleaded on behalf of a poor woman who was in the last stages of pregnancy, for a few extra rations to be given to her, which request was granted, subject only to Isabella giving them to her herself, before anyone else seized them in desperation.

On 19th May, during another fine day, the crew made another attempt to hack the ship out of the ice, but they were themselves suffering from lack of food and had to give up the attempt, after making virtually no impression. Although the sun shone, and the surface ice was melting, it had as yet little effect on the thick ice beneath the water.

On 24th May, the prayers of the *Erromanga's* passengers were finally answered. A gale blew up from the South, which began to break up the ice; there was a heavy swell beneath the ship, causing it to shake and quiver all over. The tremendous noise caused alarm among the passengers, but Isabella and the Rev. Bruce soothed their fears, saying it was only the noise of the ice breaking against the ship, as she donned more sail and cut her way through it. "We can see clear water, at last," said Isabella. "Our ordeal is almost at an end."

So it was. Forty-six days after entering the ice, the *Erromanga* was blessedly free to sail, with only some superficial damage to the bows, into clear water on her way to the Gulf of St. Lawrence and Quebec. She crowded on all sail and went driving through the water at top speed.

* * *

On shore, Alexander had simply given up hope. He was performing like an automaton, and exhausted with the effort, slept like a dead man till morning brought the horror of his existence back again. His prayers had remained unanswered.

His deputy, deeply sympathetic, unlike Fitzpatrick now at Grosse Isle, who had not mentioned the *Erromanga's* fate to his new superior, suggested a break in Pictou.

"No. I must be here to learn what happened to her. The port authorities have at last listened to all our pleas, and are intending to commission a ship to set sail for the *Erromanga's* last known position to find out what has happened. But the St. Lawrence has been free of ice for weeks. There has never been a ship delayed so long. I cannot but fear she has perished."

The Quebec Times, pursuing the story it had started three weeks previously, had, in last week's edition, criticised the authorities for not sending out a search vessel earlier. In this week's paper a score of voices were raised, some pessimistic, others angry, arguing that it was unforgivable to send 280 people to perish in an ice-trap so early in the season, and why was there not a rescue service? If the ship had beached on an uninhabited shore, there might still be survivors, it argued. But the ship's last reported position had been some six hundred miles away. Who was going to pay for a search ship, responded the authorities. They were not responsible for early sailings. The pilot boats were busy. It was too far for a lifeboat to operate.

None of this theorising helped the victims of the presumed tragedy.

At last, on an afternoon in late May, as he was working at his desk, with the window open, Alexander heard shouting from the harbour. *"Erromanga"!* *"Erromanga"*, ahoy!" it seemed to say.

He could hardly believe his ears. He ran straight out of the building and on to the quayside. "She's been sighted, Sir," exclaimed a sailor, excitedly. "At the mouth of the Gulf. The Pilot boat's going out now."

Alexander could not believe it. Six and a half weeks since last seen! And able to make her own way up the Gulf! It was a miracle!

His cautious side surfaced. Perhaps they'd made a mistake! Perhaps it was a ship that looked like the *Erromanga!* He sought out the Harbour-Master.

"It's true," said the man. "I can hardly believe it. Why did no-one spot her? But it's the *Erromanga* all right.

We've had signals. I'm sorry you've had a worrying time, Sir, but all's well that ends well, as they say."

Alexander dashed back to his own office, locked the door, and wept a fortnight's pent-up tears. That they were tears of joy, and not of grief, mattered little. His overpowering emotion just had to be released. It was too overwhelming, and too wonderful to describe. His prayer of gratitude was heartfelt but incoherent!

It took a few moments for his usual calm to assert itself. It would take them until the day after tomorrow to make their way up river to Quebec, He must warn Mary Talbot. He must tell Joanna, whom he had now established to assist Mary Talbot's organisation to keep her occupied, and prevent her moping in his own house, with no-one to console her.

He warned his Deputy to be ready to go aboard to see the Captain. He would be too pre-occupied with his own concerns to attend to *that*.

* * *

Quebec had seen nothing like it before. Thanks to the Quebec Times, the ship that disappeared had seized everyone's imagination. Its reappearance was nothing short of a miracle, and everyone had to be there to see it. Not only the relatives of passengers and crew, but the whole city seemed to be pouring on to the quayside to greet the ship.

Hooters and klaxons were sounding from every boat in the river. The *Erromanga*, bow twisted, but otherwise stately under sail, was being guided by a flotilla of small boats to the quay. She was defiantly fluttering the Ensign and a collection of bunting, and her passengers were lining the deck, and waving in a frenzy of excitement. Alexander thought he could spot the small figure of Isabella, also waving.

The crowd surged forward, pushing and jostling to get a closer view. Someone started three cheers. "*Erromanga—aa!* Hip, Hip, Hooray!" was taken up by the crowd in a mighty roar.

"Oh, Sir, isn't it wonderful?" said a small excited woman, clutching his arm, "My brother's on board – and I thought he was dead. It's a miracle!"

Someone started to clap. The sound of applause, and more cheers rang round the harbour. More hooters! More cheers! The excitement was intense. Alexander and his Deputy, who were supposed to be the first on board, strode up the gangplank, and parted at the top. His Deputy sought the Captain, and Alexander sought Isabella.

She was there, and he swept her into his arms, quite incapable of speech.

* * *

The ship got its clearance certificate and they were free to leave. Amazingly there had been little illness. No typhoid, and only a few mild cases of scurvy, which would disappear once those affected got proper food and vegetables.

As Isabella had no luggage, they could leave the ship straightaway, but first Isabella introduced Alexander to the Captain.

"You have a wonderful lady here, Sir," said Captain Oliphant. "She was a great comfort to me in my hour of trial, and without her, I don't know how we'd have coped with those crying women."

"It's thanks to you, Captain, that we are here to tell the tale," responded Isabella, shaking his hand

257

warmly. "I hope you can have a rest, while they undertake your repairs, and before you have to set off again for Scotland."

"We couldn't understand why no other ships spotted you," said Alexander. "There's been no news at all, and that is why we have all been so worried."

"Probably because we were in a bay, Sir, at least for part of the time. We'd be hidden by the headland, I daresay. There was a small boat from Cape Breton that saw us, but maybe they didn't realise we were missing – and I never thought to tell them. It was quite early on, and I kept thinking we'd break clear."

Alexander and Isabella said good-bye and made straight for a hansom cab. "I thought I'd have to carry you off the ship, at least," said Alexander. "But though you're skin and bone, you're well, I think."

"Hungry," she said. "We've been on about 6 ounces of food a day. I could eat for a week. The pilot boat brought out apples, and they tasted like nectar."

"We'll get coffee and some food while we talk," he said. "I'm taking you to Mary Talbot's where Joanna will be waiting, and Mary will look after you. All your clothes have been taken there. Oh, darling, why did you go?"

"I had to," said Isabella. "It was a spur of the moment decision. They said there were women passengers screaming and wailing, and I thought I could calm them down, and pray with them. The Captain was furious with me to begin with, but in the end, as you see, he was grateful. I had no idea it would last for so long."

"They say 46 days stuck in the ice is a record! – one which we could very well do without! It's been torture not knowing what had happened to you."

"My darling, I am so very sorry. I think it was probably worse for you than for me."

"I think one of the worst moments was when the *Albion* came in, and you weren't on board."

"Joanna told you, didn't she?"

"She said you were 'lost'. I got the full story out of Bryce Allen. At first it didn't seem too bad; your arrival was merely delayed, but when *Erromanga* got more and more overdue, I had to think the ship had perished, and you were dead."

"My poor dear. I would never have gone if I had known it would cause you such anguish." She looked at him searchingly for a moment. "Alexander, I don't remember you like this. When did your hair go grey?"

"Has it?" he said. "I didn't notice. Let me kiss you again."

Chapter 21 - The Golden Years

The Quebec press became very excited. An interview with the Captain divulged that he owed much to Isabella for tramping across the ice from the *Albion* to the *Erromanga* and the effect she had had on the passengers' morale. She became an overnight heroine. Then interviews with passengers who, excited by their escape from a watery grave, stressed how her prayers had been answered, almost gave her the status of a saint. Quebec society marvelled that this paragon of virtue had come from Scotland to marry their Immigration Agent.

Isabella's and Alexander's marriage was not long delayed. She failed to put on sufficient weight to fit the wedding dress she had brought with her from Scotland, but a few judicious darts and tucks and her own radiance did much to ensure she looked beautiful on the day.

They had chosen the Presbyterian Church in Pictou for their union, and Helen Creighton begged to be allowed to arrange their wedding breakfast. In return Isabella was happy to invite Helen's step-daughter to be her attendant, together with Neil, Nathaniel's eldest son, to be her page. Since Minette expected to be confined again, she and her younger children remained in Cape Breton, while Nathaniel came to support his brother. Of course the family from Maple Tree Grove were there, as were a large contingent of interested onlookers from Pictou.

Travelling from Quebec were Mary Talbot and the faithful Joanna. Thus in July 1831 Alexander and Isabella became man and wife.

They returned to their house in Quebec almost immediately. Isabella was eager to display the furnishings she had brought with her to make it a more comfortable home. Servants were already in place, but she needed to add polish to some of their habitual duties to raise the standard to that which she had achieved in Glasgow. She was conscious that Alexander's prestigious position as Immigration Officer on behalf of the British Government needed her support in Quebec society, and this she was determined to give. She held an early Reception to which fifty people were invited, and took Mary Talbot's advice as to which fifty should be first, and which fifty might safely be left to the next occasion.

Lady Penelope Fitzpatrick found herself among the first contingent, and arrived prepared to patronise the new bride. Instead she was forced reluctantly to admire her hostess's poise and assurance. They would never become bosom friends, and she certainly did not countenance Isabella's choice of a husband, but she recognised quality when it was presented to her. It was as well that she remained ignorant of the part Isabella had played in Alexander's appointment and the over-looking of her own husband's claims to the post.

Quebec suited Isabella well. She was at home in both Glasgow and Edinburgh, both substantial cities, and in the burgeoning country of Canada, Quebec was in the early stages of growing to be of similar importance.

The Thomsons went on the first Sabbath to the Presbyterian Church, and Isabella pledged her support to the congregation and offered active help when it should be needed. She did not consider urging that congregation to help Cape Breton, for Mary Talbot's Quebec Immigrants' Society was already fund-raising there, but she did help her new friend in the events, which were already being organised.

She and Alexander were idyllically happy together. She knew that during the day his work took preference, but his office was near enough for him to be with her most lunch-times. In the evenings, they either dined at home, or went to civic functions to which they were frequently invited, and indeed were expected to attend. The coldness shown initially to Alexander melted away, and they became the most popular of guests.

There was only one drawback to the house near the harbour, and that was its lack of a garden. Since her colourful front garden in Edinburgh, and perhaps inspired by the memory of Elizabeth's brave garden in River Inhabitants on Cape Breton, Isabella had hankered after a garden of her own. The Pictou home of Helen Creighton proved that a garden could be created, even by carving away at a hillside, and Isabella opened a downstairs window, and leaned out to discover what lay at the back of her new home.

The yard looked unpromising enough – an expanse of stone flags, and some domestic equipment, and at the far corner a door, possibly a Tradesmen's entrance.

She ventured through the kitchen and scullery to examine the possibilities from the outside. If the window through which she had been leaning was turned into a full-length one, and if the window-sills had boxes of plants upon them, and if the flag-stones at this sunnier side were lifted, and if new soil was brought in, and if colourful shrubs were planted, they would have the makings of a small garden.

She brought Alexander out to give his opinion after tea. By then the sun had come out as if to lend its encouragement to her ideas.

"It would be so refreshing to sit outside in the early evening, to enjoy the fresh air, and to have some flowers to look at," she suggested.

He could deny her nothing, but offered a few practical objections.

"There are the little black flies to enjoy your flowers, too," was one of them.

"The servants use this back yard for the laundry," was another.

"Would you want your tradesmen's goods to come in through the front door?" yet another.

Isabella was not to be diverted. "I shall make a plan," she said. "I believe we could make a small garden, for our own use, if we can alter the window."

"Indeed, my love, you can alter the window. I want you to be happy, and if a garden will make you happier, then let's do it."

Gardens, and particularly town gardens, were almost unknown in Quebec. The essentials of life, rather than its adornment, were the major pre-occupation, but Isabella tracked down the Head Gardener at Government House for his advice, and this worthy directed her to the nurseryman who was his supplier.

Scenting custom, which might grow into a fashion, the nurseryman willingly accompanied her to view the prospect of a garden for himself. So the concept was born, and it was in Isabella's character that, once conceived, it should be carried through. The small garden grew into a much larger one until even Alexander thought it time to call a halt. However, the nurseryman was right. A town garden did become the fashion, and Isabella started an Amateur Horticultural Society to encourage others to grow suitable plants in their gardens. Winter protection was needed for many plants, and so glass-houses became fashionable too.

Mortimer's List, which had haunted her for years, and had been the original reason for travelling to Nova Scotia, was finally extinguished by the writing-off of the few final debts.   Isabella then turned her attention to what to do with the capital it had produced, which was still accumulating in the Pictou bank.

"I think we should use that money to build a log-cabin on Cape Breton," she said one night, when they were sitting companionably before a log fire at home.

Alexander's eyebrows rose.   "What would we want with a log cabin?" he asked.

"It would be a summer home. I want to be able to visit the new Churches.   There are sixteen in prospect now, you know. It would be so much more convenient to have our own small home from which to do that.   You said you would be able to spare time away every other summer, and that would be a suitable distance to travel."

It was true that Alexander had made an arrangement with his deputy that they should each have some vacation time during the summer.   It could only be in alternate years, as the immigrant ships were streaming in from May to September and they were very busy, whereas in the winter there was time and enough to spare.   That was unfair to Isabella, however. She could not join him in his usual winter pursuits of trekking and hunting.

"There's no need to use your money," he said.

"But I want to.   Perhaps we would let new Ministers stay in it when we did not need it for ourselves, and I want to use my money to benefit Cape Breton."

"It would not cost so very much," he said. "If it's a summer home, it does not need to be palatial, or have you had your fill of pioneering?"

This brought back memories, which interrupted the conversation for some time.

As usual, when Isabella set her heart on something, it actually happened.

* * *

In the following year, Joanna was married to the young farmer she had met when she had been helping Mary Talbot with the staging posts to Upper Canada, during those dreadful weeks when Isabella had been trapped in the ice. Thus Isabella lost the maid she had first employed in Glasgow in 1824. The parting was a wrench. Joanna had been with her for so long and become used to her ways, besides travelling with her on many occasions. However, Isabella was pleased for her maid. Joanna would make a good wife and mother in due course, and she believed that her country upbringing would ensure that she was adaptable to the still hard life of a Canadian farmer.

Isabella decided against employing another personal maid. As a married woman again she was in no need of the chaperoning decreed by convention, and the servants already employed in the household could do all that was necessary for her.

Their household was augmented, however, by the addition of Neil, Nathaniel's eldest son. On their last visit to Cape Breton, Alexander and Nathaniel had discussed the question of Neil's schooling. Rudimentary village schooling in Mabou would restrict Neil's opportunities in future. He was a bright youngster, already day-dreaming of becoming a doctor. Only grammar schooling in a city like Quebec would equip him with the qualifications to enter the training needed for such a profession.   Isabella gladly agreed with Alexander that they should offer him a home during term-time for his years of study, and she concurred with Alexander's offer to finance him through those further years of training.   Without children of their own, while Nathaniel's brood had already reached six, quite usual for the period, it would be in everyone's interest for them to "adopt" in an informal sense at least one of the nephews or nieces.   So the fourteen-year old filled to some extent the loss of Euan, Isabella's child from her first marriage. She welcomed his friends, took him round the sights of the city, and enjoyed his confidences and companionship.

Alexander himself was concerned about his properties in the Huron Tract.   They were still being settled, and although he was careful to see that there was no conflict of interest between them and his job of Immigration Officer, it would be best if he divorced himself from their day to day management.   Nathaniel's small-holding at Mabou was unlikely ever to make him a rich man, and Alexander offered him a management role in Upper Canada, which Nathaniel agreed to accept. Richard Gordon was still working effectively in Scotland on finding immigrants, and all that remained was to put the two in touch with one another.

One day a letter arrived from Richard Gordon containing news of John Sutherland, who had been so assiduous in his attentions to Isabella, and so devious in his dealings with *The Lovelly Nelly*.

"You will be interested to know," wrote Richard, "that John Sutherland has been unmasked at last.   I had some small hand in this, because it came to my attention, via a solicitor friend, that Sutherland had acted for a couple of elderly Caithness people, who died.   They were a widow and a widower, not related, but whose estates, instead of going to the relatives as expected, were apparently willed to John Sutherland instead. One might have been greeted with raised eyebrows, but <u>two</u> were distinctly suspicious. I brought the two families together, and they compared notes. As a result, complaints were laid, and the matter was investigated. I am delighted to tell you that the case was heard last week, found proven, and Sutherland sentenced to transportation for fraud! I gather that the likely destination will be Australia – a mercy, as I think Canada would not have been big enough to contain you and him. That it will be big enough to contain my next three sailings of emigrants, I devoutly hope. There is still great interest here in taking passage. I could almost have hoped that Sutherland's plan for a harbour at Tain had succeeded, as it would have been most convenient, but we continue to use Cromarty. Your brother and I are in constant touch to ensure that people are aware of the terms of land on offer in the Huron Tract."

Isabella gave a small shudder. "A harsh punishment!" she suggested. "He was such a cultured man, and by all accounts Australia is much more primitive than we are here."

"But he was a rogue," protested Alexander. "Don't forget, Isabella, there were five deaths on *The Lovelly Nelly*."

Alexander was himself diligent in checking all complaints from passengers of faulty ships and uncaring captains, and was conscientious, as Archibald Buchanan had been, in attending the sick and dying at the various quarantine hospitals, which were opened in 1832 at Grosse Isle. Knowing what had happened to Archibald, he was scrupulous to take every precaution, and to disinfect his person thoroughly before returning home. The last thing he wanted to do was put Isabella in any danger. She was well, but remained unnaturally slim, although this could be put down to the energy she expended on her various roles, in the home and outside it.

After some three years the Fitzpatricks returned to Britain, and a new Medical Superintendent was appointed at Grosse Isle.

Alexander's main dread was that he would be called away from his blissful life to attend meetings in London. He knew the blow would fall some day, and about four years into their marriage, it did.

Isabella was philosophical. "We knew you would have to go," she said. "I have been planning what to do, and I think I shall go to Halifax while you are away, and begin a Cape Breton group there. I have been establishing some contacts by letter and the time is ripe, I think."

Alexander drew her to him. "Who's a clever schemer now," he murmured. He knew she hated the Atlantic after her last experience, and this trip would be much shorter for her. The prospect of being apart for two months seemed unendurable, but had to be faced. He would hurry back at the earliest opportunity.

* * *

In 1836 two touching little ceremonies took place. The first, arranged by Isabella, was a dinner at home, with all Alexander's favourite dishes, and unusually a bottle of fine wine. Candle-lit, of course, the best silver and napery had been used. There were only two places laid.

"Why," queried Alexander. "It's not my birthday!"

Isabella laughed. "Guess," she said. "Ten years ago today."

He thought back. "It must be about the time we first met . . ."

"Exactly so, my darling. I thought I was so horrible to you then, I had better put it right today."

He cast his mind back. He had been in the shop, in overalls and serving customers. Then this smart Edinburgh lady had come in; he had deliberately made her wait. She had said he owed her money; he had denied it, had lost his temper; they had quarrelled; he had had to apologise. How far he had travelled since then! Financially secure, even wealthy, with an influential, powerful position, and with this elegant lady as his loving wife!

"Is it only ten years?" he said slowly. "You have been so unbelievably good for me, Isabella. I would still have been in the store, I believe, except for you. I was determined to reach your level."

"It is not a question of levels," said Isabella. "You opened my eyes to all that was artificial and unnecessary in my world. I began to see the honesty and straight-dealing in yours."

"It was a lovely idea," he said. "Will you do me the honour of accepting my invitation to dine at the Clarendon, two weeks and three days from now?"

"And what anniversary will that be?" she asked.

"The day we fell in love. Or at least the day I fell in love. And, if you're honest, I think the day you also saw me as a human being and not a shopkeeper."

"I'll tell you in a fortnight when I fell in love with you! Oh, Alexander, we are being so foolish, and yet it is such fun."

Jean Lucas

They toasted one another, in total amity.

Where he found them, she never discovered, but over dinner in a fortnight's time he gave her a small package of two silver boots, mounted to add to her silver bracelet. Perhaps Richard Gordon had been pressed into service, to commission them in Tain!

* * *

The log cabin in Cape Breton took some four years to come to fruition. They chose a site on the shores of the central lake, and close to the new road, which was in course of construction. Building the cabin was a simple matter, but equipping it to Isabella's taste and standards created many problems of logistics.

The island was still backward, but had taken on a new momentum, as more and more immigrants were settling there. Land grants had been available for a time after 1817, and back in 1820 Sutherlanders from Assynt, led by Norman Macleod, had transferred from Pictou to St. Ann's, attracted by the offer of land. Links with this early group were now attracting more Sutherlanders to this destination. It was a shorter and cheaper trip than the journey to Upper Canada, for those who could not afford the better quality passages offered by Richard Gordon and Alexander Thomson. However, most of these new immigrants were still very poor. Norman Macleod petitioned the Cape Breton authorities in 1836 on behalf of one hundred and four improvident emigrants from the Highlands, recently arrived at St. Anns.

In 1837 there was a new wave of emigrants from the Western Isles, who linked up with previous Islands immigrants of ten years earlier.

Then some 400 newcomers from the Hebrides arrived to settle near McNab's Cove, and a similar number, travelling in two vessels, were expected at the Loch Lomond District of Richmond County. Five ships from Tobermory came the next year, their passengers driven out by the total collapse of the kelp industry. Being by then unable to get land, other than by squatting, they tended to add to the impoverished nature of the Cape Breton population. Presbyterian congregations were growing, and providing even more work for Isabella's Ministers. Bigger congregations tended eventually to increase Church revenues, and make parishes self-supporting.

The island's economy was changing too. John Munro, who had emigrated with Macleod, became a substantial figure in the timber trade. The Sydney coalfield, established by the British-based General Mining Association in 1827, increased production and provided job opportunities for many Scots.

There was still a need for at least three new Ministries, and Isabella, trotting from parish to parish on her pony under the escort of her Ministers, while Alexander spent his days fishing, got to know the congregations and the Clergy well. It was something in the nature of a "President's Progress" as the parishes were eager to show her what they had achieved since her last visit. She kept the Edinburgh Ladies' Society informed on the success of their mission to Cape Breton, and her lively accounts of life in the wilderness frequently adorned the pages of the Newsletter she had once founded. It brought her correspondence too, from those she had known in Scotland, and she frequently found that she was writing five or six letters a day in response.

Their holidays on Cape Breton became peaceful interludes for Alexander, but a stimulus of activity for Isabella and the mission to which she had dedicated herself.

When they returned to Quebec, the positions were reversed. For the rest of the summer and for each of the summers, when he had to stay in Quebec, Alexander was increasingly busy. Ships were coming in constantly, with their cargoes of problems. The settlers might need to be trans-shipped to Montreal en route for Upper Canada. 300 Islanders from Uist were sent on to the township of Williams; Sutherlanders tended to make for Zorra. Although in some instances their passages had been paid, many were virtually destitute on arrival and had to be provided for. 52,000 arrived in 1932, and the numbers remained high year on year.

There were problems with the shipping too. Alexander had to impound a ship whose Captain had blatantly breached the regulations, and jail another Captain for disgraceful conditions on board. He was rarely home for lunch in the summer; many days he was out from dawn to dusk at Grosse Isle. It was not unknown for him to fall asleep after dinner. The winters were much easier, of course, and it was then that he and Isabella entered into the social life of the City. The celebrations included those of the Coronation of the new young Queen, Victoria.

Conditions were changing in the colony too. A brief rebellion in Toronto showed that "Reformers" in Upper Canada were restive at the control of Westminster thousands of miles away, and were pressing for greater control of their own legislative process. As a Crown Servant, and with a Scottish-born wife, Alexander had to be on the side of the status quo, but he could not believe it would last for ever, and had more than a little sympathy with the aims of the new Canadians, some now in their third generation.

* * *

In the eighteen-forties, in Britain press unease and public clamour were developing over the clearances in

Scotland, which were alarming Ministers. Once again the state of emigration was under the spotlight, both in Britain, and in North America.

The particular incident which excited most national press comment were the clearances at Glencalvie, and the emptying of the whole parish of Croick. Virtually every able-bodied person was ready to go and their Minister had resigned his living, stipend, glebe and manse. Of the 350 people, not more than 20 had sufficient means to ensure their own passage. The Glasgow Destitution Committee agreed to pay a contribution of ten shillings per head to people willing to emigrate, provided this sum were matched by the proprietor of the land from which they were to be evicted. £250 was therefore raised charitably for this group. The scandal of Croick centred on those who were too ill to make the journey and the cruel division of families caused by the enforced emigration. The remote Church at Croick, reached only by a long, winding lane along the valley, bore testimony to the misery of families thus parted. Etched on the outside of the windows was the poignant message: "Glencalvie people was in the churchyard here May 24, 1845." It represents the pitiful resistance of those who were left behind.

The irony of the situation was that the national conscience was aroused, and money flooded into the organisations offering relief, while the worst criticism was levelled at the Government.

That summer Alexander was again summoned to the Colonial Office in London to make a report, as MPs debated the campaign of clearances highlighted by the Press.

"Would you like to come with me this time?" he asked Isabella.

She considered for a moment. "To London? I think I would rather go on to Edinburgh, perhaps," she suggested.

"No. That would mean a long and tiring journey for you. We'll both take passage to Leith, and I'll go down to London, while you stay in Edinburgh. You can look up the Ladies' Association, and your sister, and I'll come back to you, and we can come home on one of my ships. We can get Richard Gordon to come down to meet us too. Are you sure you can face the Atlantic again?"

"I think so. At least if we get stuck in the ice, we'll be together."

"We won't get stuck in the ice. This will be June. Ideal sailing weather, and we'll choose a good ship. Is that what you would like, dearest?"

"It sounds perfect. I'll write to my sister," she said.

To two people who could never have enough of each other's company, the journey over to Scotland, sped by fresh westerly winds, was unalloyed pleasure. Alexander's face lost some of its worry lines, and Isabella felt the benefit of the sun and fresh air.

It was lovely to see Edinburgh again, and Isabella had a happy time re-visiting her family and her many friends.

The journey back was less perfect. Two days out, the swell increased and Isabella stayed below, while Alexander went to dinner. Returning unexpectedly to find an immigration reference to show the Captain, he was dismayed to find Isabella face down and weeping.

"My darling, whatever is the matter?" he asked, gathering her to him.

She clutched him, but said nothing. "Are you sad to be leaving Scotland?" he asked. "I expect it brings back memories, some happy, some sad. We can always come back if you want to. Nothing is really final. I know you miss your family at times. Quebec is fine, but not the same as where one was brought up. Could you eat some food if I brought it to you? Please don't be unhappy, my love. . ."

She accepted the handkerchief he offered her, wiped her eyes, blew her nose and answered the only safe question. "No, no dinner, thank you, dearest. You go back, and I will try and sleep a little . . ."

He left, doubtfully, gathering up the book he had come for. By the following day, Isabella had recovered her composure, and was brightly discussing the shopping she had undertaken. She wrote a few letters, played a game or two of crib with him, took a walk round the deck and seemed her normal self. He dismissed the incident. Some irritation of the nerves, no doubt!

Back home, the year resumed its usual course. Neil came back after the summer holidays; they went to several dinners, but Isabella excused herself from a couple of balls. Stuffy rooms and energetic dancing were a poor alternative to a comfortable evening at home, she suggested, and Alexander was more than happy to agree. Christmas came and went. It was not their year for going to Cape Breton, so Alexander snatched a week's hunting. Isabella urged him to go. She tended her garden, planted seeds and watered them assiduously, thrilled when they came up and prospered.

In June they were sitting lazily in the garden, when the doorbell rang. The maid answered and called Alexander to deal with the caller, who had an urgent query to be resolved.

Jean Lucas

He was not away ten minutes, but when he returned Isabella was lying, slumped sideways on the flag-stones, and he knew, in a heart-stopping moment, that she was dead. No-one could lie in that position, but perhaps it was only a faint . . .he turned her over, called her name, felt her pulse, carried her into the house, held a mirror to her lips -- all to no avail. Isabella's life had ended.

The doctor was summoned, said a post-mortem would be necessary, and asked whether he would like her body removed. Alexander shook his head in total numbness. In shock, he sat holding her lifeless hand until someone took it gently away from him.

The golden years were over.

Chapter 22 - Requiem

Isabella had left a letter.

Alexander found it, addressed with his Christian name only, inside the flap of the desk on which she wrote all her many letters. He unfolded it, and noted that it was dated a couple of weeks earlier.

"My dearest Alexander,
When you find this, I shall probably have passed away, or at least be very ill. I am desperately sorry for the shock and grief I shall have caused you. I can only say that I thought it would be better this way.

Our life together has been wonderful, and I am deeply grateful to you that you have made it so. Few people can have experienced the depths of understanding, friendship and overwhelming love that has been ours over the last thirteen years. It was because I did not want to mar that perfect time that I have not told you my sad secret. You had a right to know, and I very nearly told you on the ship coming back from Leith last year, but you inadvertently gave me an excuse for my tears, and I allowed you to think that I was missing Scotland.

I accompanied you to Edinburgh because I had some minor (as I thought) health worries and I thought I would consult an Edinburgh physician while you were in London, thinking I might receive better advice there than in Quebec. I was told that it was most likely that I had a growth in the breast, that an operation might be possible but that there was no guarantee of success. This growth would spread, and would affect other organs. I could probably deal with some of the pain with laudanum, but there would come a time when it could prove intolerable.

Surgery would identify the location, and excision would remove the growth, but might also remove much of me! My love, I had no desire at all for you to have an ill, mutilated or dying wife, and if I died anyway, it would all have been for nothing.

I prayed for guidance and felt that God's will should be done. I knew that you would fight such a decision with all your strength, and I did not want to fight with you as well as with my illness. Forgive me! I decided not to tell you, at least until much, much later. I was warned that if the growth spread, it could affect my heart and that a sudden death could occur. Hence I am writing to explain, in case that happens.

The year that they thought it would take is almost up. My laudanum doses grow less effective, and have to be taken more frequently. I think we have had a peaceful, quiet and happy year, and so I hope you think I was right.

We shall meet again in Heaven, of that I am convinced. Be strong and of good courage!
Your loving wife,
Isabella."

Alexander put the letter down, and tried desperately to think. His blindness in not seeing her suffering was put aside for the moment. The letter would surely suffice as an explanation. He could not bear the idea of a post-mortem. He must find the doctor. Although the letter was personal and precious, it would have to be shown to him, and to the coroner as well perhaps, if there were an inquest. He knew something of the procedures from his work at the Quarantine Hospital. He summoned up every ounce of control and went to find the authorities.

In the end, the doctor gently advised that, with the evidence of the letter, it would be better to confirm the cause of death. "We shall know what to look for," he said, "so it will be a brief formality. But it will enable my colleague and I to issue a certificate, without having to have an inquest. Easier for you in the long run. She was a very brave lady," he added, handing the letter back.

Mingled with his overwhelming grief, Alexander was blaming himself for not seeing that Isabella was in trouble. Knowing from the letter that she would be determined to hide her problems from him, it was perhaps understandable that she had dissembled successfully. They had rarely met in the mornings because he had been up and out of the house early, and had often slept in his dressing-room in order not to wake her. Nor had she a personal maid any longer, who might have known. In the evenings, her eyes bright with the drug, she had been her usual laughing self. She had not eaten much, it was true, but then she never had. He remembered an odd occasion when she had imprisoned his hands as he had moved to caress her, but most of the time she had been perfectly normal, writing her letters, tending the garden. They had lived quietly, but he had supposed that was for his benefit, as he was so very busy. He supposed she had rested more, and spaced out her medicine carefully, so that it took effect when she needed it to. It had been incredibly brave of her, and he would not spoil that sacrifice by regretting it. Nevertheless, he ought to have known!

* * *

Letters of condolence poured in from Quebec, many parts of Scotland, and Cape Breton. The funeral service at St. Andrews in Quebec was attended by huge numbers of people.

Neil was studying in Edinburgh and could not get back. Alexander had some cards of acknowledgment printed. He could not face writing to everyone in reply –

at least not yet. The Quebec papers carried news of Isabella's death, and then more news of her funeral. Then even more letters poured in.

The Rev. Patrick Stewart had sent an urgent message asking that Alexander be good enough to attend a Memorial Service in Cape Breton some six weeks after the main Quebec service, to be held at Isabella's first Presbyterian Church in Middle River. "The Church won't be large enough for everyone who wants to come, wrote the Missionary, but we can take part of the service outside as well. It is the least people can do to honour her memory."

Alexander planned to go over alone and stay in their own log cabin on the island, but Nathaniel, who had travelled from Upper Canada with two of his younger children for the St. Andrew's service, offered to travel on to Cape Breton with him, an offer he gladly accepted. The brothers were close, as they always had been, since the days they worked together to get their father out of jail, and since they travelled throughout Cape Breton, preaching together. He was sure they would see many people they knew and had counselled in bereavement themselves.

In Cape Breton when they walked to take their places in the little Church, Alexander was impressed by the enormous, orderly queue of people, which snaked its way around the Church, and went up the lane and over the hill until it was out of sight. He knew from his preaching days that people would come long distances for the Gospel. There must be as many as 2,000 people in that long straggling queue, almost as many as lived in the western part of the island, women as well as men, and almost always with their children. In the Church itself were the dignitaries of the new Churches, which had been founded, all officially representing their congregations. The Rev. James McLeod, who had launched many of them, had come from Scotland, both to preach, and to represent the Edinburgh Ladies' Association, and he brought with him another batch of letters of sympathy. Richard Gordon and his wife had written, of course, and William Allan and Captain Kirk, from Leith.

Inside, on the offertory table, was a vase with a bouquet of bright flowers, almost the only flowers on Cape Breton, thought Alexander. "With love from Elizabeth and children," read the message, and Alexander remembered the impression the little parade of children marching to the river and back to bring water for Elizabeth's garden had had on Isabella. The children would be mostly grown-up now, he supposed, perhaps with families of their own, perhaps part of the mourning queue.

The service was partly in Gaelic and partly in English, and, understanding Gaelic as he did, Alexander could appreciate the moving tributes to Isabella's early vision in understanding the need, and her energy in raising money to ensure that the Mission could be started and continued successfully.

Outside the Church there had been a wave of Gaelic keening sweeping through the waiting throngs. As the dignitaries left, and it was the turn of the masses to enter the Church, Margaret Campbell, leaping on the make-shift pulpit Alexander had once used, spoke passionately of all that the community owed to Isabella.

"Anyone who has been the first in a desolate wilderness, or known the heartbreak when a relative dies, with no comfort and consolation from our Church, will know that what Isabella Thomson did for this community is beyond praise and beyond price.

I speak for the women of Cape Breton, whose wee bairns now have a chance of learning, which they never had afore, when I say this lady was a patron saint to us. Her loss is our loss. We cannot write our thoughts, but we from the Highlands and Islands can sing our lament."

When Alexander emerged he was met with a wall of sound, the hymn of sorrow, sung in Gaelic, unaccompanied save by a lone piper, and echoing in a surge of cadences throughout the village in the valley.

It continued, verse after verse, as ten by ten the vast crowd entered the Church to pray at the altar rail, and those outside, patiently waiting their turn, continued the haunting refrain. It was nearly three hours later when the last of the mourners passed the door, Alexander shaking the hand of each who entered.

The Rev. Patrick Stewart murmured that a plaque or memorial stone might be erected. Alexander said, "You are welcome to put up a plaque if you wish, but perhaps a garden would be more fitting. Isabella used to speak of the green shoots of a new garden, replacing the barrenness of what was here before. Her missionaries would plant the seeds, and if the garden were well-watered, the people would draw their strength from the fruits of the planting. She wanted people to have God in their lives, not to admire her good works. The people have testified to that, and that is her true memorial."

EPILOGUE

Hilary (with one 'l') put the cover on her word-processor with a sigh. Her Editor, Simon Fitzgerald of the Pictou Gazette, had gladly accepted her idea of a special feature linking Pictou with her book, "Isabella's Garden."

Her novel had been inspired by discovering in an old trunk in the attic the yellowing pages of a half-completed work penned in her great-grandmother's handwriting. The old lady, (Hillary with two 'l's) had told her it was there before she died. She complained sadly, that in 1900, the year she wrote it, there had been no hope of finding a publisher and it had been left in limbo, but she had not been able to bear the idea of throwing it away. Perhaps one day . . .

In the modern world of the late twentieth century, and the computer age, research was so much easier and quicker that Hilary the second had been able to amplify the story.

She had been fortunate to discover in the archives of the Quebec Times, the account in 1831 of the amazing escape from the ice of the *Erromanga* and the heroine status accorded to Isabella Liddel. She had thus been able to give the book a new twist, and when she found the written evidence of Mortimer's List, which had been the mainspring of the story, the book almost wrote itself. Her article, linked with the book's launch, had been flatteringly lifted from the Pictou Gazette by the Canadian national newspapers.

Its footnote, urging that anyone, who could trace their ancestry to the people named in Mortimer's List, should make themselves known to the local newspaper, thus had a massive circulation.

Originally, expecting the response to be small, the Editor had booked the Pictou Golf Club (and the marquee two members had planned to put up in the grounds for their daughter's wedding) for a tea-party to enable those who wrote in to foregather and meet others. Of course the resultant occasion would yield more photographs and personal stories for the Pictou Gazette!

Hilary had been left to cope (hence the sigh) with the hundreds of people who wrote in from all over Canada, claiming to be descendants of those who had featured in Mortimer's List.

Of course, the majority could not travel to Pictou for a tea-party, but on the day over two hundred turned up. They were given labels on which to print the Mortimer's List name with which they were associated, and their own names and the town where they lived.

Simon Fitzgerald made a welcoming speech, pointing out that the Club house where they were standing had its origins in the half-built house Alexander Thomson had planned for his bride, Isabella, before he had been offered the appointment which took him to Quebec. Naturally it had a superb view of the estuary to enable him to watch the sailing ships coming in, and Pictou Waterfront where the ships would berth was to the right below them.

He introduced Hilary's book, which by now had been well trailed in the papers, and the publisher's table was besieged by those wanting to buy it.

Then the Chairman of the Pictou Chamber of Commerce spoke to claim that his family had connections with Mortimer's List.

"We have to remember," he said, "that, but for the generous loans made available by Edward Mortimer and continued by William Liddel in those far-off early days, many of our pioneer ancestors would have had severe hardship and great difficulty in getting started over here. None were more deprived than the Gaelic settlers of Cape Breton, and it was in bringing religious comfort to them that Isabella found her mission. Today we have found something. We have found each other. Bound by common ties of the past, we can re-discover the proud tradition that founded this country. Isabella herself has no statue or plaque as her memorial, but in this gathering and in this book, what she gave to so many people will live for ever."

Several other people asked to speak to mention their own connection with the story. There was the head of the current family occupying Maple Tree Grove; there were two whose family sprang from Joanna and her farmer husband; there was Sarah, whose ancestor had suffered with Isabella on the ice-imprisoned *Erromanga*. There were the ones who, with a male line descent intact, still bore the surnames on Mortimer's List. A copy of the list was enlarged and made into a poster for all to see, and purchase if they wished.

Pictou had rarely seen such a gathering. The modern town was normally quiet. As steam-ships had replaced sail, the waterfront gradually fell into disuse in favour of larger and deeper anchorages elsewhere, in places such as Halifax. The railway had come to Pictou in the 19th century and departed again in the 20th. Now the motor car was king for personal travel and the trucks carried the freight. The big roads bypassed Pictou, and left it as a pretty backwater on the Sunrise Trail.

The lateral streets, terraced from the hillside still featured white wooden homes, and the Churches still testified to the strength of the various religions in a traditional society. But the gravestones almost outnumbered the present population. The Logans, Macdonalds and Devonishes had their last resting-place on the promontory jutting out to sea, and the inland cemeteries were thick with tombs of many ancestors.

The stocks, which had been a favoured form of punishment administered by the house of justice, had gone and the Police found little to concern them in the quiet backwater, which had once been a flourishing port. The panels immortalising the story of The Hector, with their attendant museum and shop featured as the Town's main tourist attraction. Perhaps the story of Isabella would one day take its place alongside the earlier epic.

The tea party stretched on into evening, and the car-park attendant was desperate to get home. Still people chatted and discovered people to whom they hadn't yet spoken. Simon Fitzgerald had vanished long ago to put his paper to bed.

Hilary mounted the platform. "It has been a wonderful day," she said. "Just before you all go home, and let our car-park attendant go to his Scottish country dancing class, and before I go back to my day job as a small town newspaper journalist, I want to say one thing. How did I find my material, you ask? I just don't know. But I believe it was not I who found Isabella -- just the reverse. Isabella's spirit found me!"

THE END

ISBN 141209536-0